LIKE GOLD
REFINED

Books by Janette Oke

*with T. Davis Bunn

JANETTE OKE
LIKE GOLD REFINED

BETHANY HOUSE PUBLISHERS
MINNEAPOLIS, MINNESOTA 55438

DEDICATION

We owe much to some very special people.
Not only have they raised children they can be proud of,
but they have willingly linked them with our family.
So to—

Koert & Carol Dieterman
Carl & Sheila Galloway
Wendall & Delores Sousley
and Olga Larimer—

Edward and I say a big thank-you.
You have given to us a priceless gift in your children
who have brought joy and growth to the lives of
Terry, Lavon, Lorne, and Laurel,
and have been loving parents to
Ashley, Nate, Jessica, Katie, Courtney, Jackie,
Alex, Kristie, Emily, and Connor
—the special grandchildren that we share.

GOD BLESS YOU.

JANETTE OKE was born in Champion, Alberta, during the depression years, to a Canadian prairie farmer and his wife. She is a graduate of Mountain View Bible College in Didsbury, Alberta, where she met her husband, Edward. They were married in May of 1957 and went on to pastor churches in Indiana as well as Calgary and Edmonton, Canada.

The Okes have three sons and one daughter and are enjoying the addition of grandchildren to the family. Edward and Janette have both been active in their local church, serving in various capacities as Sunday school teachers and board members. They make their home near Calgary, Alberta.

CHAPTER 1

$\mathcal{A}$ thankful sigh gently eased from Virginia's lips as she lifted her head for another glimpse of brightness outside the kitchen window. At long last a small beam of sunshine was pushing its way through the clouds that had blanketed the heavens for the past three days. It was good to see the sun again. "Thank you, Lord," she whispered, hardly realizing she did so. Maybe now the ground would have a chance to dry, and the children, who had become impatient and fussy, would once again be able to play in the farmyard. The gloomy weather and confined circumstances were hard enough for Virginia to deal with on her own without also trying to entertain three housebound youngsters.

Another anemic ray managed to find its way through the overcast and to light the tip of a cloud directly above. Virginia felt her shoulders lift. The Lewis family would not be facing a second flood after all. But even as she gloried in that fact, she reminded herself that it would be some time, even with bright sunshine, until the yard dried enough to allow the children out. But even as she was concluding that thought, she felt her skirt tugged.

"Mama!" Four-year-old Martha didn't even try to temper her excitement. "We can go out now."

Virginia's eyes again shifted to the window. "Not yet," she cautioned, moving with difficulty from the cupboards to

9

the stove with persistent Martha in tow.

"But you said . . ." whined Martha.

"I said we had to wait for sunshine."

"But it is shining. See."

"It's not . . ."

"It is. Look."

At Martha's insistence, Virginia glanced over her shoulder. "It's not *fully* shining," she said.

"But it's *trying*," argued Martha. "It's a little bit shining. See." She pointed again toward the window.

Virginia half turned from stirring her pot. No one was more anxious than she to have the children from underfoot. But it would be foolish to send them out to swollen puddles and everything dripping from the recent rains.

"I meant the sun had to warm the world again. To dry things," she informed her impatient daughter.

"You didn't say that. You said—"

"I know what I said," replied Virginia, trying to keep frustration from edging her voice. "You'd come in soaking wet if you went out now."

"We'd dry."

Virginia nodded. *Yes*, she thought, *you'd dry*. Was it worth it? It was tempting. . . .

"Mindy gets to go out."

"Mindy has to go to school."

"Why can't I go to school?"

"We've been through that before, Martha. You'll go to school when you're old enough."

"Go school," echoed a little voice from behind Virginia. Two-year-old Olivia had joined her older sister. Virginia turned to the child. Of the three children to whom she had given birth, Olivia was most like her father. Virginia couldn't help but smile and shake her head at Olivia, who stood with a rag doll dragging from one pudgy hand, a curl of brown hair hanging over one eye, the permanent mischievous grin on her round baby face. She studied her mother with direct, candid eyes, ready to back her big sister Martha in any argument that might get them both out of the house.

"No," said Virginia, her voice softening as she knelt to hug them both. "Neither of you is going off to school."

Olivia swung her attention back to Martha. Were they to throw a tantrum, cajole further, or let things pass and go back to playing?

But Martha was not ready to give up. "I bet Murphy has been lonesome."

"Murphy is doing just fine." Virginia rose to her feet and tasted the stew for seasoning. It was fine, she decided as she pushed the pot to the back of the stove. It would be ready for supper when the men came in from a long day of working with the horses. But she had to make the biscuits and the pudding for dessert. The clock on the wall alerted her that the baby would soon be waking from his nap and Mindy would soon be home from school.

"Why don't you play with the blocks Papa made you?" she encouraged her two daughters.

"We already did," muttered Martha.

"Then play with the dolly house from Grandpa and Grandma."

"We did that too."

"Would you like—"

"I want to go outside. That's what I'd like."

Olivia nodded in vigorous agreement.

"I understand," said Virginia as she moved to get out a bowl and ingredients for making the pudding. "But we don't always get what we want."

"I know that," replied Martha with an impatient swing of her arm. "But why can't we get what we want . . . sometimes?"

"You do. Sometimes."

"Why can't we *this* time?"

Virginia looked at the clock. It was wrong to give in to Martha's badgering. Yet it was so difficult to be harassed when precious time was slipping away. She had enough on her mind. Supper preparations were pressing on her immediately, she was tired from a long day spent doing family washing, had been up for much of the night with a teething infant, and she sure didn't feel like waging war with a persistent youngster. Yet if she gave in, Martha would think that she could always have her way.

Virginia turned. "Listen to me—carefully," she said firmly. "Mama will be as happy as you are when you are able to go out to play again. But it is still too wet and too cold to go out today. Mindy will soon be home from school, and she can read to you. But for now I want you to find something to do together. And I do not want you to ask about going out again. Do you understand?"

Virginia's eyes moved from the pouting face of Martha to the younger Olivia, who was looking to her older sibling for signals of how she should respond. Olivia's lip came out as she mimicked the face before her. "I want you to be cheerful about it," Virginia added, looking from one small girl to the other. "And, Martha, I want you to be a good example to Olivia."

Martha glanced at her chubby little sister, and her countenance changed. She obviously had lost this round. There was no use wasting further energy and time fussing about it.

"Can we have a cookie?" she said, choosing another approach.

"You may have your milk and cookies when Mindy gets home."

Martha lifted her shoulders and let them fall with an exaggerated shrug. "Then what *can* we do?" she asked, her voice and expression plaintive.

Virginia mentally scrambled for another suggestion, knowing they were as plagued by the weather as she herself. She could not blame them for feeling restless. "How about . . . how about"—she struggled to come up with something—"drawing some pictures for Papa and Slate?"

12

"Yeah," enthused Martha, clapping her hands, with a smile replacing the frown.

"Yeah," echoed Olivia, smacking tiny hands together, her face mirroring the happy grin of her older sister.

Virginia provided the two with paper and crayons and set them up at the kitchen table. "Now, don't write on the table and don't just scribble," she instructed Martha. "Draw a picture on the whole page before you go to another one. Try to color inside the lines."

The girls settled in happily, eager to fill the empty sheets with wonderful crayon scrawls. Virginia turned back to her mixing bowl. The sun was now streaming in the kitchen window. Hopefully tomorrow would be a better day. Mindy would soon be home to entertain her two younger sisters. Perhaps the supper preparations could be completed on time.

She had just placed the pudding in the double boiler when a distant wail drew her attention.

"Jamie's awake," called Martha, as though any person in the house could have missed it.

"Jamie," Olivia chimed in.

Virginia did hope that the baby would not be as irritable this evening as he had been over the past several days. If only that next tooth would make an appearance. It would be a welcome relief to the entire family.

There was no use trying to finish the pudding before getting the baby up. The girls were already climbing down from the table and heading for the stairs. Once Jamie was awake it meant an instant change of activity for the entire household. Reluctantly Virginia pushed the pudding to the back of the stove. She supposed it would be lumpy, but there was nothing she could do about it now. She was glad that neither her husband, Jonathan, nor their nephew Slate were very particular about food. There would be no complaints at the supper table over a few lumps in the evening dessert.

"I think Toby Wallace likes me," eight-year-old Mindy announced to the family gathered around the large kitchen table for the evening meal—lumpy pudding and all.

Virginia noted the twinkle in Jonathan's eyes as he lifted his head to study the freckled face across the table, framed in honey-colored braids over each shoulder.

Baby James, who had been rescued from his high chair because of his fussiness to a place on his father's knee, took advantage of Jonathan's distraction to grab at his dinner plate and nearly dump it in their laps. Jonathan's hand flashed out to avert the disaster, and he moved his body to keep Jamie's hands away from the table. Jamie was offered a piece of bread crust to chew on.

"How can you tell?" Jonathan queried Mindy when he had things under control once again.

"'Cause," said Mindy, tipping her head to one side and giving her father an all-knowing look. "He always looks at me in class and he teases me and he told Paul Conridge that he couldn't sit by me and he even chased me with a grasshopper."

"Sounds about right to me," put in Slate with a chuckle.

"A grasshopper," hollered Martha with no idea what the conversation was all about. "A grasshopper. Did it bite?"

"It was dead, silly," responded Mindy.

"Dead. Yuk."

"Yuk," repeated Olivia, placing a hand over her mouth to keep her mouthful of mashed potatoes from spilling.

Virginia let her gaze sweep around the table. The meal that she had struggled to prepare was being quickly consumed before her very eyes. A little sigh escaped her. If only she could get it to the table in as short a time as it took her family to dispose of it, her task would be much lighter. But then a smile lightened her face. She was blessed. Busy—but blessed. They were all there. Together. Sharing happenings and good-natured bantering and chuckles. All healthy. All loved. Her Jonathan, his hair still damp where he had washed the day's perspiration from his forehead. Slate, Jonathan's young nephew who had come to work with them. Virginia did not know how they would ever have managed without Slate. Their beloved Mindy, almost nine. Jenny's baby, who was one of this family as surely as if she had been born to them. It was easy to forget there ever was a time when Mindy had not been theirs. Martha, their mischievous, boisterous, funny family clown. Olivia, who spent her days watching and mimicking older sisters. Jamie, their usually good-natured little elf, whose incoming teeth had him momentarily cantankerous to the point that he would not even sit in his own high chair.

They were all there. Her family. Her family who filled her days with busyness, her heart with love. She had been blessed. She wouldn't change her lot with anyone in the entire world.

The next morning when the yard still looked muddy, she bundled up her three after Mindy left for school and whisked them off for a visit to her mother in town. It was worth all the effort simply to avoid another argument with a pleading Martha. And Virginia needed to get out herself. Belinda's warm welcome confirmed to her that she had made the right decision.

"Mama had another fall."

But Virginia's sense of reprieve for herself and her children was soon jolted back to reality by her mother's anxious words.

Belinda's solemn tone brought Virginia's head up from unbundling the small Olivia. Belinda was busy removing Jamie's wraps.

"Was she hurt?"

"She struck her cheek. Gave herself a nasty black eye."

Belinda freed Olivia to run to the back bedroom where Martha was already helping herself to Grandma's toy box.

"Is Grandma all right?" Virginia wondered in concern.

Belinda sat Jamie on the floor and offered him a ring of measuring spoons before answering. Virginia saw the troubled look on her mother's face.

"I guess she is. She'll get better . . . again. But it worries me."

Virginia nodded. They had talked of it before. It was not the first time that Grandmother Marty had fallen of late.

"Luke says she just tries to move too quickly. She thinks she still can rush around like a young woman. She doesn't wait to get her balance before she sets off."

That too had been discussed before.

"She shouldn't be alone," Belinda noted as she turned to the stove to heat the teakettle.

Virginia nodded again and pulled out a kitchen chair. They had talked about that many times as well.

"If they weren't so stubborn," Belinda went on, shaking her head. "Mama says that Papa feels much more comfortable in his own home—with his own chair, his own bed. And Papa says that Mama would miss being able to look out the window and see her birds and her garden and the fields. Each is pretending the reason to stay there is for the sake of the other—but they both know better. Neither of them wants to move."

"I can't blame them," put in Virginia. "It is a beautiful place. So . . . so relaxing. And they have been there so long—"

"I don't blame them either," said Belinda with another deep sigh as she lowered herself to a kitchen chair across from Virginia. "But there comes a time when sentiment . . ." She let the rest of the sentence remain unspoken.

Virginia could feel her body begin to tense. She hated these conversations about her grandparents. Why couldn't her mother and the rest of the family just leave them alone? They were doing fine on the farm. Of course, she admitted, they were getting old. Older. Grandpa wasn't quite the same since his stroke. And they had little mishaps . . . that frightened even her. But to even consider . . . It just wouldn't be the same—not for any of them—if Grandpa and Grandma Davis were not there to greet them when they paid a visit to the farm home. Virginia gave herself a little shake. She could not bear to think about it. It was too frightening. It meant that her world was changing. That it might change even more. That her grandparents were old, old. That she might one day need to face the fact of losing them. Virginia would not allow the thought. She couldn't.

"Mindy brought home a great report," she said quickly before her mother could say anything further about her grandparents.

Belinda managed a smile, but it was crooked and did not entirely erase the darkness from her eyes.

"Good. She's sharp."

"Yes, she is. She's a good student. Jonathan says that she has the brains to take her anywhere she wants to go."

Belinda's smile broadened, and she rose to finish making the tea.

Virginia felt herself relax. She had managed to steer the conversation in another direction. But even so she could not get over the feeling of chill that crept through her at the thought of her grandparents and her mother's deep concern.

"Have you heard from Jenny?"

The query from her mother brought further tension to Virginia. This was another topic she wished to avoid, but she did prefer it to the endless debates over her grandparents' situation. At least now her mother's attention would be on something else. Virginia answered softly, "Not a thing."

"It is strange. . . ."

"Well . . . yes . . . and no."

Belinda set the teapot on the table and went for the cups and saucers.

"Jenny has always been—you know—irresponsible. Independent," Virginia tried to explain.

"Yes," sighed her mother. "It's been costly."

For some reason Virginia felt the need to defend her old friend as she had so often in the past, even though in her heart she knew that no one was more caring, more understanding, concerning Jenny than her own mother.

"She had a tough start. Her mother running off when she was so young. Her father's grief driving him to attempt to find solace in drink. Honestly, I sometimes wonder if I could have survived if—"

"That is true," agreed her mother, "but you'd think that would make her even more sensitive toward her own child. A person who has gone through such grief should understand what it can do to another. Jenny should know that deserting Mindy could cause her the same trauma."

"Well, she didn't *really* desert her."

Belinda took her chair at the table, tested the brewing tea, and replaced the cozy. "She would have . . . had not you and Jonathan intervened and taken her. And now . . . all these years and no word from her. I don't understand how anyone—even Jenny—can ignore her own child."

I don't think Jenny thinks of Mindy as her own child. She's ours. Jenny knows that she is well cared for. Actually, I think it's better this way. It would be confusing to Mindy to have Jenny bouncing in and out of her life. Jonathan and I have talked of it. We appreciate the fact that Jenny is wise enough—maybe unselfish enough—to stay out of Mindy's life. It would be more difficult for us if Jenny kept interfering. It's much easier to raise Mindy in our own way."

"You don't think Jenny will ever want her back?"

The words hung in the air between them. Virginia didn't even allow herself to think them, much less express them aloud. She finally answered rather forcefully, "No. Never. She has said that she has no intention of taking on the role of motherhood."

"Has she remarried?"

Virginia tried to calm herself before answering. "I've no idea."

"She was a pretty little thing."

Virginia let her churning thoughts spin back to her girlhood. Yes, Jenny had been a pretty little thing. All flashing green eyes and tossing bright hair. The entire classroom of girls had vied to be her best friend as the boys stood back and ogled or tried, usually in vain, to win her favor through some male exploit. Jenny, the most popular girl in the school, had chosen Virginia as a soul mate. Virginia had never understood it. Not even now. But the friendship had not been without its ups and downs. They had fought almost as much as they'd been buddies. It was usually Virginia who gave in. That too, had been costly, getting her into more than one scrape and causing a great deal of friction with her parents.

Things had changed after Virginia had finally given over her own stubborn will and invited the Lord to take over her life. Then Jenny became a primary concern. Virginia had attempted to save Jenny from a life of destruction and grief, for even in her youth, she could see that her school friend was heading in that direction. But Virginia had failed. Pray as she did, try as she might, she was never able to convince Jenny that her behavior and choices would eventually bring her to harm. Jenny was determined to go her own way. Her way of parties and so-called good times. Of marrying a selfish man. Divorce. Then her ex-husband's tragic accident and death. Nothing . . . nothing in life had seemed to work out for Jenny. But Virginia had never ceased praying. Hoping. Surely God, who loved Jenny more deeply than she herself ever could, would not give up. Her sigh seemed to come from someplace deep within her.

Jamie had lost his rattling measuring spoons, and in the effort to retrieve them tumbled over on the linoleum floor. He rolled harmlessly onto his side and looked up at Virginia with a grin as though to say he had accomplished exactly what he had set out to do. Virginia reached for him, sat him back up, and offered him the spoons again, jingling them temptingly so he would reach for them.

"He is growing so quickly," Belinda remarked from in front of the cupboard where she was arranging cookies from the jar on an old-fashioned flowered china plate. She smiled at her daughter and the small baby.

"Isn't he? And he's been such a good baby. Well . . . when he's not teething, he's good. He's been a little bear over the last few weeks. The tooth finally came through yesterday. I hope it means we'll get more sleep. But I noticed the gum on the other side is swollen. I suppose we'll go through the whole thing all over again."

Belinda nodded and set the cookie plate on the table. "When they are little it's one worry. When they are old it's another."

Virginia's stomach churned. Her mother's attention had not been distracted for long.

"They shouldn't be alone. It's too risky. Having family members drop in is not good enough anymore."

"What about the neighbor lady you made arrangements with?"

"She comes only twice a week to do the washing and cleaning. That's not enough. Anything could happen in between times."

"But Clare's family—"

"They drop by. Check in fairly often. But Mama and Papa need someone with them all the time now. There's simply no one to just move in with them. It's unreasonable to even think of it. Each one of us has our own responsibilities—"

"So what are you suggesting?"

"They need to move. Leave the farm. It's the only thing that can be done."

"But you know how. . . ." Virginia couldn't even say the words. Her whole quivering insides were making her feel ill. "It's not what they want," she finally finished lamely.

"It's not what I want either," Belinda reminded her.

Virginia accepted the teacup from her mother. She wondered if she would be able to drink it.

"Can't you wait, Mama? Just . . . wait . . . and see? They . . . they take care of one another. They—"

"That's just it. They can't take care of one another anymore. Pa is so shaky he spills his soup down his shirt front. And Mama has lost her sense of balance. It's the blind leading the blind now, Virginia. We can't take the chance."

"Just . . . just give them a little more time . . . please, Mama. They . . . they've had that flu that's been going around. They'll . . . Grandma will soon get her strength back again. Just give them a little more time. Please." Tears had gathered in Virginia's eyes as she pleaded for her grandparents. "If we . . . if we make them move, they might just . . . just decide that . . . that their days of usefulness are . . . over. They might . . ." But she couldn't finish that thought either. It was far too painful.

Belinda reached for her hand and squeezed it. For a few moments neither spoke. It was Belinda who broke the silence. "I don't want to be the one with the heavy hand, Virginia. Believe me . . . this is one of the hardest decisions I have ever faced. But no one else wants to make the decision either. I'm afraid we might wait too long and be sorry for it."

Virginia swallowed hard. She reached in her pocket for her hankie and dabbed at her tear-filled eyes. Surely it wouldn't come to that. Surely. She'd pray harder. "Please, Mama," was all she could manage.

Belinda squeezed her hand again, her own cheeks moist with tears. "We'll see," was all she could promise.

CHAPTER 2

$\mathcal{J}$onathan agreed that he could spare some time to watch the children while Virginia made a quick trip to her grandparents' farm under the guise of delivering fresh strawberry jam. James and Olivia were down for afternoon naps, and Martha was more than happy to have her papa all to herself. Virginia was tempted to protest as she watched Jonathan drag some tack into her kitchen and set up to oil a bridle at her kitchen table. But she bit her lip and packaged up the jars of jam in a basket.

"I won't be long," she said for the fifth time.

"Don't rush yourself too much. Slate is working the animals, and I've been looking for time to attend to these bridles."

Virginia grimaced again, kissed both Jonathan and Martha, and hurried out the door to the motorcar.

It was not a long drive to the farm, but Virginia did not enjoy it as she usually did. Other times she savored each silent moment, each breath of summer sun, each expanse of blue sky draping over green fields. But her thoughts were not on the quiet nor the scenery. Her thoughts were on the words of her mother. Surely, surely they would not have to forcefully take her grandparents off the farm they loved. Surely there was another way. They were still able to care for themselves, weren't they? Virginia blinked back tears as she grasped the steering wheel. She would not be content until she saw for herself how things were with her grandparents.

She was walking up the rock-hard dirt path that led to the fenced yard and the house when the door opened. Her grandmother stood there, silver hair reflecting the afternoon sun. A smile shone from her face, and one hand held the door wide open as though she couldn't wait for Virginia to reach her.

She'll be letting in the flies, Virginia thought and hastened her step. Her grandmother had always detested flies in her kitchen. Pesky, filthy things, she called them. Virginia almost ran up the walk.

"Now, isn't this an unexpected blessing?" greeted Marty. "Said to Pa jest this mornin' we hadn't seen ya fer a spell."

Virginia smiled, carefully concealing her concern at the bruise still visible under her grandmother's eye. "Yes," she said, "it has been a while. I've been busy with all the little ones—"

"Yer all alone? How'd ya manage thet?"

Virginia placed a kiss on her grandmother's wrinkled cheek and received a moist one in return. "Jonathan is working inside while the babies nap."

"I'm sorry ya didn't bring 'em. They grow so fast. Last Sunday I says to Pa, 'Jest look at thet little Martha. Growing like a weed. An' Olivie jest a chasin' her.'"

Virginia smiled again. It was only her grandmother who called the young child Olivie.

"Bring her in. Bring her in" came a call from inside the house. "Don't stand there a-hoggin' her to yerself."

Her grandfather's voice held a tone of lighthearted teasing. Marty began to chuckle and moved Virginia from the porch into the kitchen. Virginia noticed at least two flies sneak in with them.

Clark sat smiling at them from his favorite chair in a corner of the room. He did not rise to meet her as he had always

24

done, and Virginia felt a knot somewhere deep inside. Was her grandfather ill?

"S'cuse me for not gittin' up," he apologized. There was still a twinkle in the faded blue eyes.

Virginia placed the jam on the cupboard counter and crossed to where he sat. She kissed his brow and let her arm linger around his stooped shoulders. "Aren't you feeling up to snuff?" she asked, borrowing one of his own expressions.

"Fine. Jest fine. Jest lazy, thet's all. Body gits lazy jest sittin' around. I should be out hoein' corn. Then I'd have a bit more spunk."

Virginia patted his shoulder.

"We're both of us gittin' lazy," her grandmother put in. "Neither of us much good fer hoein' corn anymore." She chuckled as though the thought was a good joke on the rest of the world. "But sit ya down," she hurried on. "I'll fix us some tea."

She spun on her heel to head for the cupboard, and Virginia saw her teeter, then put out a hand on the back of a chair to steady herself. *Yes*, thought Virginia with another tightening of her stomach muscles. *I can see why she falls. Uncle Luke is right. She darts around like she was still a young woman.*

"There's no hurry, Grandma," she found herself saying as she moved toward her grandmother. "Jonathan said I'd have time for tea. Just . . . just . . ." She wanted to say, just slow down. Take your time. Catch your balance before you take off on a near run.

Her grandfather said it for her. "Yer grandma—she doesn't know how to slow down. I keep tellin' her to take her time, but she jest gallops everywhere she goes. She's too used to havin' to run to git everything done—an' now thet there's nothin' to do, she can't break the habit."

"Listen to him talk," Marty said, but Virginia noticed that she was grinning. "You who always insisted on runnin' round this farm on one leg an' a hobble stick. If I learnt to run, I 'spect I learnt it from you."

Virginia heard her grandfather's chuckle. She looked his way to see him smiling broadly. "We got nothin' better to do anymore than to try to git a raise outta one another. Be pretty dull around here iffen we didn't. Yer Grandma—she keeps things lively."

Marty changed the subject with, "Did ya see this, Pa? Fresh strawberry jam. My—I miss the cannin'. Not the work of it, mind ya. Jest the taste of it. Nothin' like fresh strawberry jam. How 'bout let's have some? I'll make up some biscuits."

Seeming to anticipate Virginia's protest over the work of making biscuits, she hurried to add, "Won't take but a few minutes. I still do make biscuits. Nearly every day."

"An' ain't nobody makes better biscuits than yer grandma," put in Clark.

Virginia had always loved her grandmother's baking powder biscuits. Had even attempted to copy down her recipe and learn her method, but the ones she drew from her oven were never quite the same.

"Did I ever tell ya about her first biscuits?" her grandfather went on, chuckling as he spoke. "Well . . . they weren't much like she makes now, I can tell ya that."

"My first ones," Marty called from the pantry. "Ya didn't even git to try my first ones. I throwed them out. Dog wouldn't even eat 'em."

They were both laughing now and Virginia felt free to join in.

"Ah, memories," said Marty, sobering as she moved to the kitchen table, arms laden with biscuit ingredients. "So many, many memories."

"An' good ones too," added Clark. Virginia watched as he removed his spectacles and wiped them on the checkered handkerchief from his pocket. There were tears glistening in the corners of his eyes. She found herself fighting back her own tears.

"I jest hope thet when yer life settles to a more serene

pace, thet you and thet fine man of yers will have as many good memories as yer grandmother and me," Clark went on, his voice quivery with emotion. "Treasure 'em. The days when yer young and spry—an' hardworkin'." He chuckled again as he added the last words. "Ya don't really have time to treasure 'em when yer rushin' about. But at least set 'em down as memories so thet ya can pull 'em out an' treasure 'em later."

Marty, measuring flour into her favorite blue mixing bowl, nodded her head in agreement. "Memories are good things," she said. "I take mine out every day. Like a . . . like a string of pearls . . . almost. An' I count 'em an' work 'em through my . . . well, not my fingers . . . but my mind an' heart. They're good things . . . memories. When God blesses ya with a good life, then ya got good memories."

Virginia nodded. She'd try to remember the words. In spite of her busy days that left her exhausted by the time the sun retired and soft darkness engulfed them, she'd try.

"Now while I fix these here biscuits, ya sit on down and bring us up-to-date on everything," Marty invited.

Virginia did not realize until that moment that she still had not taken a kitchen chair. She had stood poised beside her grandmother, ready to catch her should she move too quickly and need assistance. She felt warmth flush her cheeks and quickly moved to a chair at the table.

"Well, things are pretty much the same as always," she began. "Jonathan and Slate fill their days with working horses and doing chores."

"An' fine horses they are too," her grandfather put in.

"Martha and Olivia got a mite restless being cooped up in the rain."

"Wasn't thet some rain?" said Marty, shaping biscuits for the baking pan. She wiped the flour from her hands onto her apron. "Clare's boys said we needed it."

"I suppose we did," agreed Virginia, "though I'd begun to think it was never going to stop."

"Always stops. Always stops," said her grandfather. "God's never forgot to shut off the tap yet."

Virginia smiled.

"I bet you was as anxious as the younguns to have it over with so thet they could git out," said her grandmother knowingly.

Virginia's smile broadened. "You can just bet I was," she agreed.

"I often think thet things didn't git balanced too well. There are days I long so to have my little ones back so's I could enjoy 'em. When they was here I was jest too busy to do the things I woulda liked to have done. But o' course, iffen they was back—all thet work would come along with 'em an' I wouldn't git to have the time to enjoy 'em any more than I did at the time."

Clark snorted playfully from his corner chair. "Yer grandma talks in riddles. Half the time I need to sort through what she's sayin' 'fore I can make the least bit of sense of it."

"I understand—perfectly," replied Virginia stoutly.

"Guess it's a woman thing, then," laughed Clark. "Sure don't add up to a full column fer me."

The teakettle began to hum. Marty, who had placed the biscuits in the oven and taken a chair beside Virginia at the table, rose quickly—much too quickly—from her chair and went to fix the tea. Virginia held her breath as she watched her stagger, then reclaim her balance.

"Slow down, old woman."

Virginia heard the love and concern in her grandfather's voice, but Marty did not even change her stride. Without looking toward him, she answered with a light tone, "Hush, old man. Don't you be policin' me from yer easy chair."

But you must, Grandma. You must, Virginia longed to say. *You could fall again. And the next one might be more serious than the others have been. Don't you know? Don't you understand that you are on the verge of losing your home? Your snug, cheery kitchen with the kettle singing and the biscuits filling the room with fresh-*

baked aroma? Grandpa's corner chair easily accessible to the kitchen table. Your combination living-room-bedroom so you no longer need to climb stairs. All the familiar things that bring to you those memories you spoke of. Please—please slow down. But she couldn't say the words aloud.

She forced her attention back to her grandfather and managed to converse about everyday happenings, one ear attuned to her grandmother's footsteps and one eye watching her unsteady movements. At length Marty removed the golden brown biscuits from the oven and set them on the back of the stove. She moved to pick up the plate she had taken from the cupboard in preparation for their readiness. "Jest git the cream from the pantry, Virginia. Pa still likes a little in his tea."

Virginia arose to do as bidden. "Bring out the butter too," called her grandmother after her. "It's in thet yella dish with the cover."

By the time Virginia returned with the cream and butter, Marty was placing the biscuits and the teapot on the table. A shuffling noise to her left drew her attention. It was her grandfather pushing his way up from his chair. Virginia watched as he heaved, his once strong arms now straining with the effort of lifting up his body. His face was contorted by the effort the simple task was demanding. It took three attempts before he was able to gain a rather stooped standing position.

How long has he been like this? Virginia found herself wondering. His arms had always been so strong. So muscular. He had learned to make do with the strength of his arms what most men did with the strength of two sturdy legs.

He carefully lowered himself to the kitchen chair, and the look of serious intent left his face as he smiled her way again. "Mindy still likin' school?"

The question caught Virginia off guard, but she quickly regained her concentration and answered evenly, "She loves it. Mindy is a good student. Brought home a real good report the other day."

"Strawberry jam—fresh," her grandmother was saying as she crossed to the table with jar in hand. "Now, Pa, ya savor every mouthful of this. Here—could ya open it fer me, please?"

She passed the jar to Clark. It wasn't until then that Virginia noticed how shaky his hands had become. He took the offered jar and attempted to open the lid, but it was plain to see that the strength had gone from the once powerful wrists.

"I 'spect yer gonna have to stick it in some hot water fer a spell," he said after several attempts to open the jar.

"I'll do it," offered Virginia quickly. Taking the jar from him, she moved toward the stove for the kettle. With her back turned to the table, she deftly opened the jar on her way but managed to stall a bit, hoping they would think the hot water was needed.

But it was not really the jar that detained her. It was her emotions. Fight them as she would, it was true what her mother had said. Her grandparents were getting old. Old. She couldn't bear the thought. They had always been there. Always in their sunny kitchen. Sitting around the worn table where many years of meals had been served to hungry offspring and unnumbered guests. They had always offered their little bits of gathered wisdom in a homey, caring way. She always left with a fresh outlook on life. On living. On faith. Whatever would she do? How could life go on without them here? It wouldn't be the same. Not the same at all.

———

"How were your grandparents?"

Jonathan asked the question casually when Virginia entered her own kitchen. She wasn't sure how to answer—or even if she could answer. She had battled with the question herself all the way home. How were they? Really? Was there need for concern? She had gone to visit them today to prove to herself that her mother was wrong. That they were just fine. That they would still be fine for many years of living on their own. Her mother's nursing background made her simply too protective. But she'd had to ask herself if her mother was right. Were they in danger if they continued on their own?

Virginia certainly did not wish to endanger them any more than her mother, but her whole being rebelled against the idea that her grandparents were so old and feeble as to no longer be able to care for themselves. It was just too difficult to accept. To admit that would mean having to face the truth that the day might come when she would need to relinquish them. Virginia could not even think about a world without one or the other of her grandparents. It was too painful. Too frightening. They had been her rock, her mooring. She needed them.

Now she thought carefully before answering Jonathan's question.

"They were pleased about the fresh jam," she said evasively.

"Good."

"The children are still sleeping?"

"Not a peep." Jonathan gave a little wave of his hand toward small Martha, who insisted upon holding a rein to the bridle that he worked on as her share of the task. "Except this one. Not a quiet minute from this one. She chatters nonstop." He grinned.

"I'm helping Papa," said Martha seriously. "I keep the weins from hanging on the floor."

"Reins," corrected Jonathan good-naturedly.

"Reins," echoed Martha with great concentration. Martha often had trouble with the sound of *r*, transposing it to the twenty-third letter of the alphabet.

"That's nice you've helped Papa." Virginia placed the now empty basket that had transported the strawberry jam on the nearby cupboard. She winced as she looked at her kitchen table, spread with bridles, reins, and the oil that Jonathan was using to thoroughly work the leather. She was glad for lye soap and hot water.

"Papa says I'm a good helper," Martha said, clearly wanting further recognition for a job well done.

"I'm sure you are," smiled Virginia as she looked at the small figure proudly holding the leather thong. Jonathan reached out a hand and tousled the hair of the child. Virginia winced again, hoping that his hand had not transferred oil to her head. *Treasure the moments*, her heart whispered. *If you don't learn to treasure the moments, you'll never be able to treasure the memories*. Her lesson of the day from her grandparents. Her aging grandparents.

A tear threatened to form, but Virginia determinedly blinked it back. Her grandparents may indeed be getting old. True. But they still knew much about life. They still could teach, could exemplify lifelong values, and seemed to manage to do so with every breath they took. Virginia could not resist the urge to fight against the inevitable. Someday . . . someday they would have to face losing them. But not yet. Surely not yet. They needed them . . . so much. They all really needed them.

———

"Mindy has her eye on that young sorrel mare."

"Mindy has her eye on each and every horse in the pasture," replied Virginia, removing her apron and tossing it on the chair by the bed. She was tired. It had been another long day of many tasks. Her bed looked most inviting. She could hardly wait to lay her head on the pillow.

"No," said Jonathan. "This is different. She really loves this horse."

"Yes?" prompted Virginia, wondering where this conversation was leading.

"I've talked to Slate. He's the one who's worked with the

little filly most. He says he thinks she will make a good horse."

"They all make good horses," replied Virginia, slipping out of her shoes.

Jonathan's back was to her as he removed his soiled work shirt and tossed it in a corner. "Slate says this one has a very gentle disposition. Tries her best to please."

Virginia straightened from removing her stockings and looked toward her husband. "Are you saying that you are thinking of giving the filly to the child?"

Jonathan turned toward her. "Thinking of it."

"She's awfully young for her own horse."

"Now, Virginia. You know Mindy's been around horses ever since . . ." He stopped. Virginia wondered if Jonathan, on one of the rare occasions of remembering, was recalling that Mindy had not always been theirs. That she had come to them through circumstances that at the time had brought pain. Jenny's child. Jenny. Where was Jenny? And how was she? They had not heard from her for ages.

"She can handle a horse very well," Jonathan went on.

"She's only ridden the well-broken horses," Virginia reminded him.

He swung fully to meet her, his eyes reaching out to lock with her own. "And this one will be well broken before she is given over. You can count on that. I'd never put a child on a horse that might spook."

Virginia knew that to be true. Jonathan might love his horses, but he loved his children even more. He would never jeopardize their safety.

"I know," she nodded. "I'm sorry if I sounded . . . anxious."

He smiled. "I knew it was the mother speaking."

They finished their preparations for retiring in silence, then knelt for their prayer time together. It wasn't until they were tucked between the cool sheets that Jonathan spoke again. "Mindy has another birthday coming up soon. I thought the little mare might make a nice birthday gift."

So that's where this is going, thought Virginia, but she made no comment.

"Slate says he can have her ready by then. She's coming along real nice. Be fun to see our daughter's eyes."

Yes, it would be fun to see Mindy's eyes, Virginia agreed silently. The girl would be so thrilled. She loved the horses. But a child of nine? Was she ready? They were not speaking of old, plodding farm animals. They were talking of a high-spirited horse.

When Virginia did not speak, Jonathan asked, "Is it okay with you? Are you comfortable with that?"

In the darkness Virginia's eyes narrowed. She was not sure. If Mindy had her own horse, she would feel much more inclined to ride. Everywhere. At every opportunity. They would lose a bit of their control of her life. Were they ready for that? Was she responsible enough to be trusted with such liberty?

Even as she fought against it, Virginia knew she must let go. She could not always keep her children tethered to her apron string. Little by little she had to learn to release them. A wave of fear, followed by resignation, swept through her body, but she said quietly, "If you are sure."

Jonathan sounded pleased as he answered with one word, "Good." He turned to kiss her good-night, then lay back on his pillow with a contented sigh. "You know," he said with satisfaction filling his voice, "they are really growing up—our little ones. Before we know it, they'll be off on their own."

That was hardly the thing to say to Virginia in her present state of mind. Her grandparents. Now her children. . . .

CHAPTER 3

$\mathcal{V}$irginia decided to make the most of the upcoming birthday celebration and invited all the grandparents and as many of her family members as could accept the invitation to the dinner party. The birthday was to be celebrated on a Saturday afternoon, which didn't seem to make much difference to Mindy. They weren't sure of the exact birth date anyway.

I wish Jenny would contact us, Virginia found herself fretting as she basted the turkey and returned it to the oven. *It isn't right that this child is growing up not even knowing her own birth date.*

But Jenny had not been in touch. Not for years. Virginia alternately felt concern, anger, fear. Was Jenny okay? Or was she just too busy with life—whatever it was that her life held now? *Maybe she has married again*, thought Virginia. That would not be unthinkable. In spite of her faded condition and her loss of bloom, Jenny was still an attractive woman in her own way. Perhaps with her errant husband gone, Jenny had even managed to recover some of the old vitality.

But Virginia did not have long to dwell upon her troubling thoughts. There was much to be done before the birthday guests began to arrive.

"Mindy, could you set the tables, dear?" she asked the girl who came bouncing into the room, then quickly added,

"I know it's your party and I hate to make you help, but I'm afraid—"

"I don't mind," enthused Mindy, too excited about the coming celebration to mind much of anything.

Virginia was relieved for the extra pair of hands. Once the tables had been set, Mindy asked for the next task that she might do. Soon they were working side by side. *My, she is growing up*, thought Virginia as she watched her oldest. *I hadn't even realized how much I depend upon her help.*

When the first motor was heard coming down the lane, a loud cheer went up from excited children. Mindy and Martha both ran to the door, and Olivia, who always watched them closely to learn how she should respond to each event in her world, took her cue from their actions and began to clap her hands and cheer along with them, trailing along behind as fast as her little legs could carry her.

"It's Grandpa Woods," shouted Mindy back over her shoulder.

"Gwampa Woods," echoed Olivia, turning to wave an excited hand at Virginia.

"Bring him in," advised Virginia, busy mashing the potatoes in her largest cooking pot.

Before the children could even usher in Jenny's father, another car was pulling into the driveway with Virginia's parents, along with her grandparents in the backseat.

"Look," Virginia heard Martha shout. "The other grandpas and grandmas."

It sounded like joyful bedlam in the yard outside. Virginia pushed back the potato pot, wiped her hands on her apron, and went out to greet the family members. Mindy was busy accepting birthday hugs along with congratulations, and Martha was getting hugs just because, and Olivia, who would not as yet stand still for hugs, was jumping up and down, then twirling round and round in her effort to express her excitement. And in the middle of it all was a tail-wagging Murphy, apparently as pleased as his small owners to be honored by so many guests all at one time. He bounced around the cluster of people, swiping a moist tongue at any hand that for a moment was exposed to his generous welcome, tail whipping back and forth, ears flipping with each muffled whine that came from his throat.

Virginia pushed him aside so she might receive and give a few hugs of her own. "Come in. Come in," she managed to say over the din. The clump of merry humanity moved toward the wide porch, and Murphy fell back, his tail still wagging but his eyes saying he was terribly disappointed that they had decided to take the party inside.

Before following her guests, Virginia turned toward the barn. She was about to request that Mindy run on down to call Jonathan and Slate when she saw the two moving quickly toward the house. Virginia stopped and waited for them. When they were near enough, she called softly, "I was about to send Mindy to tell you the folks have arrived."

Jonathan laughed. "I expect the folks in the next county will know that fact," he called back. "Never heard such a commotion."

Slate was grinning.

"Clara's aren't here yet," Virginia went on unnecessarily. If she would have stopped to think about it, she would have realized that Jonathan would be well aware of who was there and who wasn't. He knew the sound of every motorcar in the area.

"Nor Francine. I'm not sure whether she will be here or not. She wasn't too definite. She said Dalton may have other plans for the day."

Jonathan just nodded. Virginia often was impatient with her younger sister, Francine, and her steady beau, Dalton Chambers. She knew now was not the time to discuss the merits of this relationship.

They had hardly entered the house when they heard another vehicle pull into the driveway. Virginia cast a glance out the kitchen window expecting to see her older sister Clara and her little family, but she saw that it was Francine and Dalton instead. *So they did come*, she said to herself. *Guess Dalton must have run out of things to do.*

Quickly she chastised herself. That was not fair—nor was it charitable. Nor would it enhance the atmosphere of Mindy's party. She went to welcome her younger sister and her friend.

Dinner was waiting to be served and children were beginning to tire of the wait when Troy and Clara finally arrived.

"I'm so sorry to keep everyone waiting," were Clara's first words. "We had—well, we had a bit of an accident."

She may have dropped the subject right there, but everyone in the room was family and no one was willing to let it go without full details. It seemed that the boys had been playing ball and a window had been broken. Anthony, being the oldest, had assumed the responsibility of cleaning up the shards of glass and in the process had cut a finger. He had tried on his own to wrap the bleeding finger with a piece of cloth from his mother's rag bag. Clara had discovered the boy cowering in his room when she trailed drops of blood that had appeared on her linoleum floor. The finger had required four stitches, and Uncle Luke had combined a doctor's and an uncle's sermonette as he stitched it up.

"It's good to be brave," he reportedly had told the young boy. "It's good to take responsibility for mistakes we make. But sometimes it is not wise to try to handle it all yourself. Sometimes we need to tell our parents. Or our teacher. Or the minister. Someone . . . big. Someone who knows what should be done about the situation." Clara finished the matter-of-fact recounting of the incident with her arm lightly around her son's shoulders.

Anthony still looked a bit pale to Virginia's thinking. She noticed that he carried the bandaged finger deep within his pants pocket. He seemed embarrassed by the whole episode.

They were soon seated around the ample tables enjoying the feast that Virginia had worked so hard to prepare. The children behaved admirably. Even baby James spooned in his mashed potatoes without getting too much on the floor. His hand was more help than his spoon, however, and Virginia knew that he'd need a good washing once the meal had ended. Thankfully he was in between cutting new teeth and was good-natured and enjoying all of the hubbub.

As the last piece of birthday cake was served with home-made ice cream, Jonathan managed to catch Virginia's attention. "Do you want to clean up before Mindy gets her presents?"

Virginia knew he was anxious to share his surprise. She shook her head in answer. "I guess we don't need to make her wait," she responded with a smile. She wondered if it was Mindy who would suffer—or Jonathan—if she decided to wait. He looked relieved.

As soon as the guests began to push back their chairs, Jonathan rose and held up a hand. "I think it's time for the birthday girl to open her gifts."

Mindy began to eagerly squirm on her seat.

"Let's just clear a spot on the table in front of her," Jonathan went on. Virginia had her lap full with the now sleepy James, and Francine jumped up to remove the dishes.

The parcels were then placed in front of Mindy. With a flushed face she looked toward Virginia for permission to begin. Virginia nodded. Martha crowded in close to Mindy's elbow, as anxious to see what the packages contained as Mindy herself. Olivia pressed against the other side, her little face just barely able to peek over the tabletop to observe the proceedings. Virginia guessed she was standing on her tiptoes.

The first present was from Grandpa Clark and Grandma Marty. A new hand-knit sweater. Virginia's eyes lifted to her mother's face. *See*, she wanted to say, *she is still able to do things for herself*. Mindy "oohed" over the sweater and pronounced it her favorite color.

Francine's gift was next. The package was very small, and

Mindy's hands fairly trembled in her excitement as she opened it. It was a cameo. Elegant and expensive looking. Virginia's breath caught in her throat. Francine had been the one family member who never seemed to forget that Mindy was Jenny's child. Virginia had often wondered if her sister had ever really accepted Mindy as a niece. But the cameo was beautiful. Virginia blinked back tears.

Mindy expressed her warm thanks, accompanied by an even warmer hug, and Francine's eyes became a bit misty.

Mindy moved to open the gift from her grandfather Woods. It was a desk set. "If you're going to learn to help your ole granddaddy with the newspaper business, you need to start getting some ink on your fingers," he teased. Mindy beamed, then turned to another parcel.

Out of the corner of her eye, Virginia saw Jonathan shift on his chair. He was impatient for the girl to get to his surprise. But Mindy was taking her time, savoring each moment of unwrapping her birthday delights.

Martha was not always so patient and now and then reached out a helping hand to tear back some wrap to expose the gift more quickly. Mindy seemed to understand. "Hurry up," Martha prompted on one occasion and was echoed by Olivia, "Hu'wy up."

At last the final package was disclosed. On the table before Mindy were all the new treasures. Beside her on the kitchen floor were remains of the wrappings. A wide smile played across the young girl's face. "This is my best birthday ever," she exclaimed.

"But wait," said Jonathan, standing up, a pretend frown on his face. "There seems to be something missing."

Mindy looked up in surprise, then back at her display of gifts again. *What could possibly be missing?* her eyes seemed to ask.

"I don't see any gift from your ma and pa. Nor Slate. Slate—didn't you get the birthday girl anything?"

Slate scratched his head. "Now . . . how could I have forgotten that?" he replied, as though deeply perplexed.

But Mindy was taking the little charade seriously. "It's all right, Papa," she was quick to encourage him. "I don't need anything more." Her arms went out to encircle what she already had. "I've got lots of nice things."

But Jonathan looked again to Slate. "Do you suppose we might be able to find her something?"

Slate stood up. "I'll take a look around," he said and reached for his hat. "Seems to me that I saw somethin' down in the barn with her name on it."

Jonathan's grin nearly split his face. "Check it out," he said with a nod toward the door.

Everyone in the room appeared to be enjoying the little game—except Mindy. She looked totally puzzled by it all.

Jonathan turned to her. "I think your mama would give you permission to change from your pretty birthday dress to one of your play outfits," he prompted. "Why don't you run do that?"

Mindy looked again to Virginia. Her mother nodded. Still with a puzzled look, Mindy went to change her attire.

"I smell a surprise coming," Clark whispered loudly as soon as the girl had left the room.

Jonathan just kept smiling. "Let's all move out to the porch. Slate should be back shortly."

Even though the porch was roomy, the group filled it to overflowing. Chairs were placed for Clark and Marty at the front so they would miss nothing. Drew and Belinda helped them to make the short walk and be seated. Just as the milling crowd settled itself, the barn door opened and Slate moved out, two horses moving obediently behind him. Both animals were saddled and bridled, ready for riding. At his command they stopped and waited for him to reclose the door. Then he turned and mounted the black, picking up the reins to the sorrel. Virginia spotted the bright red ribbon that decorated the smaller horse's mane. The saddle was also bedecked. In big black letters on bright white paper it declared,

Happy Birthday, Mindy! In spite of her hesitation in agreeing to the plan, Virginia felt her heart pounding in anticipation of Mindy's delight.

Mindy would be so thrilled to have her own horse.

They did not need to wait for long. Slate just barely had time to position the horse beside the front porch, red ribbon and birthday greeting showing, when Mindy hurried out to join them on the porch, still frowning over her strange orders.

She was gently nudged forward. But it was Martha who could not wait. "Look, Mindy," she squealed. "It's a horse."

Mindy stood transfixed, her eyes traveling over the entire length of the sorrel. She did not seem to be able to believe what she was seeing. "Do I get to ride her?" she finally managed to say.

Jonathan, whose arm had not left the small child's shoulders, beamed down upon her. "As much as you like," he said. "She's all yours."

"Mine?"

The girl still did not appear to understand.

"Yours."

"My very own?"

"Your very own."

"To keep?"

Jonathan began to laugh, a strange-sounding laugh. Virginia wondered if his throat was as tight as her own. He pulled the little girl close to his chest as he knelt down on the porch boards. "She is yours, Mindy. Yours. To keep. Always."

The child threw her arms around her father's neck and burst into tears. It was hardly what Jonathan or any or them had expected. He held her while an emotional family looked on, and Slate shuffled his feet and cleared his throat as he toyed with the leather reins.

At last Mindy lifted her tearstained face. Her chin was still wobbly, but she managed a smile. "You are the best papa in the whole wide world," she said, and she leaned over to kiss his cheek. It was almost too much for Jonathan. He pulled the little girl back into his arms and held her while he fought for composure. That was too much for Virginia. She buried her face against small James and wept silently. But no one was paying much mind. They were all too busy wiping their own tears.

"Well, now," said Jonathan at last. "Are you gonna ride this here horse of yours—or just look at her?"

Mindy smiled her answer.

"Come, then. I'll boost you up."

From her place in the saddle, Mindy beamed at her gathered family. She was too happy to even speak.

"Now, the horse and bridle are from your mama and me, but the saddle—that's from Slate," said Jonathan as he passed her the reins.

Mindy turned her eyes to Slate. "Thank you, Slate. I like it—I love it."

The young man looked pleased but also a bit embarrassed.

"You're ready now?" asked Jonathan, giving the horse's neck a pat. Virginia was relieved to see that the animal had stood quietly through all the commotion. It did appear that Jonathan had been right. Slate did have the animal ready for a young rider. Mindy gathered up the reins and urged the horse forward. She responded without question. Virginia felt further relief as Slate moved his mount beside the young girl. He would accompany her on the maiden excursion. Perhaps Virginia's mother-heart could relax and she could start breathing again.

They stood and watched the two riders until they disappeared behind the trees of the lane; then one by one the group began to filter back into the house. There was still the cleaning up to be done. Virginia, who felt suddenly drained and tired, was glad for many helping hands.

"It was a good birthday, don't you think?" Jonathan expressed when they were finally retiring for the night. Virginia could only nod her agreement. It had been a good birthday.

Mindy was still too excited to settle down even as she was tucked into bed for the night. Virginia was thankful that the morrow was Sunday. That Mindy would not need to be awakened early to prepare for a day of school.

"Slate said she handled the horse like an expert."

Virginia smiled. "She is your daughter. What did you expect?"

Jonathan chuckled, looking pleased with her comment.

"And the horse responded to every command she gave," Jonathan went on.

"Slate does a good job."

"Slate does an excellent job. Boy, did we luck out when we got that boy."

Virginia smiled. "I was just thinking as I looked at him today. He's not such a boy anymore, Jonathan. He's grown up. Right before our eyes . . . he's grown up."

Jonathan seemed stilled by the thought. "Reckon you're right," he said at length.

"Won't be long until he'll be wanting a place of his own. What will we do then?"

His hand stopped on the way to removing a sock. "Don't rightly know," he said a last. "I've never thought on it, I guess."

"Well, seems to me that we're going to have to think about it one of these days," responded Virginia. "It's going to come all too soon."

The observation put them both in a pensive mood as they continued to prepare for bed. Another looming change.

———

"Mama . . . I can't sleep."

Virginia managed to open her eyes. Mindy stood by her bed, one hand clutching a well-worn rag doll. It had been some time since the little girl had brought the doll to the bed-side.

"What is it?" asked Virginia sleepily. The room was lit by

a full moon that cast soft yellowy light upon the child's features. Virginia saw the girl's chin tremble.

"Are you sick?" asked Virginia, a hand going out to feel the child's cheek.

"No," replied a trembling voice.

"What's the matter?"

"Can . . . can you get up so we won't bother Papa?"

Virginia threw back the blankets. "Of course."

With one arm about the little girl's shoulders, she ushered her from the room. "Can we go downstairs?" Mindy was asking as Virginia gently eased the door closed behind them.

Virginia felt panic. Something was wrong. Mindy had never made such strange requests. "Let me light a lamp," she responded. "It's too dark on the steps."

She retrieved a lamp from the girls' room and watched as the small flame grew into a light that would guide their way. All the way down the stairs her mind kept wrestling. *What is wrong with the child? Why this strange request in the middle of the night?*

When they reached the living room she put the lamp on a small table and pulled the little girl to her side. She eased them both onto the couch and hugged the trembling child close, one hand fingering the hair of the head that rested just beneath her chin. "What is it, honey? What's troubling you?"

Then a sudden thought buzzed through Virginia's mind. "Is it your new horse?"

"Sort of" came a shaky whisper.

Virginia was silent. Why was the gift troubling Mindy? She had always loved animals.

"Don't you like her?"

"I love her." The little girl was crying. Softly. Up against her mother's breast.

Silence again.

"Is there another horse you like better?"

"No."

"Then what is it?"

It took Mindy a while to gather enough control to answer. "I need to pray," she finally managed.

"Pray?" The answer caught Virginia by surprise.

Mindy's tears increased. Virginia felt the child's head bobbing up against her in her reply of yes.

When she could finally speak, the child pushed back and looked up into her mother's face. "I asked God for a horse," she disclosed. "A little while ago. But I didn't get it. So I told God . . . I told Him that I didn't believe that He really . . . is. That I didn't believe He could do good things . . . that I didn't believe His Book. That the stories were all just . . . made up. I even told Him that . . . that I didn't like Him. I told Him that I didn't want to be His girl." The last came out in a rush of tears and the weeping of a broken heart.

Virginia held her close for a long time. Her own thoughts were busy. What if she had insisted that Mindy was not ready for the horse? What if?

"And now?" Virginia prompted when Mindy seemed to have control again.

"I do want to be His girl, Mama. Honest. So now I need to say I'm sorry," the child sobbed.

"Yes . . . yes I think you do. We all—at one time or another—need to tell God we're sorry. When we doubt Him. When we realize we haven't believed that He is really who He says He is. When we refuse to accept His Word. I had to ask God to forgive me too."

"You did?"

"I did."

"When you were a little girl?"

"I was older than you. I thought that I knew better than God how my life should be lived. I thought I knew better than my folks too. But then I realized God was right. That my own way was wrong. Selfish. Willful. I had to admit to God that I was disobedient. Disobedience—doubt—that's what we call sin. I had to ask God to forgive me."

"Did He? Did He forgive you?"

"Oh, yes. He did. Just like He says in His Word. He always forgives the repentant heart. He always hears us when we say wc're sorry."

"Can we pray? Now?"

Virginia kissed her child and hugged her closer. "We can. And we will . . . but first . . . first I think that I'd like to go get your father. I think this is one prayer he wouldn't want to miss."

CHAPTER 4

$\mathcal{V}$irginia didn't think the name Buttercup suited the horse at all and wondered where Mindy had ever gotten the idea that a yellow flower was fitting for a sorrel, but no one protested. Olivia had a difficult time with the name, and after her childish tongue tripped over it several times, she settled on Bubba. Virginia smiled, and Mindy, after attempting a few corrections, good-naturedly accepted Bubba as the pet name for her beloved mount.

Over the days and weeks that followed, Virginia detected subtle changes in their oldest. She wasn't sure if they came simply from the birthday and another year of age, the horse, or the fact that Mindy had prayed her prayer of forgiveness and now was consciously thinking about her relationship with God. It both sobered and thrilled Virginia. Their little girl was growing up. She was now accepting responsibility in a new way. She was more patient with the younger ones. She appeared cheerful, settled, and content in some unexplainable way. A real joy to have in the household.

Mindy loved her Buttercup and rode and groomed her whenever she had opportunity. After the first few heart-wrenching times of solo ventures, Virginia was able to relax. Mindy did not go far and rode with good judgment—not pressing her horse to do anything like jumping fallen logs or wading swollen streams. Jonathan or Slate went with her whenever it was possible, tucking either Martha or Olivia into their arms on the front of the saddle.

But Mindy's captivation with her new horse did not interfere with her household chores. Virginia did not need to prod or scold with directives to do the chores first. She was thankful for this additional signal of Mindy's growing maturity and right choices.

"You know," said Mindy one night as they worked together doing up the supper dishes, "Buttercup is one of the best things to happen to me. I think"—she paused a moment—"about sixth best."

"Really?" said Virginia, wondering how Buttercup had managed to come in that low in her priorities.

"I was thinking about it last night after I went to bed," Mindy explained. "It's kinda hard to sort it all out but . . . I think I got my list figured out now."

"You have a list?"

Mindy nodded. "The very best thing is asking God to forgive me and letting Jesus into my life."

Virginia wiped her hands on her apron so she could give her daughter a hug and a whispered "I'm so glad, dear."

"The next best is being born—because if I wasn't even born . . ." She shrugged as if that should be self-explanatory. Virginia smiled. "The next is coming to live with you and Papa. 'Cause if I didn't come here—" She broke off, then finished lamely, "I was sad before."

"You remember?" Virginia was surprised. Mindy had never spoken of her life before she came to live with them as a tiny little girl of three.

Mindy shook her head. "Not much . . . I just know I was sad. I'm not sad anymore."

This time Virginia disregarded her dishwater wet hands and reached out again to draw Mindy close. She kissed the top of her head. "Oh, Mindy," she said, her voice choked.

But Mindy was anxious to continue her list. "Then . . ." she said, and Virginia released her. "Then . . . I'm happy for

Martha and Olivia and Jamie. And Murphy." She giggled. "All that counts as four."

Virginia nodded.

"Then—number five—I'm happy that Slate came here."

"Slate? I'm happy Slate came too."

"And then Buttercup." She seemed so pleased to have made it through her carefully ordered list and looked to Virginia for her approval.

"That's a good list," smiled Virginia and Mindy nodded.

The small figure reached for another dinner plate and began the drying process, but her mind seemed distracted as the towel went round and round, drying the same spot over and over. Virginia thought she must still be contemplating her list and was totally unprepared when the little girl looked up and asked, "Did my other mama love me?"

Virginia felt the air leave her lungs. What in the world could she say to that? She could not—would not—lie to the child. They had never lied to Mindy. She had grown up knowing that she had another set of parents. They were never referred to as the "real" mother and father but always the "other" mother and father. It had been explained that her father had been killed in a car accident, that her mother was living in another city, very sad over the loss, even though her father was married to another woman at the time of his death. Jonathan maintained that the child had a right to know her parentage, and Virginia agreed. The facts, after once presented, were never discussed unless Mindy brought them up; then her few questions were answered in a matter-of-fact, nonevasive manner. But this? This had never come up before.

Mindy must have read the doubts and confusion in Virginia's eyes. She shrugged those little shoulders again and attacked the plate more vigorously with the dish towel. "I know my other papa didn't," she said, and her voice was a bit too firm. Too forced.

"Why do you say that?" Virginia stood looking down at

her child, wild thoughts racing through her head. She wished that Jonathan were with her.

Mindy looked up with solemn, honest eyes. "He never held me or touched me . . . or anything. Not like my real papa." There, she had said the word. But it was to Jonathan she assigned the title "real."

"I don't think my mama loved me either. Did she?"

Virginia's mind scrambled for satisfactory words. Honest words. What could she say? Would it destroy Mindy's newly awakened faith?

"Let's sit down . . . and talk," she began, her words faltering, her hand on Mindy's shoulder.

"It's okay," said Mindy. "We can finish the dishes."

So she is determined to not make too big an issue over whether she was loved—or not. Virginia felt like crying. She would have been much more comfortable sitting down, Mindy drawn close into her arms as she sought for words that might explain Jenny's situation to a little girl. *Oh, I wish Mama were here,* she found herself thinking. *Or Grandma. They'd know what to say. How to say it?*

Mindy placed the thoroughly dried plate on the stack and reached for another one. *Say something,* Virginia prompted herself. *Don't let her shut the door on this. It has to be dealt with now—while she's open and honest.*

"Honey . . ." she began and swallowed. "There are lots of different kinds of love. Different ways to . . . to express it. Some people . . . some people find it difficult to show love to others because . . . well, because something has . . . happened in their life to make them . . . to hurt them in some way.

"Your mama was deeply hurt . . . when she was a little girl. Her . . . her mama left. Left her with her papa, your grandpa Woods. Grandpa Woods didn't know about Jesus then. He was angry . . . and bitter . . . and he didn't . . . wasn't able to show much love to your mama. So your mama didn't grow up learning . . . knowing much about how to love others."

Mindy's hand had ceased its circle of wiping the plate. She listened carefully, her eyes intent on Virginia's face. "Do you understand what I'm saying?" asked Virginia softly. Mindy nodded. Then she spoke.

"You have to learn about love . . . from family."

"Yes," Virginia hurried to agree. "You learn about love. Or at least, you learn how to express love. How to be . . . loving. You need to learn that. And practice."

Mindy nodded again.

"That doesn't mean that you will always . . . always like what another person does . . . or says. But if you love them . . . then you are able to forgive them and . . ."

"Like Martha," Mindy said with a grin. "Sometimes she's a real pest."

Virginia smiled in spite of herself. But the smile quickly faded with Mindy's next comment. The girl's thoughts were back to Jenny again. "She didn't love me . . . or she wouldn't have given me away . . . to you and Papa."

"She gave you away. . ." Virginia quickly backtracked to restate the unwelcome phrase. "She let you come to live with us because . . . because she was afraid. She thought that . . ." But it was hopeless. How could she explain to a child that her mother had abandoned her because her father had? "She didn't know what else she could do," Virginia finished lamely.

"And she didn't know how to love," Mindy said in almost a whisper. Virginia did not argue the statement.

"Was that why my other papa didn't love me? Didn't he know how to love either?"

Virginia took a deep breath. "I know nothing about him. I only know that your mama loved him very much." The statement was meant to assure the young child, but it had the opposite effect.

"She loved him . . . but not me?"

Oh, dear, now I've got myself in a corner, mourned Virginia silently. *How do I get out of this?*

"Your mama . . . your mama met your papa at a time

when she really needed someone . . . to love her. She'd had a very bad accident and needed special care. Your papa was the one who . . . who helped her get better. They learned to love each other . . . and got married. They . . . they had a good time . . . living together . . . having fun."

How could she explain their life to a child? Their way of living and acting that she herself did not begin to understand? "They . . . they liked to have fun. Go to parties . . . and things," she stumbled on.

"But they didn't go to church."

Virginia was surprised at the child's perception. She was somehow separating the way her birth parents lived from a life of faith.

"No. No, they didn't go to church."

"Didn't they know about God?"

"Your mama used to go to church . . . sometimes . . . with me, when we were growing up."

"But she didn't tell God she was sorry? Didn't ask Him to forgive her sins?"

"No. No, she didn't do that."

"We need to pray for her," said Mindy seriously, concern darkening her eyes.

"Yes," replied Virginia, her eyes filling with tears as she drew Mindy up against her aproned front. "We need to pray. We need to continue to pray for your mama. I've been praying for . . . for years."

"But we need to pray more than just, 'God bless Mama Jenny,' " went on the girl who had been taught to remember her other mama in her evening prayers along with the rest of the family members on the list.

"Yes . . . we need to pray more than that."

"Do you pray more than that?"

"I do."

Mindy looked relieved. Virginia's hand stroked the child's hair, brushing it back from her forehead. She held her close, the plate pressing awkwardly against her hip bone. For a long moment Mindy snuggled close, then she pushed back.

"Mama," she said, her eyes solemn but determined. "It doesn't matter that Mama Jenny doesn't love me. I love her anyway."

Virginia nearly choked as she stifled her sob. She pressed the child more tightly to her. "I love her too, honey," she managed to say in spite of her tears. "I always have."

Mindy seemed to put the conversation behind her, but her evening prayers from then on were filled with pleading to her God to remember her other mama and to help her to know that she had to say she was sorry for all of the wrong things she had done. Virginia's heart ached for the child. Was it fair for such a heavy burden to fill such a young heart?

"Perhaps God will answer her prayer . . . more quickly than He has mine," she said to Jonathan one evening as they retired.

Jonathan looked surprised at her statement. "God has not been ignoring your prayers," he said quietly.

Virginia was quick to amend her comment. "I didn't mean that. It's just . . . just that I've been praying for Jenny for such a long, long time . . . and there has been so little happening."

"How do you know what's been happening? On the inside? You haven't even heard from her . . . in years. Maybe God is doing terrific things in her life. Even now."

Virginia nodded. "Oh, I pray so."

But Virginia did not feel reassured. *If it's not already too late*, she found herself thinking. *I don't even know if Jenny is still alive.*

———

"I think I've found a woman to stay with the folks." Belinda sounded excited as she welcomed Virginia and the children into her kitchen. Virginia responded with a quick smile, a flood of thankfulness washing over her.

"You did? How?" She knew her mother, in one last, desperate effort to allow her parents the privilege of remaining in their own home, had been searching out someone who was willing to be a live-in.

"I put a notice in several papers. I finally got a response. It looks quite promising. Papa and I are taking the train into the city tomorrow to interview her."

"That's wonderful," exclaimed Virginia. "I'm so glad they won't have to move off the farm."

"Now, don't get your hopes too high—it isn't finalized yet," cautioned Belinda.

Virginia nodded, but she could not let go of the hope. "It's an answer to prayer," she said with confidence. "Even the children have been praying."

"Children are wonderful little prayer warriors," agreed Belinda. "I sometimes think they can understand the mind of God better than we cynical, practical adults."

Virginia looked out the window to the backyard where Martha and Olivia were busy with pails and shovels in the sandbox that Drew had built for his grandchildren. Perhaps it was true. Children had such simple, complete faith.

"Well, I do hope that is true," she said sincerely. "Mindy has been pouring her heart out to God every night. She is so concerned for her mama. The mama she doesn't even really know."

"She might know more than you realize," Belinda said softly. "Sometimes children remember more than we think."

"Perhaps she does. It's all so strange. Memory. Perhaps our past affects us far more than we think it does."

Belinda turned to look at her daughter. "You're worried about Mindy?"

Virginia stirred. "No . . . not worried. Not really. At least not at this point. She seems . . . seems to have things well sorted through. For being a child of nine, her perception astounds me at times. But I . . . I guess I worry that there may come a time when things . . . sort of pile up. She's had a rough start in life, Mama."

"She's been more blessed than some. At least she was put on the right track early on. She has a family who loves her. She knows that."

"I think she does. But she also knows that she wasn't loved in infancy. That's got to affect a child. Knowing you were unwanted. No matter how brief the time. She asked me about it the other evening."

Belinda looked surprised. "Were you able to quiet her fears? Give her assurance?"

"I'm not sure." Virginia placed James in the high chair and brushed her hand over his disheveled hair. "What could I say? I fumbled around for words. I couldn't just blurt out that her folks had decided she was a . . . an impediment to their life and activities."

"Of course not."

"But it is true—nonetheless."

"Because her parents were two selfish people who never allowed themselves to grow up has nothing whatever to do with who Mindy is. Her worth as an individual. She is a very special little girl with a . . . a sensitivity and awareness beyond her years. The world is a better place because of her being in it."

"I know that . . . but does Mindy?" Virginia was on her way to the cookie jar to get a cookie for James. She turned to her mother. "I had never given it any thought . . . before Mindy. Does one ever fully get over rejection? I don't know. Is the knowledge—the hurt—a tear that always remains? Is later love enough to erase all that? To undo it? I don't know, Mama."

"Mindy seems fine to me," her mother replied, no doubt trying to ease her daughter's mind.

"I pray that she is. I pray that she will remain so. But it . . . it still troubles me some. I mean . . . does one really ever know what is going on in the heart and soul of a child?"

"There are indicators. Signs."

"But by the time the signs show up—on the outside—is

it too late for the inside? I don't know."

"God can do miracles, Virginia. Even in the healing of a child's heart."

Virginia sighed. "Yes . . . I know He can," she said with deep feeling. "I'm counting on that . . . because, quite frankly, I admit that I'm not up to the task. I have no idea how to help her. Really help her. I can't see what's going on inside that little heart."

The entire household was astir. Their very own telephone was being installed. Henceforth no longer would trips to town be required to make a telephone call. Virginia could hardly believe it. What a blessing it would be to be able to dial the phone and speak to her mother anytime she chose. How nice to ring up Rodney and Grace or Danny and Alvira. To call Francine or have long chats with Clara. And her grandparents. Her grandparents, too, had just installed a telephone. That in itself had greatly reduced Belinda's concern. At least if they needed help they would be able to call a family member.

Even the small children skipped around in excitement, seeming to understand that this gadget on the wall would change the life of the family. Virginia had to keep shooing them out of the way so the workmen would not be tripping over them.

The negotiations with the woman from the city to stay with the Davises were still ongoing. Belinda was quite comfortable with their interview and the prospect of her coming, but the woman herself had not as yet given them a definite yes or no.

"I think she's holding out until we'll be desperate enough to promise her the moon," Drew had remarked dryly. "And, quite frankly, I am getting very close to that point. Your mother is beside herself with worry. I don't think she's had a decent night's sleep in months." Virginia had not realized it was that serious a matter for her mother and was sorry she had not been more empathetic. Her only thought had been to keep things as they had always been.

But the phone would help. It would ease the burden. At least they would feel like they had some kind of connection with the folks on the farm.

Virginia could hardly wait until the man in charge stepped back and said with satisfaction, "It's ready to go, ma'am."

"Now?" It was almost too good to be true.

As soon as the crew stepped out her door, Virginia checked the phone list they had left, lifted down the earpiece, and with a trembling hand cranked out two shorts and a long. Would it really work? Would she really be in touch?

The receiver lifted on the other end and she heard her mother's voice. It sounded strange. Muted. But it was definitely her mother.

"Mama. It's me. Virginia. We have our phone."

"Virginia." Her mother sounded as excited as she felt. But now that they were speaking over the miles, Virginia did not know what else to say. They had been together for tea and a chat just the day before. There was no new news.

But the children were jumping up and down and tugging on her skirts, and Virginia decided that it was time to introduce them to the modern technology of this new world. "Here," she said to Martha. "Say hello to Grandmother Belinda."

Martha, a grin on her face, eagerly reached for the earpiece and pressed it to her ear as she had seen her mother do. But the moment Belinda's voice came crackling through the strange new instrument, her eyes grew big and she threw the receiver back at Virginia. Virginia lunged to catch it. She was unsure of the damage it would cause if the piece fell to the floor. She need not have worried. The attaching cord was far too short to let the piece actually drop.

Olivia was braver than her big sister. She had to be placed

on a kitchen chair in order to reach. When the voice of Belinda greeted her, she giggled, then began to babble back in her childish prattle. But she had no idea where to speak. Much of her conversation was buried in Virginia's bib apron or spoken to the wall. She did not want to relinquish the new toy, and Virginia had to pluck it from her hand amid protests.

Martha stood by, watching it all as though waiting to see if any harm would actually be done through the strange new instrument. When Olivia was disentangled from it, still crying to have it back, Martha reached out and pulled her away. "That's enough, Olivia," she informed the howling child. "You might get sick if you talk more."

Virginia was still on the phone and could not correct the misconception, because her mother was saying that the woman had sent word she was willing to come out and look things over. That was one more forward step, and Belinda sounded very pleased.

Olivia stopped her crying and stood staring at the phone. How long would it take for her mother to begin to feel the ill effects that her sister had described? When the conversation continued and nothing happened, she lost interest and wandered off.

"When will she come, Mama?"

"Next week. She didn't give a firm date—yet. She'll let us know when she has made her arrangements. Your father says we might as well be prepared to make some adjustments. Coming from the city, she might not be taken with farm life."

"Adjustments? Like what?"

"Well—for one thing—there is no inside plumbing. She may object to that."

Virginia thought about it. "I suppose," she admitted at length. "If she does, what can be done?"

"At this point, I'm not sure. We'll have to deal with it when the time comes."

It was all they could do.

CHAPTER 5

$\mathscr{T}$he new telephone proved to be a continual source of pleasure for Virginia. Even on her busiest of days she could take a moment or two, if she so desired, to get in touch with family or friends. Even when it rang in the middle of some task that was difficult to drop, she found this addition to her rather isolated farm life a distinct advantage.

It was through the telephone that she first got the latest news concerning her brother Danny. Her mother called, breathless with excitement.

"Danny is coming home."

"Home? When?"

"Next week."

"Why?"

Not that Virginia wasn't as pleased as her mother to hear that they soon would see Danny, but her common sense told her that Danny would not leave his job at the city zoo to travel the long distance home without some good reason.

"Listen to this," explained her mother. "The zoo wishes to send Danny to Kenya for two years to study wildlife there."

"Kenya?" It was only an exotic name to Virginia.

"Kenya. He is so excited that he hardly made sense on the phone."

"But why Kenya? Isn't that . . ."

"There are huge tracts of land teeming with wildlife.

Lions, elephants, hyenas, jackals, elands, rhinos . . ."

"You sound excited too."

Belinda laughed. "I guess Danny's enthusiasm was a bit contagious."

"But isn't it . . . dangerous?"

There was a moment of silence except for the soft static of the phone line. "I guess it is," said Belinda finally. "Some. But Danny assured me he will be in good hands. They will place him with a game warden who knows the land and the animals."

Virginia wasn't sure if that made her feel any better about Danny's situation, but she did not wish to upset her mother. "I'm sure they will . . ." She wasn't sure how to finish so took another direction. "What is Alvira to do in the meantime?"

"Alvira? Oh, she's going with him, of course."

"With him? To Kenya?" It sounded preposterous to Virginia.

"Danny said he would not have agreed to go if they had suggested otherwise."

"No . . . I don't suppose he would have."

"He'd never leave her here alone for two full years."

"But what if. . . ?" Virginia stopped.

"What if *what*?"

"What if . . . if she . . . if a baby . . ."

There was silence again on the line. Virginia wished she had not raised the question.

"I don't know, dear" came Belinda's voice at last. "I suspect that babies are born in Kenya too."

Yes, with a high mortality rate, Virginia could have said. But her mother already knew that. Virginia decided to return to the original piece of information.

"So when is he—are they—to arrive?"

"Next Thursday. He thinks they will be here on Thursday. They have so much to do before leaving, and they will depart directly from here."

"How do they go?"

"They take the train to New York—then catch the ship."

Virginia drew in a deep breath. "Well . . . they certainly will have lots of experiences to share when they get back home."

"Yes. Yes, they will. I told him to be sure to keep a diary. He said that will be Alvira's job—while he's out tracking animals."

"I guess it will give her something to do."

"Oh, she's going to take her sketch pads with her. She is quite good at it, you know. Says she will enjoy having some new material to work on." Her mother barely stopped to catch her breath. "Well, I must ring off. I want to phone Clara."

Virginia said good-bye and stepped back from the phone. She wasn't sure whether to rejoice with Danny over his upcoming adventure or pray with every waking breath—maybe both.

————

The Miss Groggins from the city who was considering the live-in position with the Davises arrived on the same train as Danny and Alvira. They all had hoped to give Danny and his wife their undivided attention for the few days the two would be with them. Instead several members of the family were tied up with ongoing discussions and negotiations, trying to impress a city woman with the fact that country living was neither impossible nor unsatisfactory. She was not responding with much enthusiasm.

"You will have your own room, of course," Belinda informed her as she showed her about the house. Virginia, who had gone out to the farm with her mother for moral support, stood back and observed. The woman's face had not brightened.

"In fact," Belinda went on in her cheeriest voice, "you may have your pick of the bedrooms upstairs. The folks have their bed in the living room now."

"I noticed," said the woman, her tone indicating that she was not particularly taken with beds in living rooms.

Virginia was glad that her grandparents were not at home. Belinda had wisely arranged for Uncle Clare to take them for an afternoon drive. They, as yet, knew nothing about the proposed new arrangement. "There will be plenty of time to inform them of the plan when we know it's going to work," Belinda had stated. "No use stirring things up for nothing."

Virginia had secretly wondered, but she had not contradicted her mother.

Now, as Virginia stood and studied the straight-backed, stern-faced Miss Groggins, she half hoped that her grandparents need never know of the plan. She was not at all taken with the woman. In fact, she didn't like her at all. Miss Groggins was too stiff, too superior, too self-imposing, to her way of thinking. Why, she would take all the fun out of the household. Her grandparents would not survive without their little jokes, their teasing, their sense of humor. Her grandmother had always maintained that a sense of humor was as necessary to get one through life as a strong back or a right hand. Miss Groggins appeared not to share the sentiment in any way.

"Will I be expected to do the cleaning?" she asked brusquely.

"A woman comes in twice a week for the laundry and cleaning."

The woman's eyes did not even flicker.

"And the cooking?"

"Mama still does the cooking."

No glimmer.

"You say your father has only one lower limb?"

Virginia was not used to hearing one's leg referred to in that impersonal manner.

"Yes."

"So I'm expected to be a nurse?"

"No. He is self-sufficient—still."

What is this woman supposed to do? Virginia found herself

wondering. *No cleaning, no cooking, no nursing care. What do we need her for?*

"I do have a cat. Cleopatra goes everywhere with me."

"A pet would be welcome."

The woman studied the house with a critical eye. For the first time in her life Virginia also looked at it in that manner. It had always seemed a perfect place to her. A place where love was freely given, where real people lived. Really lived. Now she could see that it was a bit shabby. A bit used. The wallpaper was faded. The doorframes worn. A spot of bare brown showed through the pattern of linoleum in front of the stove. The cupboard was tightly crammed with odd bits of china and silver, gathered as gifts from loving family members over the years. Knickknacks occupied every available space on stands, shelves, and windowsills. One might even say that the house was cluttered. But it had always been homey. Always been a haven of sorts. Virginia did not like how the woman carefully peered around through narrowed eyes, studying, assessing, judging without knowing anything about this home or the people.

"I assume that is the bathroom," the woman said at last as she pointed to a door.

"No," answered Belinda. "That is the pantry."

The woman's face changed its expression for the first time.

"I must have missed the bathroom."

"There is no bathroom," said Belinda without batting an eye or altering her voice. Virginia was proud of her mother.

The woman appeared to be totally caught off guard. "I don't understand," she said, flustered. "How can civilized persons manage to live in a house without . . . without a *bathroom?*"

"We use the bedrooms for bathing, the outhouse for . . . other purposes."

"But . . . *Outhouse?* Good heavens!"

"And we do not say 'good heavens,' even though we believe the heavens to be good," Belinda went on softly but firmly. "If I didn't alert you to this, my mama certainly would correct you the first time you used the term." She turned abruptly as though to dismiss the matter. "Your main concern will be the health and safety of my parents. As I have told you, they are elderly. Mama has taken a few falls. I don't expect you to altogether prevent that from happening. Such incidents can happen too quickly. But we do hope that your presence here might help her to feel she can slow down. And if something should happen, you can call quickly for help. My brother Luke is a doctor. He would come immediately."

The woman seemed to have not been listening. "No bathroom," she said again.

Belinda's voice slowed so that each word she spoke was clear and distinct. "We need someone to stay with my parents, Miss Groggins. Someone dependable. Someone who will place their safety and well-being first above all else. There is no inside bathroom. There will not be—at this time. I have stated the salary that we will be offering. You may have the weekends off. Your—Cleopatra is welcome to join you. You may take the job—or leave it."

The words were spoken with a decisiveness that surprised Virginia.

Miss Groggins was still flustered. She reached up a nervous hand and began to finger her lace collar. Her face flushed slightly, bringing a bit of color to the powdered cheeks. "Well, I . . ."

"Do you wish the employment—or not?" pressed Belinda. "My son and daughter-in-law will be out of the country for two years. I do not wish to spend further time on this now. Either you are interested—or you are not. And if not—I will continue to look elsewhere."

"I . . . I need some time to think," the woman finally managed.

"Very well. I will take you back to town. You may catch the afternoon train or spend the night at the boardinghouse, as you choose. I will expect your answer by tomorrow afternoon."

The ride back to town was a quiet one. Even Belinda and Virginia did not chat. The woman did decide to spend the night at the boardinghouse. There was no use traveling all the way back to the city if there was a chance that she might be staying, she said stiffly. They said their good-byes and moved on. With all of her heart Virginia hoped the answer would be no and that the stuffy woman would pick up her Cleopatra and head back to the city.

"Well," said Belinda when they were alone. "That didn't go so well, did it?" She gave her shoulders a bit of a shake as though to remove the agitation of the afternoon.

"No," agreed Virginia, easing the Ford out from the parking area.

"Rather like an iceberg, wasn't she?"

"Icebergs *must* be more warm and pleasant than that," quipped Virginia.

"Stiff as a barn fence rail," continued Belinda.

Virginia had never heard her mother use such expressions before. She cast a sideways glance at her to see if her ears were playing tricks. At the same moment Belinda turned to her. They looked at each other for a moment, then both burst into laughter.

"Well," Virginia offered when she could speak again, "at least we have had an experience."

"Mama and Papa would enjoy this," added Belinda. "It's a shame we can't share it with them."

They stopped by Clara's so Virginia could pick up her children and then drove on to the Simpson home. All the family was gathering for a time with Danny and Alvira. Even Rodney and Grace had arranged for three days with the family and were motoring home with their little ones. Belinda was beside herself. It had been some time since she'd had her entire family together. The nice weather meant the little cousins could play outside in the fenced yard. Grandpa Drew and Grandma Belinda had over the years added to the play equipment. Swings, a teeter-totter, a full sandbox, plus various smaller toys soon scattered across the yard, kept them all happy and busy. The fathers were stationed on the back porch to oversee the activity while the mothers busied themselves in the kitchen preparing the bountiful meal.

Miss Groggins and Cleopatra offered no further interference. After reporting her change of plans by phone, the woman and cat took the afternoon train back to the city.

Belinda expressed both relief and disappointment. The woman would not have been satisfactory, but now they would have to start the search all over again.

Virginia felt nothing but thankfulness. She would not have wished to impose someone with such a sour disposition on her grandparents. *They deserve much better than that*, she thought as she looked over at them sitting side by side across the room, smiling at the joyful commotion.

The evening was full of good-natured banter and chatter as the group filled one another in on what had been happening in their lives. And the remembering. So much remembering. Laughter and camaraderie and love spilled over and poured out on all present. Virginia found herself wishing she did not have to go home at day's end. That she could just stay and soak it all in. That they could all stay. That things could remain like this. Family together. Love and laughter. The whole outside world shut away.

But even as she wished it, Virginia knew that the dream was unrealistic. There was a world out there. Responsibilities for each one around the table. They were not children anymore. They were all adults. Adults with lives that called them away from this home where they had grown up. Away from this haven of safety and security. It was their job now to supply the same kind of haven for the children in their care. Virginia looked around at her little brood and prayed inwardly that they—each one of them—would have the same warm feelings about the home they would one day leave. *Lord, may it ever be a nice place to come back to*, she silently entreated.

All too soon they were pushing back chairs and commenting about getting children home to their own beds. Little James already slept in his father's arms, and Olivia, who had been determined to keep up with the older siblings and cousins, had finally succumbed, curled up against her grandfather.

"Before you all go," said a shaky voice, sounding squeaky with nervousness, "I'd like . . . I'd like to say something."

Virginia looked over to where Francine sat with Dalton. He had stood to his feet, face flushed, mouth twitching. Virginia had never seen the self-assured young man look so nervous before.

"This . . ." He tugged at his shirt collar and took another deep breath. "This seems to be a good time . . . a good place to . . . to . . ." He flushed a deeper red and reached for Francine's hand and pulled her up beside him.

"Francine and I . . . Francine has honored me by promising to become my wife. I have her permission—in fact, it was her idea that we announce this to the family tonight." Once he finally got started, he seemed in a big hurry to get everything said. He did not even pause when the family members began to clap and cheer. "We are planning to be married at Christmastime, and we know that Danny and Alvira will be many miles away. We will be thinking of them, but I'm not prepared to wait longer than that for this lovely young lady"—he turned to the blushing Francine—"until they get home again. I've waited much too long already." He pulled her closer.

At another round of clapping, he fished in his jacket pocket and came up with a black velvet box. Then he turned to the young woman beside him.

"Francine," he said, and his voice was now steady and mellow. "I love you. Have loved you since the day we met, I think. I have appreciated getting to know you over the many months we have been keeping company. My love has continued to grow. And I know that it will not stop growing in the many years we have together—whatever God blesses us with. I'm . . . I'm so happy that you have already accepted my proposal of marriage. But now . . . I am asking you again in the presence of your family, whom I have also learned to love and respect—my future family—will you marry me?"

Francine, whose lips were curved in a trembling smile, leaned against the man beside her, her hands clutching his arm. "Yes," she said, and her voice was strong and sure. "Yes. I will."

Dalton removed the ring from the box he held and slipped it on Francine's outstretched finger. Then he kissed her gently. Right in front of the entire assembly.

"Are they married now?" Martha's clear, puzzled question broke the spell. Laughter rippled around the circle until it was magnified and shared by all.

"No, they are not married yet," answered her Uncle Danny.

"Then why did they kiss?"

There was more laughter. Martha's frown deepened.

"That's just a . . . a silly thing that grown-ups do," teased Danny, ruffling her hair. "You'll understand . . . someday."

Virginia looked at her child. *Oh, please God, not for a long time*, she found herself praying silently.

Then she turned her attention back to her younger sibling. Francine was passing around the room, proudly giving a close-up look of the new ring on her finger. She looked so happy. So radiant. So beautiful. Virginia's breath caught in her throat. Her little sister. To be married. Imagine.

Her eyes went to the young man who followed closely at Francine's side. He looked . . . triumphant. As though the most exciting thing in the world had just happened to him. The most priceless gift just placed within his possession. Virginia blinked back her tears. *Yes*, her heart responded as her gaze again fell on her little Martha. *I would wish this for you . . . someday. The happiness. The sharing. The blending of two lives. Nothing is more beautiful. Nothing. But please, my darling . . . please don't be in any hurry. Your mama needs you.*

CHAPTER 6

$\mathcal{T}$he Simpson family's few days together ended all too soon, and the group gathered on the platform of the train station to bid farewell to Danny and Alvira. There were no tears. Danny was far too excited to allow the family to express sorrow over his departure. Virginia guessed that there may be more than one damp pillow that night after he had gone. But not now. Now there were only well-wishes and promises of letters and prayers. The happy bedlam of everyone seeking last-minute hugs and giving last-minute advice gave way to the train departing eastward, billowy plumes of smoke wafting a long tail behind as it curved its way out of town. The Simpsons stood and watched until it disappeared; then they turned slowly away, each one with private thoughts centering on the long time that stretched ahead until they welcomed the young couple home again.

Virginia slipped up next to her mother and placed her hand into the hand she had held since she was a tiny infant. Only now she was the comforter, not the comforted. She said nothing. Didn't need to.

"Well . . . I guess it's back to the ordinary again," Drew commented as they left the station.

"The ordinary," echoed Belinda. "I guess it is."

"For me, that begins with a long motor trip," said Rodney. "I'm not looking forward to that."

Belinda seemed to shake herself from her reverie. "I wish you didn't have to go. So soon."

He looked at her fondly. "I wish I didn't too, Mama, but it was pushing things a bit to get the five days off. We're awfully busy right now."

Virginia felt her mother's fingers tighten over her own. "I'm glad you made the effort to come," Belinda said to her older son. "We all would have been so disappointed. Certainly Danny."

There didn't seem to be much more to say.

Olivia begged to be carried, and since Jonathan already had his arms full with James, Virginia released her mother's hand and reached for her little daughter. She walked along, in step with Rodney, who carried his youngest. "When do you leave?"

"First thing in the morning. It's a full day's trip."

"How did the children manage the drive?"

"They did very well—considering. I hope it goes just as well going home."

"I'd hate to travel with our babies. It's bad enough just driving into town."

"They sleep. At least for part of the time, and Grace is terrific about keeping them entertained."

"Please be careful," whispered Virginia, not wanting her mother to overhear her admonition. "There are more and more motorcars on the roads. I don't trust some of those drivers."

Fall was approaching before Belinda found another person interested in staying with her parents. A widow lady from a small town nearby was looking for something to fill her lonely hours. It sounded like a good prospect, and Belinda could hardly wait to have a visit with the woman.

Drew took a day off and drove her for the interview. She was well satisfied with the results, and the woman agreed to come look over the situation for herself within the next week.

Virginia wasn't sure if she wanted to be involved this time. Besides her uncertainties about the whole arrangement, she was busy with fall canning and a small James, who had decided it was time to learn how to walk. Virginia felt she had to watch him every waking moment. Her baby girls had been active and inquisitive, but James was a living cyclone. And he climbed. Continually. He seemed to have an uncanny gift for being in two or three places at the same time. She would just remove his hands from the butter crock when he would be emptying out the sugar bowl. No sooner had she cleaned up that mess than he would be dumping over the washbasin.

So this time Virginia remained at home, busily engaged, while her mother took the widow out to the farm home. Again, Clark and Marty were busy with a visit elsewhere. Belinda reported the outcome later over the telephone.

"She wasn't so shocked that there was no indoor plumbing."

That was a plus.

"She wasn't so quick to define what she wasn't going to do either."

"You mean she actually plans to work for her pay."

"It seems that way."

"Does she have a Cleopatra?"

Belinda chuckled. "No Cleo."

"Was she friendly?"

"Oh, yes. Very warm."

Virginia was puzzled. Her mother didn't sound as excited as she had expected.

"So what is the problem?"

Belinda hesitated. "No problem," she said at last.

"Mama . . . something is troubling you. I can tell by your voice."

"Well, it's not a problem. Not really . . . it's just . . ."

"Yes."

"She's a little domineering. A touch . . . pushy. And she

loves to talk. No wonder she's missing her husband. She doesn't have anyone to listen to her anymore."

"Maybe Grandma will enjoy having someone to chat with."

"Maybe."

"But you're worried."

"Not really . . . worried. It's just . . . you know how Mama is about her kitchen. And Pa . . . he isn't so fond of continual chatter since the stroke. Mama says he needs his quiet times . . . to sort of . . . regroup."

"I see," said Virginia. "So what do you plan to do?"

"She's staying over. She's off to check out our town shops at the moment. I'm going to see the folks in the morning. If they agree, I'll take her on back to see them in the afternoon."

"Don't they nap?"

"I'll give them time for that first."

Silence.

"Virginia . . . pray. Pray that they'll be reasonable about it all."

Virginia swallowed but could not answer immediately.

"I'm sure they will, Mama. They have always been reasonable people."

"But this . . . this will be hard for them. They could be stubborn about it. It's . . ."

"It's a whole change of life for them, Mama. You can't blame them if they resist. It won't be easy for them to have a stranger in the house."

"Perhaps . . . perhaps if they realize the alternative . . . they may be a bit more pliable."

The words brought a chill to Virginia's heart. She did not need to ask what the alternative might be.

She wanted to hang up. To end the conversation. But she wasn't sure that her mother had said all she needed to say.

"She's . . . she's a pleasant enough person, Virginia," Belinda said, as though to convince herself. "She seems energetic and . . . and personable. I'm sure Mama could enjoy sharing tea with her. Exchanging knitting patterns. She'd like her as a neighbor."

Virginia had no reply. Yet she couldn't just hang up. *Say something*, she scolded herself. So she said the only thing that popped into her mind. "What did you say her name is?"

"Iwanna. Mrs. Iwanna Gobble."

Virginia was sure she had heard wrong. "What was that?"

"Yes . . ." replied Belinda with a sigh. "You heard correctly. It is Iwanna Gobble. I thought it a unique and rather pretty name—Iwanna—until I heard the surname. I'm sure her maiden name must have been something more appropriate."

"Iwanna Gobble," repeated Virginia, but already the two of them were laughing.

It felt rather good.

————

Her grandparents were not pleased about the interference in their lives. They should have been told, they maintained. This sort of thing was not a trivial matter. It hurt to know that it had been going on behind their backs. They had been doing just fine on their own.

Belinda was crushed. That afternoon they drove Mrs. Gobble back to her own town. It seemed they would not be needing her after all. Virginia knew just how hard this was for her mother and was sure she must have spent the night in tears.

But the next day Marty rang Belinda up and apologized. "We know you were jest thinkin' 'bout us. We didn't mean to be ungrateful . . . it's jest . . . it's hard to grow old. One has a tendency to fergit how yer kids worry 'bout it. We've been talkin' and prayin', and iffen it'll ease yer mind, we'll give it a try."

Belinda, elated, immediately phoned Mrs. Gobble and gave her the good word. The woman declared that she would be ready by Friday. They could motor over and pick her up then.

It was Clara's Troy who made the trip the second time. Drew had an important court case and could not get away. Belinda rode along, directing her son-in-law to the woman's small brownstone house.

Mrs. Gobble was duly established in the Davis farm home, and the family held its breath. They hoped and prayed that it would work well. Clark and Marty seemed more than willing to give it their best. At least for a time.

Virginia met the woman for the first time at church the following Sunday. She was a pleasant-looking woman. Not stiff and distant like Miss Groggins had been. In fact, she was a matronly looking woman, whom Virginia thought would have made a good grandmother and felt it a shame that the woman and her deceased husband had never had children.

Mrs. Gobble was indeed talkative. And she was a bit loud. It made Virginia wonder if she might have a hearing problem. And she laughed a lot. Not always at the appropriate times, to Virginia's way of thinking. But laughing at the wrong time was certainly better than not laughing at all.

The woman joined in heartily in the singing, and her voice seemed to bolster the entire congregation, everyone singing with just a little bit more volume and enthusiasm.

"She might work out okay," Virginia dared to venture to Jonathan on the way home from church.

"I think she's rather a cute old thing," he responded, and when she frowned her disapproval at his description, he laughed.

"Did you notice the attention she got?" he went on.

"Attention?"

"Tom and Harry both had their eye on her." He chuckled again.

"Tom and Harry? Our Tom and Harry?"

Tom Crow was a widower who had lost his wife two years earlier. He looked lonely and forlorn, and Virginia had often wished that there were a suitable widow in the congregation. Harry Simcoe was a bachelor farmer. The fact that he had never married did not seem to be preplanned. And certainly it was not because he had no interest. He openly eyed every new available woman in the congregation no matter her age, but he never did seem to be brave enough to speak to any of them.

"I wonder which one will win," mused Jonathan and was rewarded with another frown.

But Slate seemed to think it was a good joke. From the back seat between Mindy and Martha, Virginia could hear him laughing heartily. "Well . . . if it's to be Harry Simcoe, he's gonna have to get up his courage and do more than just stare," he ventured. "I'm no expert on the matter, but seems to me it takes more to convince a woman than just moon eyes." He laughed again, and Jonathan, to Virginia's annoyance, joined in.

———

It was Tom who won the contest. Mrs. Gobble had not been there for two months when she announced that she and Tom were planning to marry. She would no longer be available to care for the Davises.

"So she's going from a Gobble to a Crow. Iwanna Crow. Has a nice ring to it," laughed Slate, and he and Jonathan had another good guffaw. Virginia had to smile in spite of herself. But she sobered again quickly when she remembered how hard her grandparents had tried to make the situation work. Her grandmother bit her tongue when the woman stepped over boundaries in her kitchen. And her grandfather took himself out to the porch—even on chilly days—to escape Mrs. Gobble's nonstop chatter.

"Can't you please wait until after Christmas?" Belinda pleaded with Iwanna when the woman announced she was leaving. Belinda was busy with preparations for Francine's wedding and knew that she would have no time to hunt for a replacement. And now she felt even more uncomfortable leaving her parents on their own.

"We're not young anymore," Iwanna responded, "and Tommie is most anxious to have a woman in the house. He has five grown children, you know, and their younguns are praying for a grandma. I've never been a grandma, and I've a notion that Christmas is about the best time to be one."

Belinda knew that she could not press further. She reluctantly let the woman go with her blessing and best wishes.

————

A cold November wind was blowing, causing disruption and crackling on the telephone line, but Virginia was able to hear Belinda's words, and her heart felt as though it were being squeezed.

"Was Grandma hurt?"

"I don't know. Pa phoned. He seemed quite upset. I'm going right out."

Virginia cast a glance toward the table where her family still sat at dinner. "Just a minute," she said to her mother and turned to Jonathan, placing one hand over the receiver. "Grandma's fallen again, and Mama is going there right away. She sounds quite upset. Is there any chance—?"

"Do you want me to go with her—or do you want to go?"

"I . . . I'd like to . . . if you can watch the children."

He nodded.

"Mama," she said, speaking into the phone again, "can you stop by for me? I'll be ready."

Belinda sounded relieved as she set a time.

She was there within half an hour. Virginia stood, coat and hat in place, her gloves in her hands. She would not keep her mother waiting this time.

"What did Grandpa say?" she asked as soon as she had pulled the car door behind her.

"Just that she had fallen. He said that she seemed to knock the wind out of herself. Was having a hard time catching her breath. Oh, I'm so worried. I should never have let them—"

"Mama," Virginia scolded softly, "it won't do to punish yourself. You've done all you could do. None of the others will be—"

"That's just it." Belinda's voice took on an impatient tone. "No one else is willing to do anything. They let me be the one to make the decisions, break the news. I just wish someone else would take some responsibility for a change. Missy and Ellie so far away. And Clare and Arnie might as well be for all the help they are. I can forgive Luke. He's so rushed off his feet that he doesn't even have time to take a decent meal most days. But the others. They have nothing pressing. They could at least take some interest."

Virginia had never seen her mother so upset, nor heard her speak so forthrightly about her family members. It was not at all like her. *It's the worry*, she told herself. *She's sick with worry*.

They pulled into the yard, and Belinda was opening her car door before she had rolled to a complete stop.

She rushed to the house with Virginia close on her heels, fairly ran across the porch, and threw the door open. Her father sat in his usual chair, facing the door.

"Where's Mama?" Belinda asked, her eyes casting wildly about the kitchen.

"She's in there." He nodded his head toward the living room, where a curtain had been pulled across to give them a private dressing area.

Belinda moved forward.

"Don't come in." Marty's voice halted her.

She stopped, confused, casting a glance toward her father. "Mama . . . are you all right?"

"No . . . I'm not all right. I stink to high heaven."

"What?"

"I stink to high heaven," the woman repeated. "Stay where ya are."

Belinda turned to her father and Virginia moved up beside her. "What's going on?" Belinda asked. "Did she strike her head?"

When Clark began to chuckle softly, Virginia feared that both her grandparents had lost their senses.

"Papa . . . what's going on?" Belinda repeated. "Has Mama. . . ?"

"She'll be fine," he managed. "But she's right. She does stink to high heaven." He chuckled again.

"What's she doing?"

"She's scrubbin'. With lye soap. That's her third time."

"Papa . . . please . . . tell me . . ."

"She took an unexpected bath, that's all."

Virginia moved closer. "Grandpa," she said in a voice that she hoped wasn't as demanding as her mother's, "tell us what happened."

He looked up at them, but a twinkle still lit his eyes. "She was on a trip—out to the outhouse with the slops. She slipped on a patch of ice . . . and came in wearing the whole thing. Don't know iffen it was the fall or the smell that took her breath away. She's been scrubbin' ever since. Emptied every pail of water in the house, and the boys had 'em all full this mornin'."

Virginia heard the air leave her mother's lungs in a heavy sigh. "She's all right, then?"

"She's fine. Least she will be iffen she doesn't scrub her skin off."

Virginia turned away, weak with relief. "I'll put on the kettle."

"You'll hafta go to the pump first. She's emptied everything in the house."

Virginia picked up two pails and headed for the door.

Eventually they were able to have a good laugh over it. Thankfully, Marty truly had not been seriously injured. All the scrubbings had taken care of the odor, and her clothes were soaking in the washtub, after having been rinsed out in bath water. They would wait there until the neighbor lady arrived the next morning and the week's washing was done.

"It could have been worse," Virginia said as they drove home together.

"Yes," agreed Belinda. "I don't dare leave them on their own anymore. It's too dangerous. Mama . . . on that icy path. She could have been badly injured. I'm going to have to insist that they leave the farm."

Virginia felt an icy hand reach in and squeeze her heart.

The situation seemed serious enough for the family to gather for a discussion of what could be done. Virginia was worried about her mother. She knew that Belinda would not sleep with her parents' lives in peril. And Virginia knew that was her mother's sincere assessment of their present situation.

There were many plans, many suggestions, any number of *what-if*s and *could-we*s put forth. They all eventually came to a dead end. "We are going to have to insist on moving them," argued Belinda once again.

"Moving them—where?" asked Drew. "We have no facility for people who need their kind of care."

"Moving them here."

"My dear, we've been through that a dozen times. We've invited, we've asked, we've pleaded—we've even cajoled—all to no effect. They have refused every time."

"This time we won't accept no for an answer. They must move. We'll move them."

"How?" asked Drew. "Bodily?"

"If we have to."

Belinda seemed most determined. Virginia inwardly cringed.

"Would they . . . would they be able to stay on there if . . if someone was with them?" It was Francine who spoke up, her voice breaking. Virginia lifted her head to look at her younger sister. Her eyes were flooded with tears. Virginia blinked. It was like looking at the little sister again. The one who cried over everyone else's problems.

Belinda softened and reached for Francine's hand. "Yes, of course they could, honey. That's what we've tried. I've run ads in every paper I know. I thought Mrs. Gobble was the answer. . . ."

"Mrs. Crow," offered Jonathan. "She didn't get a Tom Turkey. She got a Tom Crow. And now she Wanna Crow."

After a moment to smile at the attempt at a touch of lightness, Belinda continued. "I wish I could find someone. I . . . I wish they would move in here. I can't understand why—"

"I think I can," Luke broke in. "They have survived by being independent. You can't expect them to change now."

"It makes it so difficult. I really don't know—"

"I'll go." The quiet voice was filled with emotion. Francine's lips trembled, and her eyes spilled over as tears ran unchecked down her cheeks.

"Francine, honey. . ." Belinda reached for her hand.

"I'll go," the girl repeated.

"You're about to be married. . . ."

"I'm planning to quit work anyway. Dalton doesn't want me to work once we're married. He's already said so. He can drive back and forth from the farm—to see me until we're married, and then he can move in too."

Virginia felt weak. Francine had no idea what she was offering. How difficult it was to start a marriage in that way. Perhaps they would survive . . . but it would not be easy. Virginia knew that firsthand.

"I don't think that's a good idea," she began before she could check herself.

Francine's chin came up. She sniffed. "I can take care of them," she countered. "I know that I haven't cooked . . . and cleaned and . . . done the housework like the rest of you, but I know how . . . and Grandma can teach me her way. I can learn."

Virginia quickly amended, "I didn't mean that I thought

you couldn't do it. It's just . . . it's . . . it's hard to start out like that. I know." She cast a glance toward Jonathan as though to apologize for what she was going to say. "There are enough adjustments for a new couple without . . . without being in another's home . . . caring for elderly. It's . . . it's hard, Francine. I . . . I don't want to see you go through that."

A fresh spate of tears washed down Francine's cheeks. "They're my grandparents," she whispered. "I love them. If it won't work to . . . to do that, then . . . then I'll ask Dalton to postpone the wedding."

CHAPTER 7

$\mathcal{V}$irginia felt the little shock wave traveling round the circle at the large kitchen table in her parents' home. It was several minutes before Drew, her father, broke the silence.

"Seems to me the young man is a bit anxious to marry," he said, his tone reasonable.

"He'll . . . understand." Francine's voice was choked. She twisted her lacy handkerchief into a damp ball.

"Honey . . . we can't ask you to do that." Belinda had finally found her voice.

"You aren't asking me—any of you."

"But we . . . we can't allow it either."

Francine looked up, her long lashes still damp. But her voice was now steady as she said, "Look what Virginia gave up—for the family. She missed college—had to change all of her plans—without a single complaint. I know how much it meant to her. She used to cry—at night—when she thought no one was listening, but I heard her. I cried right along with her. She was so unselfish."

She fidgeted with the hankie while all eyes now turned on Virginia, making her squirm in discomfort.

"Well . . . I've been raised in the same family," Francine continued. "With the same principles. I may have been more . . . spoiled, but I'm not totally insensitive. They are my grandparents. And I love them. And I—we can postpone our marriage for a few months so I can help take care of them."

A hush fell over the little group. No one spoke. Virginia wondered if anyone even lifted eyes from the checkered cloth on the table, but she did not look up to see. She felt like weeping. It was all so complicated. So emotional. Did other families face such tough decisions?

"I don't think your grandparents will let you do that." Belinda's voice sounded weary. As if she had just put in a long, exhausting day.

"We can try," insisted Francine. "I think I can convince them. . . ."

"There must be another way."

"And if there isn't?" Francine no longer looked young and agitated. She looked mature and confident.

"I don't want you to have to sacrifice—"

"Sacrifice strengthens the soul. You have always told us that, Mama."

"Would they come to my house?" Virginia asked. She couldn't stand this cloud of doubt. Of uncertainty. This wrenching apart of family plans.

Belinda shook her head slowly. "Virginia . . . you've done enough."

"If they won't come here, I don't expect they would consider moving anywhere else," said Drew.

"But they would still be out in the country," argued Virginia.

"I don't think they have anything against town. It's the leaving that bothers them. The moving from the familiar and loved," her father explained.

"It's the feeling that they are intruding on their family's lives," Luke put in. "They don't want to be a bother."

Belinda nodded. "Yes, that's likely closer to the truth."

Virginia felt there must be something she could do. But what? She couldn't pack up all her little ones and move in with them. And Jonathan's horses. . . . It seemed totally out of the question.

"I still think I've the only answer," Francine said quietly but firmly. "I'll talk to Dalton."

"No, I'll go out to the farm," said Belinda, her face brightening. "There's no reason to talk to Dalton. Your papa can drive back and forth for a while. We'll just shut the house up—oh, no—we can't do that," she caught herself. "You'll still need to live here until you're married, Francine. But we will move on out there." She looked toward her husband and got his nod.

"Mama, if you go, we won't be ready for the wedding anyway," said Francine.

For one moment Belinda's expression was doubtful; then she spoke again. "Yes, we will. I don't expect to be busy every waking moment with the folks. I can still work on wedding plans. Mama would love to help. She's never happier than when she's sewing or cooking for one of the family."

Belinda seemed so pleased with the solution. "I don't know why I was so thickheaded not to think of it sooner," she muttered to herself as she rose to her feet and moved toward the stove. "Refills, anyone?" She poured coffee around the table.

"Then after the wedding—after Christmas—I'll see what I can do about finding someone else again."

Virginia sighed and shifted James in her arms. It seemed that the crisis was again solved—for the moment.

———

Clark and Marty looked surprised when Belinda arrived with bag and baggage and announced that she planned to stay. Belinda couldn't help but laugh when she told Virginia about it later on the phone.

"You and Drew had a set-to?" queried her mother, looking uncertain as to whether it was a serious question or not.

Belinda chuckled and replied, "Of course not. He'll be out in time for supper."

"He's comin' too."

"He is."

It finally began to dawn on Marty what was happening. She stopped, one hand going to the countertop to steady herself. "Now, look here," she said, her voice shaky with emotion. "No one needs to leave home or family to come in here and tender-care us. We're jest fine on our own. Sure, I had me a few falls. Yer pa is better on his one leg than I am on my two. But a few bumps never hurt none. Can't even see the marks. You git back on home and care fer yer own household."

"I'm staying here," said Belinda, ignoring the outburst. "I need your help with Francine's wedding—sewing and all. Since you won't come in to me, I've come to you." She put down her suitcases.

Marty seemed to consider the words. The frustration left her eyes. Her entire demeanor changed. "Well . . . in thet case . . ."

From the corner of the kitchen, Clark chuckled. "Ninety-two years old and ya still got her sewin' weddin' dresses."

Belinda had no intention of passing on the sewing of the wedding dress to her elderly mother, but she didn't say so. "Which room do you want us to use?" she asked instead.

"You can take your pick. Mrs. Gobble said she left 'em all fit fer company."

Belinda was appreciative of that kindness. She picked up her things and moved toward the stairs.

She chose her old room. Her parents' bedroom would have given them more room, but it didn't seem right somehow to be taking over their bed. Well . . . it wasn't even their bed. That had been moved down to the living room. This was a new bed, purchased to fill up the empty space. But, still, it was their bedroom . . . of more than seventy years. . . .

It felt strange, and rather nostalgic, to be in her old room again. Nothing had changed. The wallpaper was the same pattern she had chosen and she and her mother had hung together. She had been fourteen then. Fourteen—with all sorts of ideas of her own. The curtains at the window were curtains she had brushed aside many times to look out at the new day, or to catch the first wishing star of the evening. The same pictures were on the wall. The same pine bed with the handmade hooked rug before it. The same dresser with the telltale gouge on top from when she had broken a small mirror and a piece of glass had scratched its mark.

Belinda unpacked the suitcases and hung her clothes in the closet. She arranged other items in the dresser drawers, careful to leave room for Drew's things. She found herself humming softly as she stacked the last bit of clothing and shoved the suitcases under the bed.

─────────

After the good start and Clark and Marty's acceptance of the new living arrangements, the transition turned out to be not as easy for any of them as Belinda would have hoped.

"I wonder if they have picked up a number of little idiosyncrasies since I left home, or if I just never noticed them before," she noted in one of her frequent conversations with Virginia. "They do seem to have some strange ways of doing things. Little things. Things that shouldn't matter, but I find myself getting annoyed."

And she knew, by their expression and often their silence, that there were things she did that irritated Clark and Marty.

She had been right about one thing. They did need someone with them. She'd had no idea how much they now depended on one another. Her mother's eyes were not as keen as they had been. Even with the reading glasses, her seams were not as straight and even. And her father, who seemed fairly steady once upright, had to have his wife's help to get up from the chair. Belinda watched, her heart stricken, as her mother, her strength nearly spent, awkwardly tried to help lift her husband. On the third attempt they both tumbled into the chair. Marty eventually struggled back to her feet, but it was a moment before the two of them stopped their chuckling and were ready to try again. They made it that time. Belinda wondered how many times in the past they had gone through this little scene.

And Marty was very unsteady. She'd even tied a cord from the bed to the kitchen so she had something to hang on to as she walked. Belinda knew that the cord would not be strong enough to hold her should she fall. But it did give her a measure of balance and confidence.

"I hadn't known they were quite so needy," Drew observed as they prepared for bed.

Belinda nodded, her eyes shadowed. "Even I didn't know it was this bad."

"Maybe after Christmas we'll have to insist they move into town with us."

She said nothing. She hated to think of the emotional toll it might take on all of them. She certainly had no intention of raising the question now. It was going to take all her physical and mental reserves to care for their needs and get ready for the coming wedding.

———

Everyone said it was the loveliest wedding ever held in their church. Francine was certainly the most lovely bride, Virginia was quick to agree. Dalton seemed to think so as well. His eyes never left her face during the entire ceremony.

But it was Belinda who held Virginia's attention. She looked drawn and pale in spite of her brave smile and her braced shoulders. *She's worn out*, thought Virginia. *Something is going to have to be done. She can't carry on like this.*

Virginia arranged a few "trades" with her mother, and Belinda would come to the Lewis farm for an afternoon with her grandchildren while Virginia took over the responsibilities with the Davises. They both knew Belinda was simply providing care for a different, much younger set of people, but she said it gave her a break and time with her beloved grandchildren.

It was well into the new year before a more permanent answer came—from a most unexpected source. No one—not a solitary family member—had even thought of such a solution to the problem. Belinda could still scarcely believe it herself when she excitedly told Virginia about it.

"He came for coffee. Mr. Simcoe. Sat right there in the folks' kitchen—looking around as though sizing up the place—then I saw him give a little nod and he cleared his throat.

" 'We been good neighbors for a lot of years,' he said, and Pa nodded. 'I've been thinking,' he went on. 'I'm not so fond of being alone anymore. I'm a sight younger than the two of you—but I play a fair game of checkers and I've been cooking up my own grub for thirty-odd years. I been hearing about your family's looking for some help for ya, so I figured maybe we ought to join forces.'

"Mama looked a bit suspicious. But she didn't say anything. Just waited.

" 'I lost my best friend—my dog Raider this past spring, and I've been lonely ever since. I wondered if it would work out if I moved in here and helped out some—for the company—and the Simpsons here moved on back to their house in town.'

"Well, I couldn't believe my ears. I started to open my mouth to say it would never work, but Mama spoke up. 'Don't know why we couldn't give it a try,' she said. 'Never know about anything 'til ya try it.' "

"I can't believe it," responded Virginia. "She was willing for a bachelor to move in with them?"

"A bachelor."

"Do you think it will work?"

"I don't know." Belinda's initial excitement seemed to have waned. "But like Mama says, 'You'll never know until you give it a try.' " The two chuckled at the familiar homey wisdom.

"So is he—are they going to do it?"

"He's moving in tomorrow."

"And you and Papa are moving home?"

"As soon as he is settled."

Virginia sighed. "I'm glad," she said at last. "You know I've been worried about you."

Belinda smiled weakly. "Well . . . I'll be the first to admit that it has been a bit of a strain. I think I can empathize a little more with the folks. It will be so good to get back to my own house. My own bed. At least for a while."

"What do you mean—a while?"

Belinda sighed again. "We have to be realistic, Virginia. Even if this works, it won't be for long. The folks are really failing. Even Mr. Simcoe—bless his heart—will not be able to care for them for long."

———

Virginia absently fingered through the morning's mail as she stood at their mailbox. There was not much. A few advertising flyers put out by Mr. Woods for the town merchants, a bill for feed grain for Jonathan. A letter. Her hand stopped. A letter, addressed to her. The only letters she ever received were from Jonathan's family. But she did not recognize this writing.

Or did she? Puzzled, her eyes scanned the envelope for a return address. There was none. She checked the postmark. *It's from Jenny*, she thought, her heart suddenly beating faster.

She did not wait to slit the envelope carefully open but tore at it with trembling fingers. Jenny, after all this time, in touch with them again.

The brief note told her very little. Except for one very important fact. Jenny was coming. "I plan to come see you on Thursday's train," the letter read. "Talk to you then. Jenny."

That was all. No information as to how she was doing. No inquiry about her child. Not even a greeting, asking how they had been or hoping that they were keeping well. Nothing like that.

Virginia smiled ruefully. It was typical Jenny. She turned and started for the house. Thursday was only two days away. She had much to do before Jenny arrived. She and Mindy . . . Virginia stopped short. Mindy. What would Mindy think about Jenny showing up out of the blue? How would she respond? Would two days give them enough time to prepare the child for the upcoming visit of her mother? It had been years since Mindy had seen her.

Then Virginia moved forward again, a smile on her lips. Mindy faithfully had been praying for Jenny each night. Perhaps this was God's answer to those prayers. Maybe Jenny already had good news for them. Mindy would be so excited.

By the time Virginia reached the house she was so keyed up herself she could hardly wait for Mindy to get home from school. She had to share the news with someone. Letter in hand, she headed for the barn to find Jonathan.

He was not there. She felt keen disappointment but pressed on to the corrals behind the barn. Slate was working with a young stallion, putting the horse through a brisk trot. Jonathan was watching with a critical eye.

"He does toe-in that left front foot," he called to the young man. "We'll have to work on it."

Virginia moved up beside him and leaned on the rail. "Guess what?" she said as he turned to her. "I just received a letter from Jenny. She's coming."

"Here?" A frown deepened the slight furrow of his brow. He lifted a hand and removed his brimmed hat and ran fingers through his thick hair. "Why?"

Virginia felt her own feelings turn uncertain. "Well, to see us all, of course. Does she need a special reason?"

Jonathan did not reply for a long moment. He stood watching the young stallion, but Virginia knew his thoughts were not on the horse.

"You don't sound pleased," she said.

"I'm not." There was no apology in his tone.

"Why? Mindy will . . ."

"Mindy. That's why. Mindy has not seen her mother since she was—"

"I know—and she will be so excited."

"Will she? Or is it you who'll be excited?"

He turned to face her, his eyes probing hers.

"What . . . what do you mean?" she stammered.

He ran his hand through his hair again and pushed the worn hat firmly down on his head. "Jenny is your friend," he said at last. "I respect you for sticking with her . . . all these years even when she has done nothing to deserve your loyalty. I was . . . I am able to . . . to give her free rein where your friendship is concerned. But Mindy? That's different. You know how much it took to get her to where she felt loved . . . accepted . . . able to face life. She's settled in with us now. She's doing fine. I don't want that woman coming in here and upsetting everything."

"But she won't—"

"How do you know that?" He swung around to face her with his full attention. "How can you be so sure? Mindy's just a child. An emotional child. She can't help but be thrown off balance, coming face-to-face with a mother she knows only by name. It's bound to do something to her, Virginia, and I don't think it will be for her good."

Virginia bit her lip. She had never seen Jonathan's face so set, almost angry.

"You're saying she can't come?" she asked at last.

He did not answer for a long time. His hand moved to his hat, but he did not remove it, just tugged on the brim. Finally he looked at her again. "I'm not saying that," he answered. "You are my wife. This is your home. I am not ordering you as to what you can or can't do. But I will say that I don't like it—not one bit. I think it will upset our Mindy."

"We've been praying," pleaded Virginia. "Don't you think this could be the answer to our prayers?"

He hesitated again. She watched his eyes soften. "Look," he finally said. "She's coming. I don't expect you'll be able to turn her away. We have no idea why she's coming. We have no idea how Mindy will react. But I'll tell you this—if she starts making waves . . ." He left the sentence unfinished.

Virginia nodded. The letter hung limply at her side. All of the anticipation had gone from the coming visit. She was no longer anxious to share the news with Mindy. Had Jonathan spoiled everything? Sometimes she thought he could be a bit narrow, overly protective. He certainly was protective where his children were concerned. And Mindy was as much his— theirs—as any of the little ones who shared his home.

———————

When Virginia did tell her, Mindy's reaction was difficult to interpret. One minute she seemed excited about the fact that Jenny was coming. The next, she seemed quiet and with-drawn—probably frightened about the prospect of meeting this woman who had brought her into the world and then brought her to Virginia.

"Perhaps God is working to answer our prayers," Virginia murmured to Mindy as she tucked the child in for the night. She hoped the words would settle Mindy's doubts. She did manage a smile.

"We'll just keep on praying. Pray that God will use this little visit to open your mother's heart to Him."

"She's not my real mother, you know," said Mindy. "She's just my birth mother."

"Well . . ." began Virginia, and then let it drop. "We'll keep praying," she said instead. She leaned over and kissed the child on her forehead.

She was at the door before Mindy spoke again. "Mama," she asked, "will I need to kiss her?"

Virginia stopped, one hand on the doorknob. She turned back to the child. "No," she said quietly but firmly, remem-bering Jenny's last visit when she had almost totally ignored her own daughter. If Jenny had not changed, she would not wish to be kissed. "No . . . you won't need to kiss her. Unless you decide that you want to. Unless she asks. . . ." But Virginia did not expect Jenny to ask.

"Good," said Mindy.

Since making those initial adjustments into the Lewis family, Mindy had been free with her affection. Every visiting grandparent, aunt, uncle, or cousin, were always given a hug and welcoming kiss. *Why is she hesitant about kissing her own mother?* Virginia puzzled.

Then Mindy enlightened her with, "I don't think that I want to kiss someone I don't even know."

"I see." Virginia waited.

"Mama, what should I call her?"

Mindy sounded so worried that Virginia's heart twisted inside, and she went back to sit on the edge of Mindy's bed.

"I don't want to call her mama," Mindy said, her voice low.

"We'll figure out something that will feel right to you," Virginia comforted her, smoothing back the tangled curls from the small face.

"Will she stay long?"

"I . . . I don't expect so," said Virginia, remembering Jenny's last visits and her restlessness.

Mindy seemed to relax. "Do you think she'd like to see Buttercup?" she wondered.

"I expect she would."

"Do you think she would like to ride her?"

"No," said Virginia, smiling at the thought. "I don't think Jenny will be interested in a ride."

"I'm kinda glad," said a sleepy Mindy with a half smile. " 'Cause Buttercup doesn't know her either."

CHAPTER 8

"We have a letter from Danny." Belinda's excitement seemed to have erased the many difficult weeks without hearing anything at all.

"It was posted four months ago," Virginia's mother continued on the other end of the telephone line.

"Where has it been?"

"On the ship, I guess. Takes a long time."

"But surely not that long."

"I was worried," Belinda admitted. "I thought we'd hear sooner. According to this letter, he'd already written twice."

"What happened to the other letters?"

"I've no idea. But it's a relief to know they are okay. They say it's dreadfully hot—but they are managing."

"Have they received any of our letters?"

"Yes. He said the post had brought one from Clara, two from you, and four of mine to this point. But I've mailed a dozen or so. And Rodney says they have written a number of times, and I know that Francine has posted a couple. And Mama has sent off several as well."

"It's truly awful. The mail situation."

"Well—he is out on the plains. I guess one can't expect hand delivery."

"And how are they? Is Alvira managing?"

Belinda hesitated. "She is expecting—just like you supposed she might be."

"Do they have medical facilities there?"

"Danny didn't seem worried."

"Why should he worry?" Virginia said, rolling her eyes. "He doesn't have to go through delivery."

"Virginia, I don't think that's fair. It's his baby—and his wife. Of course he'll worry."

Virginia was contrite. "I was sort of joking. But I shouldn't have said that. It's just that—sometimes I don't think men understand what birth is really like. They just seem to assume that everything will be fine—that it's part of life."

"Well, I guess it is."

"You know what I mean, Mama."

Virginia decided to change the subject. "I got a letter from Jenny."

"Jenny?"

"She's coming. Tomorrow's train. It seems—unreal."

It was a moment before Belinda spoke. "Does Mindy know?"

"Of course. We told her right away."

"How did she respond?"

"Well . . . she had to do some sorting through on it. I think she's excited . . . but she is hesitant too. That's understandable. She really doesn't even know her. Jenny. Even if she is her mother. She has very few memories."

"Yes . . . this could be hard for her." Belinda's voice was very solemn.

"You sound . . . like Jonathan," Virginia stated softly.

"Jonathan? Doesn't he. . . ? Isn't he . . . pleased?"

"No. Not really. He surprised me with his reaction to the news. I thought he would be glad. But I think it would be fine with him if we never saw or heard from Jenny again," Virginia said slowly.

"What does he have against Jenny?"

"Nothing. Really. He's just . . . just . . . you know Jonathan. He's so protective of his children. He's like an old mother hen hovering over them, clucking away."

"Virginia!"

"Well, he is . . . in a way. Anyway, I'm sure he will thaw out once she gets here. Jonathan has always been courteous and kind."

"Yes, I know. He's a good man, a good father."

The conversation turned to other things. Virginia felt somewhat better as she hung up the phone. Jonathan *was* a good man and father. He would do right by Mindy—and Jenny.

Virginia was glad too that word had finally come from Danny and Alvira. But that thought sobered her again. Would Alvira really have the care that she needed to take her through her pregnancy—through the delivery? It would be a dreadful thing if something happened. She resolved to do some serious praying for her sister-in-law.

———

The rest of the day did not go so well. Virginia had made herself a mental list of all of those things that she needed—or wanted—to get done in order to be ready for Jenny's arrival. She had been sidetracked early on when Olivia had come to her with a sliver in her finger. If there was anything that upset young Olivia, it was the sight of blood. Even a drop of blood could send her into terrified shrieks. It took some time to get the sliver extracted, the finger bandaged, and the child calmed down again.

Virginia was just ready to resume her tasks when James upset the pail of feed waiting to go out to the chickens. Not only had he spilled it, he was sitting there eating it when Virginia went to investigate.

She had to clean it up—and then clean him up, and by the time that task was complete she could smell her pies. She had quite forgotten them in the oven with all the distractions. And the crusts were burned. Virginia could have wept. She decided to serve them to the family for supper and start over on the morrow. The worst places could be cut away; then she'd whip some cream for the top. Jonathan and Slate would not complain. They never did.

By the time Mindy arrived home from school, Virginia was hopelessly behind in her self-imposed schedule.

"Bundle the girls and take them out to play," she said, agitation in her voice. "I'm not getting anything done with them underfoot." Then quickly followed another order. "I need more wood for the fire—and another pail of water."

Mindy looked confused. Virginia did not improve things when she quickly followed up with, "Hurry and change your school dress so you don't get it dirty."

Martha trailed her older sister from the room. Virginia heard her say as they climbed the stairs, "Mama's flustated. Jamie's been bad again. He ate too much chicken food. Now he'll die, I s'pose."

He's not going to die, Virginia almost called out. Surely the child did not think she would be standing over a hot stove mourning over burned pies if there was any danger that her baby had been poisoned.

Virginia put a hand to her forehead, brushing back damp hair. No wonder Martha was confused and Mindy had looked at her as if she had taken leave of her senses. That's exactly the way she had been acting. All agitated and muddle-headed. What did it matter if Jenny found her in her usual situation? She was not a perfect homemaker. Did not have a perfect house—nor a perfect family. She was putting far too much pressure on herself. On the entire family. She was being ridiculous.

She moved to the table and took a chair, her shoulders lifting and falling in resignation. She'd forget the list. Entirely. Jenny would arrive—when she would arrive. What got done would be done. And if it didn't, who was likely to notice or complain? Least of all Jenny. The only thing she would be sure to get done would be to bake a loaf of that oatmeal bread Jenny loved from their childhood days. She'd have to call her mother for the recipe.

When Mindy and Martha came back down the stairs, Virginia greeted them with a smile. "Why don't we all go out to get some wood from the shed and a pail of fresh water? Then we'll make some hot cocoa to take the chill off our bones."

Everyone seemed to agree that was a wonderful idea.

They never had the hot chocolate. Before they even returned to the kitchen from their errand, Jonathan came from the barn, helping a limping and pale-faced Slate. He had been kicked by a yearling. He insisted that he wasn't badly hurt, but Jonathan was determined that a doctor should decide. He loaded the boy in the motorcar. "I don't know when we'll be back," he called from the open window as he swung the car around. "Don't wait supper on us."

It was a sober little group that moved on to the house, arms laden with wood for the cookstove. "Will Slate die?" sobbed Martha, who seemed of late to be overly obsessed with the thought of someone she loved departing this life.

"'Course not," said Mindy. "The worst that could happen is for his leg to get cut off."

Virginia didn't think that thought was likely to bring much comfort. "He won't get his leg cut off," she corrected. "If it's broken he will need it to be in a cast until it gets better. That's all."

"Oh, yeah," said Mindy, her eyes brightening. "I remember when our old grandma had one of those."

If you remember Grandma Withers and her cast, you should be remembering your mother, thought Virginia, but she said nothing.

They held off supper until the children started to complain, and Virginia decided that they must go ahead on their own after all. Mindy, who said the grace, also said a prayer for Slate. "And God, help Slate's leg not get ampu'ated like Grandpa Clark."

When she opened her eyes, she looked very solemn. "I

asked Grandpa Clark about his leg one day, and he told me that he got hurt and they had to ampu'ate his leg."

"What's amu . . . amu. . . ?" asked Martha, frowning as she worked with the strange word.

"Ampu'ated," said Mindy knowingly.

"Amputated," said Virginia, fixing a plate for the impatient James, who was pounding his spoon on the high-chair tray.

"It means chopped off," Mindy explained to her younger sister. Martha made a face, which Olivia copied.

"When things like arms or legs or fingers get hurt really bad, they chop them off."

Martha made another face.

"That's what happened to Grandpa Clark's leg. And that's what happened to Grandpa Drew's arm too."

"That's yuk," said Martha, and Olivia repeated the word several times.

Virginia could not dispute the facts, even though she did not appreciate the terminology. She tried to divert the attention of the children round the table.

"Tomorrow your mother Jenny will be here," she said to Mindy.

Martha's face immediately brightened. "Tomorrow our Jenny mother will be here," she repeated to Mindy.

"It's not your mother," responded Mindy. "Just mine."

"Is not," argued Martha.

"Is too."

"Mine too," said Olivia.

Oh, dear, thought Virginia, *why did I bring that up?*

"She's just mine—isn't she, Mama?" asked Mindy.

"Yes, she is just Mindy's."

"Why?" Martha's whine clearly said that she didn't think it fair that Mindy had something she didn't.

Virginia had neither the energy nor the words to explain.

"She's mine," said Mindy, with a tip of her head as she reached for the gravy. Then added with a flip of her braids,

"But you can have her if you want."

Martha looked puzzled—then pleased.

———

Much to the relief of all of them, Slate's leg was not broken, though it was badly bruised. The limp signaled the damage, but he insisted upon walking. "It'll just stiffen up if I don't" was his comment to Virginia as she busied herself with warming up some supper for Jonathan and Slate.

"I thought you might get it chopped off—like Grandpa Clark," said Martha, who seemed just a bit disappointed.

"You don't have a cast either," noted Martha. It seemed that Slate had really let them down.

"No chop off. No cast. Nothing," said Slate with a shrug. "Guess that colt will need to try harder next time."

"Don't joke about that," cautioned Virginia from her place by the stove.

She turned to Jonathan. "Who treated Slate?"

"Luke."

"No wonder it took you so long. His office gets more and more crowded. One of these days he will decide to retire, and then what will the town do?"

"I don't think he'll be retiring for a while yet. He has more energy than fellas half his age. But it's true. The town does need another doctor."

Virginia dished up the men's food, and the two made their way to the table, Slate hobbling some but refusing help.

"Come on—let's get you to bed," Virginia called to the girls. "It's already past your bedtime."

They made their rounds of good-night kisses and turned to follow her. Just before they left the room to follow Virginia up the stairs, Martha turned to her father. "Mindy gave me Mama Jenny," she said with satisfaction.

Jonathan frowned, and Virginia knew she would be asked to explain. But she would not do so now. "Come," she said to her little brood. "You're long overdue at the pillow station."

They trooped along after her, she cautioning them to be quiet since James had already been put to bed.

When Virginia looked in on them later, Martha and Olivia were already sleeping. But Mindy lay, eyes wide open, seeming to be in deep thought. Virginia lowered herself onto the bed beside the girl.

"Can't you sleep?"

Mindy's answer was to reach out and finger Virginia's dress pocket as if she needed something to hang on to.

"I'm just thinking."

Virginia brushed the hair back from the child's face. "Happy thoughts . . . or scary thoughts?"

"Sort of . . . both."

"Do you want to talk about them?"

Mindy hesitated and took a firmer hold on the dress. The wind had risen outside and the tree close to the house swayed, causing light and shadow from the window to alternate across the child's face. Virginia thought that it must reflect what she was feeling inside.

"I feel happy that my Jenny mama is coming. But I feel kinda scared too."

"I understand. I feel like that too."

"I want God to answer my prayer. I want Mama Jenny to ask Him to forgive her for not loving Him and doing . . . what's right. I really want that a lot. But . . ."

She was silent again.

"But. . . ?" prompted Virginia.

"But . . . I don't know her, and I'm scared."

"Scared of what?"

"That I won't like her. That she won't like me."

Virginia waited. "Is that why you gave her to Martha?"

The head on the pillow nodded. Then she said slowly, "I shouldn't have done that, should I?"

"Well, probably not. But Martha was just—"

"Do you think Martha would give her back if I asked her to?"

Virginia groped for words. "Honey, Martha won't need to give her back. She is still yours. You . . . you can't just give away . . . people."

"She gave me away," said the child simply.

Virginia's breath caught. What could she answer?

"In a way," she admitted honestly. "In a way she did. But that doesn't mean she is no longer your mother. That you are no longer her daughter. The . . . the tie is still there. The relationship. It stays."

The words did not seem to comfort the child.

"What if she wants me back?" Her voice was little more than a whisper. The thought chilled Virginia to the very core of her being. *What if she wants me back?* swirled through her mind and emotions. She drew the little girl close to her bosom and the child clung to her. "Honey . . . you are ours," Virginia said. "You have been with us now far longer than you were with Mama Jenny. You are ours."

Gradually Mindy's grip on Virginia lessened. Virginia eased her back and kissed her forehead. "Do you think you can sleep now?" she whispered.

Mindy nodded and even managed a smile.

"I think I can."

But Virginia's troubling thoughts descended the stairs with her.

"I suppose I'm the one who will need to go pick her up." Jonathan did not sound one bit happy as they prepared for bed.

"If you don't mind," responded Virginia.

"And if I do?"

He cocked his head to one side and gazed at her face. She knew he was not expecting an answer.

"I wish . . . I wish you didn't feel so . . . so negative about this," she said, her voice sounding tight and forced.

He made no reply. But after they had slid beneath the

warm blankets, he reached over and drew her close to his side. "I'm sorry," he whispered against her hair. "I've been pretty difficult about this whole thing. I'm sorry. She's your friend . . . I know that. And you've prayed and tried to share your faith with her for . . . how long? Maybe you're right. Maybe God is at work. I'll . . . I promise you I'll try."

It was enough for Virginia. She returned his kiss, then sighed. "This has been one awful day. I'm glad it's finally over. I feel all wrung out."

"Well, some good has come of it." She heard the teasing in his voice and wondered what was coming next.

"And that would be?" she asked, already feeling drowsy.

"We get to have pie two suppers in a row."

She gave his ribs a playful punch. "Don't you count on it, my dear," she replied in kind.

———

Jonathan came from the barn in plenty of time to clean up before meeting Jenny's train. True to his promise, he did not make any more negative remarks. "Is there anything you want me to do or pick up while I'm in town?" he asked.

Virginia shook her head.

"Then I guess I'll be off. Are you sure you don't want me to take Martha? It would be nice to have some company." They had already decided that Mindy should go to school as usual and see Jenny when she arrived home in the afternoon.

"It's too cold, Jonathan. That wind has been blowing all night. There will be drifts. . . ."

He conceded with a nod.

"By the way," he said carefully, "have you explained to Martha that mamas are not something you can give away? I wouldn't want her to say something embarrassing. For our sake . . . and for Mindy's."

"I . . . I hardly know what to say . . . but I'll try. She was so disappointed when Mindy claimed to have something she didn't."

"So Mindy generously offered her the privilege."

Virginia did not wish to go into that now. Mindy's comment had surprised her too. Now, after their little chat, she felt she understood Mindy's feelings. But now was not the time to explain it to Jonathan. She said instead, "I called Mr. Woods this morning and invited him for supper."

"Is he coming?"

"No, he said not."

"I suppose it would be a bit awkward."

"Maybe. He gave me another excuse, but I got the impression he really doesn't care to come."

"If Jenny has chosen not to let him know she'll be in the area, he can hardly just show up. The surprise might not be a pleasant one."

"I can't imagine . . . I can't imagine anyone not wanting to see her own father."

"Maybe she will. Before she goes back, maybe they'll get together. That would be another part of the answered prayer."

"It would."

"Well, I'd best get going. I don't want that train to beat me to the station. Keep an eye on the barn, will you? If you don't see Slate now and then, check on him. That leg is bothering him more than he'll admit."

The door closed and Virginia was alone. Alone except for chattering Martha, who was busy drawing a picture at the kitchen table while her younger siblings had their afternoon nap.

Virginia felt her stomach tighten as she gazed out the window. It would not be long now, Lord willing. And no problem with snowdrifts across the roads. Jonathan should be back within the hour, and she would see Jenny again. It had been so long. What would Jenny be like? Would she still be hard and bitter—or were Mindy's fervent prayers having an effect?

In the meantime she had a job to do. A job that she really

didn't know how to tackle. She crossed to the table and sat down opposite Martha.

"Do you like my picture?" asked the little girl, cocking her head to one side.

"It's very nice."

"It's a snowman."

"Yes, I could tell."

"He's got Slate's hat on his snow head."

"Yes, I can see it's Slate's." Martha was surprisingly artistic for a child her age. And she had a pronounced sense of detail.

"Martha . . ." Virginia took a deep breath. "I know that Mindy said that you could have her Mama Jenny. But mamas . . . mamas are not really something that we can pass on from one to another."

"I can't keep her?" Already the eyes were darkening.

"No . . . no you can't keep her."

"Can I pretend?"

"Mama Jenny—" She stopped and started over. "You see . . . mamas and children need to agree on things like that. Mama Jenny might think that one little girl is enough."

"But she does just have one little girl. Me. Mindy doesn't want her anymore."

"But Mama Jenny might still want Mindy. Don't you see?"

Martha thought about that for a moment.

"You are my little girl. I would be very unhappy if you tried to give me away," Virginia went on.

"I wouldn't do that," said Martha.

"But you can understand how Mama Jenny might feel. If she thought that Mindy tried to . . . to give her away . . . she might feel sad too."

Martha considered the words carefully. "Maybe we better not tell her," she said at last, nodding vigorously.

Virginia felt relief wash all through her. "I think that's a good idea. I don't think we should tell her."

CHAPTER 9

Virginia looked at the wall clock so often it seemed the hands were not even moving. She felt agitated and nervous and found herself doing more pacing than actual work. You've got to stop this, she scolded herself. *You're acting like a child—with no good reason.*

Her mother called. Virginia did not know whether or not to be thankful for the distraction.

"I was out to the farm yesterday," Belinda told her. "My, I'm glad I went before the wind started blowing. The roads will be nasty today. I was really pleased about how things are going with Mr. Simcoe. I had been worried, but it seems—to this point, at any rate—that things are working out well. He's even taken on the chores that Clare's boys had to do. Hauling the wood and water and emptying the slops.

"Pa appears to enjoy having a partner for checkers. Mama—I do worry a little about Mama. She seems to feel she needs to be cooking for a guest now. Mr. Simcoe has a hard time getting her away from the stove. But maybe keeping busy—in moderation—will be good for her.

"While I was there Pa wanted to move from his chair to the table, and it was quite an easy thing for Mr. Simcoe to just take his arms and help him up. So much different than when Mama tried to boost him. I think it was easier on Pa too. Mr. Simcoe is a fairly big man, used to hard labor, so he is strong enough. Poor Mama. It was a major task for her."

Virginia decided her only role at the moment was to listen. Her mother seemed so relieved about the situation at the farm and she just wanted to talk.

"And he can drive the car too. They won't need to worry if supplies are needed from town. Or if for any reason a fast trip has to be made—an emergency—or anything. And if the weather is bad, he can use a shovel. Papa would have never been able to do that if they had gotten stuck in a drift."

Virginia was able to offer little more than an occasional murmur to let her mother know she was still listening.

"Oh my. I forgot," Belinda said suddenly. "Today is the day Jenny is coming. Is she there yet?"

"No—Jonathan has gone for her."

"I hope they won't have any trouble with the roads. Your father had to make a trip out in the country, and he just called and said the roads were really bad in spots."

"Jonathan took the shovel."

"Well, I won't keep you. I know you must have work to do to be ready. Just wanted to let you know that things seem to be going well at the farm."

Virginia thanked her mother for calling and turned back to the tasks at hand, her eyes once more on the clock. At least the hands had moved forward.

She remembered Jonathan's request that she keep an eye on the barn. Slate was just moving one of the mares into the warmth after taking her to the watering trough. Thankful, Virginia turned back to the stove.

The rhythmic chug of the car's motor finally announced they were back. She hurried to the window, trembling, and watched as Jonathan opened the passenger's side door and a woman stepped out. Her face was hidden beneath the brim of a green felt hat. Jonathan closed the door and opened the trunk to retrieve a suitcase. They were talking to each other as they moved up the path to the porch. Jonathan looked pleasant enough, and Virginia found herself whispering a little prayer of thankfulness. She was so glad he had been able to lay aside his misgivings and be courteous to their guest.

Virginia wiped her hands on her apron, removed it, and tossed it on a nearby kitchen chair. She had the door open before they reached it and stood back, giving a little wave to welcome the woman inside.

"Jenny," she said, trying to keep her voice from sounding as nervous as she felt. "Come in out of the cold. It's freezing."

She dared not say, *How good to see you.* Nor, *It's been such a long time.* Jenny would find that maudlin. Neither did she dare move forward for a hug or a kiss on the cheek. Jenny abhorred emotional scenes.

Jenny moved in, brushing the snow from her shoulders as she did. Martha, at the table, had stopped her coloring. She stared openmouthed at this stranger who was Mindy's Mama Jenny.

"I've got the coffee on," said Virginia for something to say. Then rushed on, "Take Jenny's suitcase up to the first bedroom, dear." The three girls had been moved to make room for the guest. They would be spending the next nights on makeshift beds on the floor in their parents' room. Slate had volunteered to give up his room for the barn loft, but with the colder weather and Slate's injured leg, Virginia would not hear of it.

Jonathan moved to do as bidden, and Virginia stepped forward as Jenny shrugged out of her heavy coat.

It was the first that Virginia had gotten a good look at her friend, who still had not said a word. It appeared that Jenny's health had not improved. She was even thinner and paler than before, making Virginia even more nervous. She reached to hang up the coat and motioned Jenny toward the table. Martha still stared, absentmindedly sucking on the end of one of her coloring pencils.

"Jonathan will be right down," said Virginia in an effort to find something to say.

Jenny moved forward slowly and sat gingerly across the table from the little girl who had followed her move closely. Martha's eyes were big, her curiosity piqued.

At last she could hold back no longer. "Are you Mindy's Mama Jenny?"

Jenny looked from the small child to Virginia and back again. She said nothing.

"Yes," said Virginia, reading Jenny's uncertainty. "We have no secrets around here."

Jenny seemed to sag in her seat. She nodded. At least she was not going to make a fuss about the fact that they had been honest with Mindy.

Virginia poured the coffee. She was tempted to ask Jenny how she had been, but she didn't dare. It was quite obvious that Jenny had not been doing well. If she wished to disclose that information, she would do so in her own time. Virginia was relieved to hear Jonathan's step on the stairs. It would help to have another person at the table to make conversation.

"How were the roads?" she asked almost before he was in the door.

"Not good—in spots. But I only had to get the shovel out once. That patch of open land by the Blais farm. It blows pretty bad across there."

He took a seat beside his young daughter, who was busy studying the woman across from her. She did not even seem to notice her father's presence.

"So . . ." he said. "You've been making another picture."

She did manage a nod, but her eyes never left Jenny's face.

"Looks like Slate's hat."

She nodded again.

"How is poor Slate going to keep his head warm when his hat's in here?" Jonathan's voice was teasing. Martha at last turned to him, her eyes twinkling. "That's not his real hat. That's silly." She giggled.

Virginia was thankful for the bit of lightness in the room. Bless Jonathan for trying.

————

Jonathan eventually drove the team and cutter to the school to get Mindy. He didn't want to chance the motorcar on the roads, and it was too cold for her to walk the distance. Virginia could not help but wonder what the conversation would be on the way home. Would they speak of Jenny?

And how would the two respond when they finally met again? Virginia's nerves were so tight she jumped when Olivia called out that she'd had her "good sleep time."

Jenny had been nearly mute. She seemed even more morose than in the past. Virginia did not want to press. But she did wish the tension in the kitchen would be reduced.

Martha had at last lost interest in the newcomer and gone back to her play. It must have seemed to the small child that Mindy's Mama Jenny was not going to bring much excitement to the house—in fact, she was rather dull.

Virginia picked up Olivia, still rosy cheeked and bright-eyed from her nap. Olivia gave Jenny her full attention, eyes large with curiosity, then grinned.

"My," Jenny surprised Virginia by commenting, "that one sure is Jonathan's." Her voice sounded husky, probably from her years of smoking. She put her hand to her mouth and coughed. Her entire frail frame shook, and by the time the spasm had passed, she looked watery eyed and spent.

"Does talking bring on a coughing spell?" Virginia asked with concern. If so, no wonder Jenny did not speak much.

"Not always," said Jenny with a shrug of the thin shoulders. But she coughed again.

Virginia settled Martha and Olivia with milk and a piece of sugared bread. Then James announced his return from dreamland with some banging on his crib. Virginia hurried to get him. If she didn't, he'd be trying to crawl over the side again. He'd already had two tumbles.

He too studied the woman at the table, then clung to his mother. James, their adventurous little troublemaker, was the most timid with strangers. Virginia was afraid he might start to howl.

"Look," she said to distract him. "Martha and Olivia are having milk and bread. Would you like some?"

He still had his fists filled with her dress, one hand pulling at the bodice, the other tightly tugging on a sleeve. He lifted his head for one more look at Jenny, then buried his face against his mother's shoulder.

"He's a bit shy," explained Virginia, though she knew his response needed no explanation.

She disentangled his fingers and placed him on the floor. He grabbed handfuls of her skirt and leaned into her so she could not even move.

"He'll be fine—once he gets to know you," Virginia explained. She attempted to pry him loose. "Papa and Mindy will soon be here. Listen. Can you hear the team?"

But even that would not distract baby James. Virginia was forced to pick him up again. She fixed his milk and bread with him in her arms.

The jingle of the harness did seem to catch his attention. His head came up and he forgot the danger of the woman at the table. He even pushed away, wanting to be set down again. Virginia lowered him to the floor and watched as he raced toward the door on sturdy legs.

Mindy did not appear alone. Jonathan was with her, one hand resting lightly on her shoulder. Mindy's eyes traveled the kitchen until they rested on Jenny at the table. Neither said a word.

Say something, Virginia wished to scream at the woman. *This is your daughter you're facing.*

Jonathan urged Mindy forward. "Mindy," he said, his voice firm but low, "say hello to your Mama Jenny."

Without smiling, Mindy responded, her back obviously pressing hard against Jonathan's hand. "Hello."

Jenny nodded. Just nodded, her eyes scanning the young girl before her and then returning to her coffee cup.

"Mindy—change your school dress, and I'll fix your hot cocoa," said Virginia, trying to keep her voice matter-of-fact. Jonathan cast one glance Virginia's way, then turned to go out to care for the team.

Mindy turned to the stairs, and three eager younger siblings followed along behind her. To the children, Mindy's return from school was the highlight of the day.

"Did you see her?" Virginia heard Martha say excitedly. "She's here. Your Mama Jenny."

Virginia did not hear Mindy's answer.

She turned to Jenny. "Mindy's a good student," she began, hoping to make some kind of connection—draw some kind of response from Jenny. "She always brings home a good report card."

Jenny stirred. "I don't suppose you're going to let me smoke in front of the kids," she said and coughed again. "Where am I to be exiled this time?"

"Jonathan has the heater going in the shed where he keeps the car. It'll be warm. I've asked him to put a chair in there for you."

Jenny gave a wry smile. "Planned ahead—did you?"

Virginia nodded. She had to admit it. Jenny left her seat and crossed to where her coat hung. She shrugged into it, coughing again.

She was going out the door when she turned back. "She's grown" was all she said, but Virginia was thankful for the two simple words.

————

The children had been put to bed and the house was quiet. Virginia heated some apple cider and joined Jenny near the front-room fireplace. Even through the walls, the chill of the winter's night could be felt. They stretched their feet toward the flicker of flame and sipped at the spicy cups.

Both Jonathan and Slate had retired early—something Jonathan hardly ever did. Virginia knew it was not fatigue that had taken him up the stairs but that Virginia and Jenny needed some time alone.

"You haven't gained any weight," Virginia dared to comment. "Have you not been well?"

Jenny shrugged.

"How have things been since . . . since. . . ?" She wasn't sure what to say.

"I'm doing okay."

"Good."

Silence again.

"Are you still living in the same place?"

"No. I moved. A couple of times."

"You're still . . . alone?"

"Yeah. I'm alone."

"Your friends . . ."

"What friends," Jenny said, sarcasm in her tone. "My former friends have forgotten I exist."

Virginia was silent for a moment. "I'm sorry," she managed at last.

"Don't be. They aren't worth missing." Jenny's words were followed with a bout of coughing.

They sipped quietly.

"She's . . . really grown, hasn't she?" mused Jenny.

"Getting to be a young lady," answered Virginia.

"I noticed she helps around the kitchen."

"She's very good at helping out. I don't know what I'd do without her." The simple phrase sent a pang to Virginia's heart.

"The kids seem to like her." Jenny coughed again.

"They adore her. They can hardly wait for her to get home at night. She's so good with them."

Again there was silence.

"You've done a good job."

This bit of high praise from Jenny was highly unexpected.

Virginia's eyes filled with sudden tears. "Thank you," she whispered, "but I haven't done it alone. Jonathan—"

"I noticed. He's good with kids."

"He's a great father." Suddenly Virginia's heart was so full that she wondered if she would be able to contain the emotion of it. She was so thankful that God had blessed her life with Jonathan. Thankful for his love for family. His deep, committed devotion.

Jenny set aside her empty cup. "I'm going out for one more cigarette," she said, "then I'm off to bed. I'm beat. It's been a long day." As she moved she went into another spasm of coughing. Virginia could not help but feel alarm.

———

Jenny did not join them at the table the next morning, so it was easy to follow the normal routine. The family shared breakfast and family Bible reading and prayer. Martha remembered Mindy's poor Mama Jenny, and Virginia wondered just what the child meant by the words. The usual morning commotion saw Slate leave for the barn and Jonathan bring the hitched team to the door to transport Mindy off to school. There was the scurry to bundle up, gather books and lunch pail, the good-bye hugs and kisses and calls of younger siblings as Mindy was pressed out the door—and then the excited clambering for the spot at the window to watch the team trot briskly down the long driveway.

Virginia took a deep breath. She had to bake bread. She'd best get the yeast set. She turned to the little ones, who were climbing down off the chair by the window.

"Martha, why don't you take James in and get him some toys?"

"Yay," clapped Olivia, seeming to think that play was a good idea.

Martha took James's hand and started toward the toy box, then turned suddenly to her mother. "Is Mama Jenny going to come back?"

"She is still here. She is sleeping. Well, I don't suppose she is still sleeping—with all the racket. But she is still in your room."

Martha's eyes grew big. She had never heard of anyone sleeping past breakfast.

"Is she sick?"

"No, she's . . ." But Virginia stopped. Maybe she was. She certainly didn't look well. "She's very tired," she answered the child.

"Do we have to be quiet?"

"It would be a wonderful idea."

Virginia turned to the cupboard to lay out the ingredients.

"Jamie doesn't know how to be quiet."

"Maybe you can show him."

She lifted down the yeast and sugar and reached for a bowl.

"I don't think he wants to learn that."

Virginia turned. James was tugging impatiently, wanting to be free from the restraining hand of his older sister. "No," said Virginia. "I don't suppose he does. But you and Olivia can be quiet anyway. That will make two less noises." She held up two fingers.

Martha disregarded the grammar and seemed to get the message. All three turned to go.

It was close to noon before Jenny made an appearance. "I hope you didn't try to hold breakfast for me," she mumbled.

"As a matter of fact, I did. For a while."

"Don't. I don't eat breakfast. I would have some coffee, though."

Virginia pointed to the pot on the back of the stove. "Might be a bit strong by now."

"Strong I like. Where's your biggest cup?"

Virginia, who was punching down her batch of bread, pointed at the cupboard door with her chin. "In there."

"Do you mind if I take it out with me?"

"No. That's fine."

"The heat's still on?"

Virginia nodded. "I'm sure Jonathan will keep the fire going for as long as you need it."

Jenny filled her coffee cup and reached for her coat.

"Why don't you just carry the pot on out with you?" suggested Virginia. "You can set it right on the stove out there. It'll stay hot if you want another cup."

Jenny nodded. Virginia thought that her eyes seemed to take on a bit of life.

"Use that potholder hanging by the stove."

Jenny poured the cup of coffee back into the pot to keep it warmer for the trip to the outbuilding.

"You'd best be careful, Virginia. I might just get so comfortable out in your shed that I won't come back."

Virginia hoped that the quip was meant as a joke, noting silently the longest sentence Jenny had spoken yet. She knew Jenny wasn't fond of being sent to the shed for her cigarettes, but she had no intention of making her family live with a smoked-filled home.

"Come back in time for dinner," she replied, smiling so Jenny would know she was teasing.

Jenny nodded, picked up the pot and her cup, and left the house, coughing again.

CHAPTER 10

$\mathcal{H}$ave you seen your father?" Virginia asked Jenny as they sat at the table following the noon meal. The men had already excused themselves and headed for the barn. Virginia was catching her breath before corralling the two youngest for their afternoon naps.

Jenny shook her head. "No, I have not seen my father." She seemed to emphasize each word, and Virginia gathered she would be wise to drop the matter. But she pushed on.

"Don't you think you should? He misses you, Jenny."

"What would give you that idea?"

"We see him—fairly frequently. At church on Sundays— and he comes out to the house from time to time."

"Well, I hope one of those times isn't while I'm here."

"Why?" asked Virginia, doggedly pressing for an answer. "Why do you feel so . . . so ill toward him?"

"Why shouldn't I?"

"Because. Because he's your father."

"And that means I'm supposed to feel something for him?"

"Most people do."

Jenny shrugged. "Well, I'm not most people. Or had you forgotten?"

Virginia rose from her chair. "I must put the children down for their nap. Do you want another cup of tea?"

Jenny pushed her cup forward and Virginia refilled it.

When Virginia came back down the stairs, Jenny was still sitting at the table, her shoulders hunched, her head down. She did not look at all well.

When Virginia began to clear the table, Martha ran to join her. She loved to gather all the cutlery, which she stacked together in a heap on the counter.

"When you are done with your job, would you like to go out with Papa for a while?" Virginia asked her small helper. "The sun is shining, and the wind isn't blowing." Martha's "Yes!" was filled with excitement at the prospect of getting out of doors. She hurried with the little chore, clattering tableware and chatting about her upcoming venture to the barn.

Virginia stopped to help the child dress warmly, then opened the door. "Remember, let Papa know you are there before you go into the barn. Make sure he sees you. You just stand and watch—don't get in their way."

Martha agreed, with many words and waving of hands.

Virginia turned to see Jenny cringing in her seat. She said some words under her breath that Virginia assumed she was glad weren't said aloud. Jenny muttered, "I don't know how you stand the racket. If it isn't one chattering away at you, it's two. It'd drive me crazy."

Virginia refused to let Jenny's words disturb her. "I don't find it a problem. Oh, I admit there are times when it would be nice for some peace and quiet—but that does come every night after they have been tucked in bed. Then the house often seems too quiet."

"I don't know how you stand it," Jenny repeated, choking back the chronic cough. "Did you set out to have three kids?"

Virginia laughed as she lifted the dishpan off its wall hook. "Set out? I guess I haven't thought about it much. And what makes you think I'm planning to stop now? Besides, there are four—not three."

Jenny gave her a cold look. "Don't forget," she said, "one of them is mine."

The thrill of fear that shot through Virginia left her weak-kneed and shaking. She focused all of her attention on the dishwashing. Jenny made no move to help.

———

When Mindy returned home from school, she gave Virginia her customary hug, said hello to Jenny, then went to change her school clothes, an excited little entourage following close behind her.

"Boy, I'd think she'd get sick of that," Jenny commented sourly.

"What?" asked Virginia, perplexed.

"All those little kids dragging along, hanging on to her hand and her skirt or anything they can get their hands on—chattering like a flock of blue jays."

Virginia smiled. "I don't think it bothers Mindy at all."

"Don't know where she gets that from. Sure isn't her mother."

Virginia let that comment pass and continued to prepare the vegetables for supper.

When the children trooped back into the kitchen, Virginia prepared their cider and put them around the table to eat. She supposed their presence there was an annoyance to Jenny, but she would not exile her family just because a visitor preferred silence and solitude.

The cheerful chatter rose in volume, and Jenny pushed back. "I'm going out," she announced, and Virginia understood that she was going for a cigarette.

Virginia continued her supper preparations. She was tempted—had been tempted all day—to phone Mr. Woods again and invite him for a meal. Surely Jenny could not object to her asking guests into her own home. But, yes, Jenny might indeed object—and in a way that could make things between the two worse than they already were. As difficult as

it was to understand, Jenny did not wish to see her father—
at all. Virginia could not fathom it. Had something happened
that she was not aware of, or was Jenny simply being obsti-
nate because of her childhood hurt?

———

"Mama would like to see you," Virginia told Jenny that
evening. "She hasn't been over yet because of the roads—and
because she thought we should have some time together first.
Do you mind if she comes out tomorrow afternoon?"

"Why should I mind?"

"I just wanted to check—that's all."

Jenny shrugged in her familiar, impatient way. "If she
wants to see me, she'd better make it soon. I don't plan to be
here much longer."

Virginia leaned forward. "But you just got here.
Surely—"

"I've been here two days already."

"That's not . . . We've hardly had time to talk—"

"What's there to talk about?"

"Well . . . you, for one thing. I . . . I don't even know. . . ."

"You know as much as you need to know."

This time Virginia would not let the comment pass. "I
know nothing," she insisted, frustration in her voice. "You've
said nothing—to speak of—since you've arrived. Only little
comments . . . mostly about the noise of my children."

"Boy, you are touchy." Jenny added some unrepeatable
words under her breath.

"I'm not touchy. I'm worried. Jenny, you . . . you look like
death itself. You cough from morning to night. I've even
heard you during the night. One can't . . . can't live like
that." She reached helplessly toward her friend, then let her
hand drop.

Finally she spoke again. "And I don't know where you
live. How you . . . manage. I don't know anything about you.

We are friends. Surely . . . surely you can be a bit more open than you have been with me."

Jenny waved a bony hand in the air. "Okay. Okay—let's stop with the theatrics. If you think you need to know what should be private and personal, I'll tell you.

"I live in a small apartment downtown. It's not much, but it's a place to stay. I get by—just fine. Hayden had a life-insurance policy—not much, but in true Hayden fashion, he'd failed to sign it over to that . . . that other woman." Jenny swore again. "Poor ole' husband-snatcher—she never got a thing. Hayden hadn't planned to die, you see. Hayden thought he'd live and party forever.

"You think I'm not well. Why should I be well? Why would anyone care? I've lost my husband—I've lost my kid. What reason do I have to even live?"

"You have me. Us. We care, Jenny. And your father. He cares. And he would show you, if you'd just let him."

Jenny swore again.

"Have you seen a doctor?" Virginia pressed further. "I'd like to make an appointment for you with Uncle Luke. I'm sure there is something—"

"Drop it, Virginia. Just drop it, okay? I've seen more doctors in the last year than one should have to see in a lifetime."

Virginia was relieved to hear that Jenny was seeking medical help, but frightened that they had not been able to help her.

"But can't they do—"

"No!" said Jenny emphatically. "They can't *do*."

"What do you mean? Have they tried?"

Jenny looked at Virginia evenly, a chilling glare hardening her eyes and stopping Virginia's words. "It's curtains for me, Virginia," she said without any sign of emotion. "My lungs are shot. Cancer."

Virginia's breath caught in her throat. She sank down into her chair, a little sob escaping her lips.

Jenny stood up. "That's the last I want to talk about it or hear of it," she said. "You had to know. You wouldn't rest until you dragged it out of me. But I want no ridiculous fussing about it. I can't stand fusses and I don't want you stirring one up now. Understand? I want this kept quiet. I didn't even want you to know 'cause I don't want any big commotion made over it—but now that you know, promise me you'll keep it to yourself."

Virginia could not speak. Could not even move her head in a nod.

"Promise?" insisted Jenny.

Virginia managed to swallow and meekly nodded her head, her eyes full of tears.

Jenny turned and headed for the stairs, a spasm of coughing slowing her progress.

————

The next morning felt more like spring than a winter's day. The icicles that had formed on the rooflines dripped into banks of snow, making strangely shaped holes deeper and deeper into the whiteness like some invisible tool. Shivers of steam rose from the dark barn roof. Chickens that had been huddling away in the henhouse came out to scratch at the frozen ground, totally ignoring the filled troughs they had left behind. The cats stretched out lazily on the back porch, soaking in sun rays as though storing them for any weather that might lie ahead. Murphy was much too busy to provoke them as he barked excitedly at a squirrel that had poked its head out of a hole in a tree.

Virginia sighed as she looked out the window, wishing spring truly had arrived. But she knew better—they were only into the middle of February. There would be more storms to come. She sighed again and took the opportunity to send Martha out to play while the two younger ones slept.

She would love to take the other two little ones out for some fresh air after nap time. It would be good for all of them. But right now she had guests.

She poured three cups of coffee and sat down at the table across from Jenny. Her mother occupied the other chair at the table. This was the first attempt of Jenny's to be hospitable. Belinda had always seemed to have that effect on Virginia's longtime friend. They were talking now of books, and it sounded like Jenny spent much of her time reading. Virginia was surprised at how up-to-date she sounded. It made her feel embarrassed that she had so little time to keep abreast of current thought.

"Do you get out much?" Virginia heard her mother ask.

"To the library," said Jenny, managing a hoarse laugh.

"Well—that's as good a place to go as any. But some companionship with real live people would be good for you too."

"I don't seem to have many of the old friends since . . ." Jenny did not finish the statement, but both Belinda and Virginia knew she was thinking back to Hayden again.

"I've been trying to talk Jenny into staying for a long visit," Virginia put in.

"Surely you're not thinking of going back already?"

Jenny toyed with her cup. "I've gotten rather used to . . . to things being quiet."

Belinda laughed. "Well, it's not very quiet here, I can testify to that. This little family is busy, busy, busy."

Jenny nodded. "One gets in rather a rut," she said, "and after a while it gets comfortable—in a way."

Virginia sat and listened to the casual conversation. She wondered what her mother would think—or say—if she knew that Jenny had cancer. Virginia had asked no further questions after Jenny's blunt announcement. She did not know how serious Jenny's condition was. She only knew that the very word itself carried doom—left her feeling chilled. There was no reversing the diagnosis.

Please, Jenny, her inner heart cried silently. *Please—stay here and let me take care of you. Don't go back to your lonely room—your library. Stay with me.*

Jenny was saying to Belinda, "I found this new author. It's the first I've read any of his work, but I quite liked it. I decided I'm going to look up more. It's very light reading, but it . . . it sort of takes you out of the world for a few hours. His . . ."

Olivia called and Virginia excused herself and went for the child. From then on there was little chance for more discussion. The child demanded her grandmother's full attention, and soon Martha was pounding on the door, wet from playing in melting snow. Then it was James who let them know his nap time had ended. Virginia's world was back to its normal chaos.

"I must get home," announced Belinda, rising from her chair. She leaned over and gave Jenny's thin shoulders a warm hug. "I do hope you change your mind and stay longer," she said, but Jenny was noncommittal. Belinda then turned to Virginia and gave her a kiss on the cheek. "Thanks, dear. Now that the weather has warmed, maybe you'll make it into town for tea. It's been a long time."

Virginia acknowledged that it had been.

"Tell Jonathan and Slate I said hello." She was about to pass through the door when she turned back. "Jenny," she said, as though she just had the idea. "If staying here is too . . . too lively for you, why don't you come in and spend some time with me? It's quiet at my house. Much too quiet most of the time. You can read all you like. I have a whole shelf of books I doubt you've read, and there are more at the library."

Jenny smiled and gave a little wave. "Thanks," she answered, but Virginia was quite sure she had no intention of accepting the offer.

"Oh, Mama, here's a loaf of that oatmeal bread you used to make." And Virginia followed her mother out on the porch. Belinda quickly turned to her. "She looks a fright," she whispered. "Is she well?"

Virginia could feel the tears gathering in her eyes. She shook her head, unable to speak.

"Has she said anything?"

Virginia swallowed away the lump in her throat and fought for control of her voice. "She's . . . she's very ill, Mama, but she doesn't want any fuss about it."

She read the horror in her mother's eyes. "What. . . ?" she began.

Virginia wished to blurt it all out to her nurse-mother, but she checked her impulse. "I can't talk. I know little—Jenny made me promise. And I have to get back to the children."

Belinda gave Virginia another kiss on the cheek and said, "Thanks for the bread," and turned to go. "Call me," she murmured. "Call me as soon as you can talk freely."

Virginia turned back inside. *That's the problem*, she thought. *Jenny has made me promise not to talk freely.*

In spite of the sunshine outside and the laughter of small children, a gloom seemed to settle over the house with Belinda's departure. Virginia went about cleaning up from the coffee time. Jenny took her pack of cigarettes and another cup of coffee and headed for the shed. *Her lungs are gone and she still insists on poisoning herself*, Virginia noted, vexed with her stubborn friend.

She tried to put aside her impatience with Jenny and went straight to her supper preparations. Mindy would soon be home. Perhaps her presence would dispel some of the heaviness.

But when the child arrived, her face was troubled. She looked around the kitchen. "Is Mama Jenny still here?" was her first question.

"Yes. She's out right now."

Mindy looked both relieved and worried. "She hasn't changed her mind, has she?"

"No. She still plans to go back home soon."

"I don't mean about that. I mean about God. She still doesn't love Him, does she?"

"I—we haven't talked about it . . . yet."

"But she doesn't even close her eyes when we pray."

At Virginia's knowing smile, Mindy rushed to explain. "Last night Jamie pulled my hair during prayer time, and I opened my eyes and Mama Jenny's eyes were wide open. She was just sitting there looking at her hands."

"Oh."

"I don't think she likes God at all."

"Mindy, honey, we mustn't judge people for opening their eyes during grace."

Mindy nodded solemnly. "But she doesn't pray to God at all."

"How do you know that?"

"She told me."

"She told you?"

"When I went to my room last night to get my school clothes ready for today, I told her that I prayed for her every night. She said I might as well save my breath—it hadn't done one bit of good. I asked her if she prayed, and she . . . she laughed and said, 'Never.' "

"She said that . . . to you?"

Mindy nodded, her eyes dark with concern. "I thought . . . I thought God answered prayer," she said, her voice trembling.

Virginia bent and gathered her daughter close. "He does. Never, never lose faith in Him. He does. But sometimes, sometimes it just takes years and years of praying. And sometimes—sometimes people resist what He wants to do."

"Mama Jenny's resisting."

"I think she is."

Mindy thought about it. "I wish she would go away again," she said quietly. "I don't like her to be here. I can pray for her just as good when she's in her own city."

Virginia did not know how to respond. Jonathan was right. Jenny's presence was upsetting the child. Just how much ground would they lose?

Again Jonathan retired early, leaving the two women to talk on their own. Virginia was not sure if it was for their sake or because he simply did not wish to play further at being the cheerful host. She knew he would spend the time reading until she came up to bed, keeping the light shaded from the sleeping children.

Slate too went to his room, though Virginia wondered fleetingly just what he would do with the long evening hours. Perhaps he would listen to the radio his folks had sent him for Christmas. Virginia had little time herself for the radio. The strange crackling voices put her on edge. It didn't seem normal that somebody so many miles away should be heard in her living room. But Jonathan seemed to enjoy it, and the children took great delight in the radio and its music.

Virginia put another log on the fire and watched the sparks dance upward. She never tired of watching the flames. They seemed alive, full of vigor and joy. Yes, joy, that was it. They always looked as though they were dancing in pure delight.

"I'm off," Jenny said with a yawn. "All this visiting exhausts me."

You ought to try running after little ones and keeping up with meals and laundry, thought Virginia but then felt guilty. Jenny was in no condition to do any of those things.

"Will Jonathan be able to take me to the train tomorrow?"

This was the first time Jenny had asked. On previous trips, she had informed them of her plans.

"You're quite sure you want to go . . . so soon?"

"I'm sure."

"Then I'm sure he will be able to arrange it."

"I'm going out for a cigarette before I go to bed."

She left, and Virginia did not even pick up her knitting. She just sat and watched the red-and-gold flames lick at the new log until charred patches began to appear on each side of it. She was deep in thought—and she was weary. In a way that she did not wish to put into words, she agreed with Mindy. She would be glad when Jenny returned to her city. As much as she wanted her to stay, she would be glad when she was gone. Her visit had been a strain on the entire family.

Jenny was soon back. Virginia smiled, then sobered to say, "Jenny, you asked for no . . . no exhibitions. But I just want you to know that . . . that if there is ever anything I—we can do, we're here."

Jenny nodded but said nothing. Instead she moved toward the stairs, then turned back. "Don't bother sending Mindy to school in the morning."

Virginia frowned. "What do you mean? It's a school day. We never keep her home from her classes even to see someone to the train."

"She'll not just be seeing me to the train. I'll be taking my daughter with me."

CHAPTER 11

$\mathcal{V}$irginia felt as if the breath had been knocked out of her. She tried to rise from her chair but fell back, staring numbly at Jenny's back as she ascended the stairs, coughing as she climbed.

As the words sank into her numbed brain, Virginia slumped forward, face in her hands, and began to weep. Surely Jenny couldn't mean it. Surely not. She had not spoken more than a dozen words to the child since she had been in the house. Mindy was their beloved daughter. Jenny had herself given the child to them. Many, many years earlier. Mindy was theirs. *Theirs*.

Then her own words, spoken such a short time ago to little Martha, rushed back to her churning thoughts. "You don't give people away. The relationship is still there."

It was true. Jenny was still Mindy's mother—though she had long since relinquished the right. She had not wanted the little one. Had been about to place the toddler in an orphanage. *An orphanage*—with both parents still very much alive.

Virginia continued to weep. How could they ever stand losing Mindy? What would those little shadows think—Martha, Olivia, and James? How would Mindy feel, bereft of all her family in one swift, wrenching choice of a selfish mother's desire? And Jonathan?

Jonathan! Virginia sat straight in the chair, beginning to come to her senses. *I must tell Jonathan.*

She managed to get to her feet and started for the stairs, tears still coursing down her cheeks. Whatever would Jonathan do when he heard what she had to tell him?

Jonathan, propped up in bed, was reading an article in *Farmer's Magazine.* He had borrowed her pillow to elevate his head. Without looking up from the page, he said in a low voice, "You're early tonight. All talked out?"

"Jonathan," she gasped and could say no more for her tears.

He looked up quickly, then thrust his magazine aside. "What is it? Has something happened? Where's Jenny?"

Virginia could only shake her head wildly.

In two long strides he was in front of her and taking her by the shoulders. "What is it, Virginia?" he insisted, gently shaking her.

Virginia fought for control. She had to talk. Had to make sense—but her whole world was whirling around her. "Let's go down to the kitchen so the children . . ."

Jonathan followed her quickly back down the stairs. Virginia turned to face him, took a ragged breath and said, "Jenny—" She took another gulp to quiet herself. "Jenny is leaving tomorrow. . . ." How could she actually say the words? "She's . . . she's taking Mindy."

Virginia had never seen that expression on her husband's face before. He pulled her tightly to his chest. His arms held her so close she could scarcely breathe. "Oh, Virginia" seemed to come from someplace deep within him. Then he said, "Shh. Shh. It's all right. We'll work it out in the morning."

It was several minutes before Virginia could get control of her emotions. She had expected Jonathan to be angry, then to grieve along with her. Was he simply going to give in to Jenny's determined plan? Had she misread him all these years? Did he not think of Mindy as their daughter? Virginia could not believe what was happening, but she let Jonathan silence her sobs and try to calm her troubled thoughts. The morning seemed to be much too far away to wait. She wanted to talk about it now.

"Let's go to bed," said Jonathan, and his voice boded no argument. "We'll get some sleep." He led her back upstairs to their bedroom and carefully skirted their slumbering brood. Virginia had to cover her mouth to stifle another sob as she looked at Mindy's face, deep in sleep. *Oh, Mindy*, her heart called out to the small figure under the blanket, *what are we going to do?*

Jonathan turned to the bed and moved Virginia's pillow back to its rightful side. She could not read his eyes, but his chin was jutted slightly as though his jaw was clenched.

Virginia started to make further comment, but he cut her off with a rather sharply whispered, "This is not the time of day to be dealing with this. Let's leave it."

He had never before refused to talk about any problems at night. They had always been able to discuss and plan and sort through what should be done in situations they faced. Virginia could only stare at him. He seemed so . . . so different than she was expecting. Was it possible that he really didn't care about what happened to Mindy? *No.* She shook her head. *It must be something else. . . .*

She mopped at her tearstained cheeks and moved to get her nightdress.

"I forgot to check the fire," she murmured as she slipped her dress over her head.

"I'll get it."

Jonathan was gone for quite a while. Virginia was about to go check when he finally came back. He said nothing, just slipped into bed beside her. She did not stir or speak. Perhaps he thought she had already fallen asleep, for he did not lean across to kiss her good-night as he always did. She lay still with her eyes closed. She feared that if he did show his usual affection, she would begin to cry again. That would never do. They both had to get some rest.

Sleep would not come for Virginia. She lay in the darkness, staring up at a ceiling she could not see. There was no light from the moon to outline the room. The night appeared to be as dark as her own soul. Her heart felt as if it were being squeezed.

Jonathan, who usually slept the moment he laid his head on the pillow, also seemed restless. Tonight he tossed and turned from side to side. She heard him sigh and was tempted to speak, but she held her silence. They would talk about it in the morning, he'd said.

But what could they say? What good would any discussion do? Jenny was claiming her child. There was nothing they could do about it. But how could they live without Mindy? How could she live without *them*? Virginia buried her face in her pillow to muffle the sound of her weeping.

Virginia's thoughts whirled—perhaps foolishly—with thoughts of Buttercup. Who would now shower love and attention on the horse? And Murphy? He waited at the end of the lane every afternoon for Mindy to come home from school and ran to meet her with joyous yips that the family was all back together again.

Virginia could not help the tears. Off and on throughout the long night she cried into her pillow. If only Jonathan were awake. If only he would talk—now. If only he would hold her and let her cry. She nearly reached for him, but she held back, uncertain about what he was feeling.

She tried to pray. Her prayers were little more than snatches of phrases, pleading for God to please, please intervene. She was far removed from the ability to say, "Thy will be done." Far too distraught to even make much sense in her petitions.

At last she did manage to fall into a restless sleep. But she did not sleep for long. She wondered if Jonathan was managing to get some rest, then realized that his side of the bed was empty.

She glanced toward the window, but there was no hint of

dawn. She propped herself up on her elbow, straining in the darkness to see the clock by the bed. She fumbled for a match, and flickering light responded to the strike against the side of the box. Virginia lifted the globe of the lamp and touched the match to the wick. A small flame grew until the room was washed in a soft light. The sleeping children did not even stir. The clock said three-twenty-five. Three-twenty-five, and Jonathan was not in bed beside her.

Virginia was stepping onto the rug by the bed when she heard Jonathan's footsteps in the hallway. He looked surprised when he entered the room and saw the lamp lit.

"I was worried," she whispered. "Is something wrong?"

"Just checking" was his noncommittal answer.

"On the fires?"

"The children. Go back to sleep."

Virginia's eyes went quickly to the little ones in various positions of sleep. They were all sleeping peacefully on their makeshift beds. Mindy's arm was draped across Martha's shoulders.

Jonathan climbed into bed again, and Virginia leaned over to blow out the lamp.

Jonathan reached for Virginia, drawing her close to him. But when she began to speak, he softly hushed her. It was clear that he did not think they should get involved in a discussion in the middle of the night. Virginia took comfort from his arms—his closeness. She laid her head against his shoulder, feeling as if she had cried all the tears from her body. She felt him kiss the top of her head as he snuggled her in against his side. "Sleep," he whispered into her hair.

But Virginia could not sleep. Over and over in her mind she fought against the realization that Mindy was leaving them. Mindy. Their oldest daughter. The one whom they had loved—had patiently waited till she could love them in return. What would they ever do without her?

And then again the even more terrifying thought, *Whatever will Mindy do without us?* Mindy scarcely knew the woman who was her mother. Jenny was only a name—a prayer request. The girl knew nothing about Jenny's outbursts and impatience. She knew nothing of Jenny's friends—if indeed Jenny still had friends. She knew nothing about that faraway apartment in the downtown of that distant city. There would be no family members to welcome her home from school each day. *School?* What would Mindy do for school? She was a good student. Now she would go to a new school where she knew no one.

And church. Most certainly Jenny would not introduce Mindy to a church.

Virginia felt panic-stricken with the continuing realizations. Life would be a nightmare for the little girl.

And Jenny was ill. She would not be strong enough, aware enough, to care for the needs of a child.

Why, oh, why does Jenny want Mindy now? Virginia's silent cry nearly tore her apart. *After all the years of ignoring her—why come for her now?*

And then the truth hit her. Jenny was dying. She was lonely—scared. Needing someone. And so she returned to see if that little girl from so long ago could fill in those empty places inside. But why Mindy? Why didn't she get a nurse? A companion? Why drag a child into such a situation? It was unthinkable. Totally unthinkable. Virginia had always known that Jenny was selfish. Self-centered. But this was too much. Just too much.

Virginia could bear the sleepless waiting no longer. She slipped out of bed and made her way downstairs, padding into the living room to stare down at the smoldering logs on the grate. They gave out little warmth and the room was chilly. She reached for the poker and stirred the logs. A brighter flame began to dance around the blackened chunks of wood, and she stirred a little more, then knelt down and blew on the flame. It fanned into life, and she threw on a few smaller pieces, then tried to block out all thought while she watched the flames build.

It would take the new flames some time to reheat the room, and she crossed to the couch to pick up an afghan. Wrapping the blanket closely about her shoulders she lowered herself to the nearby rug in front of the fireplace and tried to get her mind and emotions under control so she could concentrate. There had to be a way to solve this. There just had to.

Jenny could stay on with them. The idea hit her with a force both shocking and full of hope. That way she would be with Mindy as well as have people to care for her.

Even as she entertained the new plan, Virginia remembered how much the noise and activity of the younger children bothered Jenny. And Jenny's need for cigarettes—that would be an ongoing problem. Maybe she—and Jonathan— could consent to her smoking in her room. *Her room*—that was the children's room. They couldn't go very long with all the little ones sleeping on the floor of their bedroom.

"Lord, what should we do?" she prayed, her voice barely above a whisper. She did manage to have some coherent thoughts—thoughts she hoped would express her feelings to her loving God, her Father, who certainly understood her grief and turmoil. And she prayed for Mindy—for wisdom and the right words to tell her about this. She prayed for their other children, who would be losing a dearly loved big sister.

She prayed for Jenny—that as she faced death she would turn to the Savior. All of the anguish of her soul was poured out into her prayer. She felt spent. Entirely exhausted. And in spite of the briskly burning fire and the afghan, she still felt chilled.

She sat in her huddle listening to the ticking of the kitchen clock. Each tick-tock meant one less second of having Mindy. One less second. Oh, if only she could hold her. Whisper to her words of love. But she would not waken the child to meet her own needs.

She had to toss more logs on the fire to keep it blazing. At long last she heard soft steps on the stairs. Was he up because it was time—or because he too could not sleep?

Jonathan stood in the doorway and looked at her, one hand running absentmindedly through his hair. "Did you get any rest?" he asked at last.

"Some."

He moved toward the kitchen. "I'll get the stove going and put on the kettle," he said. "I think we could both use some coffee."

He sounded so . . . so much the same . . . and yet so different. Her whole world seemed different. She wasn't sure how to function anymore, how to relate to him. . . .

She still did not stir. Wrapped in her afghan cocoon, trying to bury herself away from reality for as long as she could. The children would soon be waking. Then, whether she liked it or not, she would need to return to the world. She was a mother. A caregiver. Her own pain would need to be laid aside.

She leaned her head forward on her knees and shut her eyes. But even then the scene would not go away. A house— their house—without Mindy. An empty chair at the table. A long, vacant lane with no little girl, braids swinging, coming home from school, book bag and red lunch pail at her side, Murphy dancing around in front of her.

You should be thankful for the years you've had her, a little voice somewhere deep inside seemed to say, but Virginia was not ready to accept that. It was unfair to be family, and then to be torn apart. It was totally unfair.

What about Jenny? Jenny had no one. Jenny was suffering, was facing the hereafter, without God. Wasn't it selfish to want to withhold her child? Virginia had so much. So many on whom to lean. So many little arms to slip around her neck in warm hugs. So many little faces to give her wet kisses. Was she being selfish?

But Virginia pushed away all those thoughts. Perhaps . . . perhaps if she were the only one to bear this loss, perhaps if it didn't mean pain for Mindy, she could endure it. But

Mindy . . . dear Mindy. What would it mean for her?

She wasn't aware that Jonathan stood beside her until he spoke. "Coffee? It might warm you some."

Virginia stirred, opened her eyes, and shook her head as though to clear the cobwebs. She stood slowly to her feet and accepted the outstretched cup before moving to the chair. Jonathan lowered his tall frame into the other one. He sipped from his own cup in silence. Then he turned to her. His voice held a tone that she had not heard before.

"The children will soon be awake. As much as possible . . ." He stopped, then picked up with, "I think it would be wise that nothing be said in front of them. That we carry on . . . as normal." He sipped from his coffee cup again.

Virginia nodded dumbly. She didn't have the strength to argue . . . and besides, Jonathan was likely right. It would be bad enough when the time actually came.

They finished their coffee in silence. Virginia stood to take her cup to the kitchen, but Jonathan took it from her. "I'd best go get dressed," she managed to say and he nodded.

As Jonathan had predicted, by the time she reached the room the children were stirring. Olivia was the first one awake, and Virginia knew she would not be content until she had rousted the others from their beds.

Martha opened her eyes, then snuggled closer to Mindy's back to catch a bit more sleep. But Mindy was already stirring—stretching. Those familiar movements brought a new wave of sadness to Virginia. She muffled a sob and hastened to finish dressing.

By the time she had leaned over to tie her shoes, James was awake. No stirring and stretching for him. No snuggling back into blankets for a few more moments of shut-eye. He was up with a flourish. Talking even before he was on his feet. From across the room Mindy giggled.

"What did he say?" asked Martha, still blinking sleep from her eyes.

"He said, 'Horsey. Whoa.' I think he wants to go for a ride," Mindy told her.

Mindy was the only family member who seemed to be able to understand James. At least she thought she could, and he usually proved her to be right.

They were all up now. Virginia pulled herself together and began the dressing chores. Mindy helped Olivia while Virginia worked on getting lively James into his clothes.

"You got your dress on backward," Mindy laughed and helped Martha pull her dress around to the front. They all had a good giggle. At last they were ready to troop downstairs. Virginia once again reminded them to go quietly so as not to wake up their guest. But she felt the irony even as she was putting a finger to her lips. Here they were trying to protect someone who was about to tear their world apart. For a fleeting moment she wanted to stand on the landing and scream until Jenny ran from the house with her hands over her ears.

The children chattered and laughed through breakfast, filling the silence between Virginia and Jonathan. Slate didn't do much talking in the morning anyway.

"We're having a spelling bee today," announced Mindy. She loved spelling bees and did very well.

Oh, but you won't be going to school was Virginia's thought. But she could not say the words. She could not even look up lest the lump in her throat explode into wild sobs.

"Spell 'cow,' " challenged Martha.

Mindy spelled "cow."

"Spell 'horse.' "

Again Mindy spelled the word. Martha seemed intrigued with the sound of the letters.

"Spell . . ." She looked about her, thinking long and hard, " 'pancake syrup.' "

"That's two words." But Mindy spelled them both.

"That's right," beamed Martha, though of course Mindy

could have spelled them backward, for all the younger child knew.

"That's right," parroted Olivia, thumping her fork on the table in excitement.

"You'd best finish your breakfast or you'll be late for school," said Jonathan patiently. "We're a little late this morning."

Virginia's head came up. What did he mean? He knew Mindy was not to go to school. She had agreed with keeping things as normal as possible for the children. But Jenny had made it very clear that Mindy should not go to school.

"Let's see," Jonathan was saying as he reached for the Bible. "Whose turn is it to say our Scripture memory verse for the week?"

Three hands went up. James mimicked them, lifting his, spoon included, and managed to spill a bite of pancake and syrup down his arm. The children all laughed in glee, and James, pleased with his performance, joined in noisily.

Virginia went for a cloth to clean him up.

"I think it's Martha's turn," said Mindy.

Martha, thrilled, needed help to get started.

"All things . . ." prompted Jonathan.

"All things . . ." She squirmed on her chair. "All things work for good together."

"Together for good."

"Together for good."

"To . . ." her father said.

She frowned in concentration, then her face brightened. "To us."

"Who love God," finished Jonathan. "Close enough." He turned to the day's Scripture passage.

Virginia, who normally listened intently, heard little of the day's reading. Her thoughts were still on the verse they had been studying all week. She had known the words for many years. Now they were seeking to instill in their children the verses that they would need for life. *All things work together for good to them that love God.* She pushed the verse aside. It was quite a coincidence that it should be the verse they had chosen for this particular week. Or was it?

For good continued its refrain in her mind during the prayer time together.

CHAPTER 12

$\mathcal{W}$hat are you doing?" Virginia asked, confused.

"Making Mindy's lunch."

Jonathan never made Mindy's lunch. Virginia shook her head, trying to understand. Then it dawned—she had not even thought about Mindy's needing a lunch for the long train ride.

"I'll do it," said Virginia, sounding as weary as she felt. "We'd better be generous."

"No, you go ahead and clear the table. Mindy will keep me on track."

So the two of them made the lunch.

As soon as the food was tucked in the lunch box, Jonathan turned to Slate, who was already putting on his heavy jacket. "I'm going to be tied up for a while this morning. After you feed and water, do you want to work a bit with the little bay? She seems a bit skittish. I wanna catch it right away. Something might have spooked her. Let her know she has nothing to fear."

Slate nodded. A chorus of good-byes followed as child after child ran for a good-bye hug. Slate stood there grinning. "You'd think I was heading off to India or something."

Then he was gone after a swish of cold air at the closing of the door.

Jonathan went to the wall phone and rang up a number.

"Mother—good morning." He was the only family member to call Belinda "Mother."

"I was wondering if you have anything pressing today. No? Well, actually—not all of us. Could we bring in the three youngest for a while? Virginia got little sleep last night. She could sure do with a few hours of rest. Good. Thanks. I'll drop them off. See you then. Bye."

Virginia found herself frowning at the mysterious call. "Why did you do that? I could have managed."

But Jonathan merely patted her shoulder and moved on. The next thing she knew he was getting coats and mittens on the children, telling them they were to have a day at Grandma Belinda's house. Squeals of excitement followed. "Would you collect the things for James, please?" he asked Virginia. "I never know what to put in the bag."

Virginia went dumbly up the stairs to do as bidden. She wasn't sure what was happening. Was everything all off base—or was it her weariness and grief that made it seem that way?

By the time she returned with the items for James, Jonathan had the children all ready. Even Mindy. *So that's it,* thought Virginia. *He does not wish them to be here when Mindy leaves.* Virginia fought hard to keep back the tears. Jonathan was right. It would be very hard for the children. Why hadn't she thought of that?

And Mindy. One last car ride with her siblings. One last ride—and the child was not even aware of it.

She kissed them all, holding back her tears until Jonathan had ushered them out the door. Then she broke down completely. She managed to cross to the table, laid her head on her arms, and sobbed.

But she could not cry for long. There was much to be done. She could not do any packing for the child until Jenny got up. All her clothes were in the dresser drawers and closet of the children's bedroom. She did do up the breakfast dishes, occasional tears dripping off her chin into the dishwater. Then she climbed the stairs and made up the beds, picked up little night clothes, and tidied the room. Mindy's nightgown was tenderly carried back downstairs. She would pack it along with the other clothing.

When Jonathan returned they would need to tell the child what was happening. She was sure there would be tears. She knew she would be unable to keep her own in check. She prayed that Mindy might not—

She didn't dare let herself even finish the thought. *Lord, please help us* was all she was able to put into words.

It seemed forever before she heard the motorcar. Had Jonathan said anything to her on the way back from town? Was Mindy fretting about missing the spelling bee? Virginia glanced out the window, her heart beating anxiously.

Jonathan was alone.

She was at the door to meet him. "Where's Mindy?"

"At school," he said as though there were no reason for her to think otherwise.

"But . . . but I said . . . Didn't you understand?"

"I think I understood."

She could not see his face because his back was turned as he slipped out of his heavy coat. "Then why. . . ?"

"Because today is a school day," he answered evenly. "Because she has a spelling bee."

It seemed foolish to Virginia to pull the girl out of class in the middle of the day to make the afternoon train.

Perhaps Jonathan had been wise enough to think of notifying the teacher so that proper preparations could be made for Mindy's transfer to another school. In her muddle-headedness, Virginia had not thought of that. "Did you speak to the teacher?" she asked him.

"No," said Jonathan. "Why?"

Virginia felt totally confused, disoriented. She wished she could go back to bed and get some sleep. Maybe then she would be able to make some sense out of what was going on.

"Why don't you lie down for a while," Jonathan suggested. "I'm going to be working around in here this morning. Take care of some of these little inside jobs I should have done long ago."

"Jenny will be up," cautioned Virginia.

"I'll call you. Anyway, she won't be making an appearance for a long time yet." He glanced at the clock and her eyes followed his. It was ten past nine. Jenny had not yet come down before eleven.

"Maybe I'll just lie down on the couch for a few minutes," she agreed. He nodded.

Surprisingly, she fell asleep. She did not waken until she felt Jonathan's hand on her shoulder. He said nothing, but she understood. She pulled herself upright and disentangled herself from the afghan. She noted that Jonathan had spread another light blanket over her as well.

Jenny was in the kitchen, already seated at the table, looking morose. A cup of coffee was before her. Virginia wondered if she had slept any better than the rest of them.

Jonathan worked on a nearby curtain rod that was loose, his back turned. He said nothing.

"Where's Mindy?" were Jenny's first words to Virginia.

Virginia avoided her eyes. "Jonathan took her to school."

"But we have to catch the train at one-thirty."

Virginia nodded and continued to the table with a plate of muffins.

Behind her she heard Jonathan approaching. He laid his hammer on the counter and reached for a chair across from Jenny. He flipped it around and straddled the seat, arms propped on its back.

"I'm sorry," he said, and there was unmistakable firmness in his voice. "Mindy will not be going with you."

Jenny stared. She seemed too stunned to speak. But Virginia was just as shocked by the words.

It was then that the truth fully dawned. Jonathan had no intention of letting Jenny take Mindy with her. He had been busy working through a plan, no doubt finalizing details as he went. That was why he had not discussed it with her.

"This is Mindy's home—and she's staying here," Jonathan said to the silence.

"She's my child," said Jenny, her voice harsh and demanding.

"Not anymore. You gave up those rights when you walked out that door many years back."

"I never, ever said that I wouldn't be coming back for her," argued Jenny, her face now scarlet with rage. It sent her into a spasm of coughing.

Jonathan waited for the worst of the coughing to cease. "Nor did you say you would," he reminded her.

"You—her parent—were taking her to an orphanage. Remember?" Jonathan had not raised his voice, but his determination could not have been more clear had he shouted.

"A parent can change her mind," Jenny mumbled.

"Not a parent with any right to a child," Jonathan said flatly.

"She's mine. I have legal claim on her and I intend to make it."

Another paroxysm of coughing.

"Have you considered what you are talking about? Do you have any idea what this would do to Mindy? She came to us scared and silent—she wouldn't talk, she wouldn't play. It's taken us years to get the fear out of that little person. That little mind and heart. Do you think for one moment that I'd sit idly by and let that happen to her all over again?"

"Things are different now," argued Jenny, obviously giving in on the point Jonathan had made concerning Mindy's past.

"Yes. Yes. Things are different now. Mindy is loved and she knows it. She is part of our family. And she is staying—right here."

"You have no right—"

"You gave us the right," Jonathan repeated.

Virginia stood as if frozen, her eyes moving back and

forth from Jenny's angry face to Jonathan's calm, determined one. She had never seen him like this. Never in all of their years of marriage. Of course they had never faced anything like this before. But Jenny *was* the child's mother. She did have legal claim. Didn't she?

"I gave you nothing—legally."

"You gave us your word."

"That will mean nothing in a court of law."

"I happen to think it will."

Virginia did not know whether to try to intervene and ask for some kind of compromise or to step aside. They seemed to have forgotten she was even in the room. No wonder Jonathan had not wanted the children present. He knew there would be a scene. One of his own making.

Jenny struggled to her feet. "You can't stop me."

"I think I can."

"I'll get a lawyer. I do have money, you know."

Jonathan also rose to his feet. He passed his hand through his hair, his fingers spread to comb through its thickness.

"Jenny—this isn't about you. It isn't about us. It's about Mindy. It would destroy her to be uprooted and sent off to live with a stranger—"

"I'm her mother," Jenny screeched, a string of profanity following the words.

"And a stranger. Mindy does not know you. Would not feel comfortable with you. And you are not well enough to care for a child."

Jenny swung on Virginia. "You promised you wouldn't tell," she shouted. "I asked you not to, and you promised," and another blast of swearing shriveled Virginia's soul.

But she had said nothing to Jonathan. Nothing concerning the nature of Jenny's illness. Now she thought she understood Jenny's insistence on her silence.

"I didn't," she tried to say over Jenny's angry accusations.

"Tell what?" asked Jonathan, turning to Virginia.

Jenny seemed not to have heard either of them. "First you

pry it out of me," she hurled at Virginia, "and then you spread it around the whole community. How many other people have you told? How many? Some friend you are—you can't even keep your word. And you're supposed to be a Christian. Well—saint you are not." Jenny spat the words at her and swore again.

Weak from her outburst, she sank into the chair, coughing so severely that her face began to lose its color.

Virginia stepped forward uncertainly. She didn't know what to do. How to help.

"Perhaps some water," Jonathan said softly. He had moved around the table to help ease Jenny to her seat, but she shook his hand off angrily. He backed away again, his eyes dark with concern. Virginia placed the glass of water on the table in front of Jenny, but she did not touch it.

When Jenny finally regained her breath and her speech, she spoke again. "Another woman stole my husband, cancer is stealing my life—and now you want to steal my child." She sounded very bitter. Very old.

"No one is stealing from you, Jenny," Jonathan said quietly. His voice and eyes had softened. "No one cares for you more than Virginia. She has . . . has been a friend to you for many years. She . . . she still cares. And because she cares, so do I." He paused briefly and his tone returned to its former resolve. "But my concern does not go so far as to let you take Mindy. The child has done nothing to deserve such a traumatic and devastating experience. We are her family. The only one she has known. To tear her away from us now would destroy her."

In her weakness, Jenny seemed to have little fight left. But the anger clearly was still there. Still smoldering. She did not have the strength left to express it.

"We'll see," she said at last. "We'll see. I'm going straight to a lawyer when I get home. I'm getting a court order—"

"You do that," said Jonathan abruptly. "If you can't think of Mindy, go ahead and find a lawyer. But until you have a court order in hand, don't set foot on my farm again. It's too disturbing—for all of us."

Jenny's head came up. She looked straight at Virginia. "I want out of here," she said. "Now."

"I'll drive you to town," said Jonathan.

Jenny swung around to face him. "No you won't," she hissed. "I'll crawl first."

Virginia cringed. She had never experienced so much raw anger in all of her life. She wanted to run and bury her head beneath a pillow to block out the angry words.

"All right," said Jonathan. "I'll get Slate."

Jenny left the room, climbing the stairs too quickly for her limited strength. Virginia could hear her stop, hear the coughing, knew she was near collapse.

Jonathan grabbed his jacket from the hook by the wall and left, the door closing firmly behind him. True to his word, he was going to get Slate. Jenny would not need to crawl to town.

Virginia wrung her hands helplessly. She didn't know what to do—where to turn. Jenny had always been her friend. Jenny was also Mindy's mother. It seemed right that a mother should have access to her own child. She herself would die if anyone took her little ones from her. But Mindy was hers too. That was what made it so hard. Mindy was hers. Hers and Jonathan's. To take Mindy from them was just as cruel as to keep her from Jenny. And Mindy . . . Mindy would suffer so much if she were wrenched from them.

Jonathan was soon back. "Slate is getting the car," he said, placing his hands on her shoulders and looking into her face. "Do you want to ride in with him and pick up the children, or would you rather have some time alone first?"

"I . . . I think I would. It . . . it would be awkward to go with Jenny now. I . . ."

He nodded his head in understanding.

Jenny was soon back clattering down the stairs, suitcase in hand. Jonathan moved forward to help her with it, but she gave him a look of pure contempt and jerked the bag away. He let her go.

When she reached the door she turned back. "You'll be hearing from my lawyer."

But Jonathan did not back down. "I'll fight you on this, Jenny," he said, and his voice made Virginia feel a chill all down her spine. "If I have to sell every horse on the farm. The farm itself. I'll fight you on it. I won't see Mindy torn from the only family she knows. She belongs here."

Virginia's knees nearly gave out on her. It was all she could do to make it back to the table and lower herself to a chair. Jonathan crossed to her and knelt by her side, putting his arms around her waist. "We'll never let her go," he said, his voice low and deliberate. "You don't think I'd let them take her—do you?"

"She is Jenny's child." Virginia's voice trembled.

"Not anymore. She is our child."

"But—"

"No buts. She's ours—and I aim to keep her. Until she no longer wants to be with us—she stays here."

"But . . . but surely . . . not at the . . . the . . ." Virginia's eyes sought out Jonathan's. A court battle would be costly in far more ways than merely dollars and cents.

"I don't expect things to go that far," he said to her unspoken fear. "But if they do . . . then, yes, we will have to weather the storm—together."

Virginia shivered.

"Why don't you lie down? Try to get some rest. Jenny is gone now—things will be back to normal again."

Virginia wondered if life could be normal again. Ever.

Jonathan stood up. "I'll be back after a while," he said. Virginia supposed he was going out to the barn, but when he reached the door he turned once more. "I'm going over to the school. I'll wait around until Mindy is dismissed and bring her home."

His words constricted Virginia's heart with new fear.

Surely it hadn't come to this. Surely they wouldn't need to spend every waking hour on guard for Mindy's safety. Was that the way they were going to have to live?

All she could do was nod her throbbing head. She just wanted the nightmare over. This horrible, horrible nightmare. She just wanted to crawl away somewhere and be claimed by dreamless sleep.

The door clicked shut. Jonathan was gone. She was alone. She would collapse if she could manage to make it to her bed.

And then the phone rang. Insistent. Making her already taut nerves jerk her body in response. She had to answer it. She pulled herself from the chair and crossed the room. "Hello," she managed, and Clara's voice came over the wire.

"Virginia, is that you? You sound so far away. I can hardly hear you. You'll never guess what just happened. Troy came home with a new motorcar. He's just dying to try it out— show it off. Is it okay if we come out tonight after supper?"

Virginia scrambled for concentration. "We . . . we need to pick up the children. They are at Mama's. We'll be driving in to get them later. I don't know—"

"Great. Call us when you get to town. We can just pop over there. We can show the folks at the same time."

"Yes . . . yes . . . I guess that . . . that will be fine," Virginia stumbled along.

She had just replaced the receiver when the phone rang again. It was her mother inviting them for supper. Virginia wasn't sure if she had said yes or no when she turned away after hanging up. She hoped she had said yes. The distraction would be good for all of them.

CHAPTER 13

"$\mathcal{I}$ am so worn out and confused it gives me a headache," Virginia confessed. The supper dishes had been done and Clara and Troy, with their excited family, had driven away after showing off the new car. Mindy had the little ones in tow in a back bedroom where Grandma Belinda stowed some toys. Now the four adults sat in the family living room. Virginia could feel her mother's eyes searching her face with concern.

Jonathan must have decided on the direct approach. "Jenny has demanded that she have Mindy back."

Virginia's eyes were on her father, the lawyer, who dropped his gaze as though to hide any message his eyes might give. Virginia thought she could see the legal wheels turning in his mind.

"Can she do it, Papa?"

Drew hesitated for a moment, then shifted in his chair. "She has the right to try."

The words further frightened Virginia.

"What would it mean?" asked Jonathan solemnly.

Drew did not take long for his answer. "A fight. Perhaps a long, costly one." He did then pause a moment before he added, "And probably an acrimonious one."

Jonathan nodded. "I guessed as much."

"Are you prepared for that?" asked Drew quietly.

Jonathan shifted in his chair. The muscles along his jaw line moved. "If that's what it takes," he answered, and his words sounded determined as they had when he said as much to Jenny.

Virginia felt the tears sting her eyes. She agreed with her husband, but the entire prospect chilled her soul. She had lived in the home of a lawyer all her growing-up years, and though her father had never discussed his cases with the family, neighbors and others did. She knew of court cases that dragged on and on, year after year—totally destroying families, sucking up everything they had in the process. And still without the intended results. Could they endure that? Should they even try?

Then there was the other side. Jenny had given birth to Mindy. Virginia's mother-heart constricted at the idea of keeping a mother and child apart. Was it morally right? And yet it was Jenny who had brought Mindy to them. . . . She debated with her conscience, not knowing what was the weightier truth. Eventually her troubled thoughts brought her back to Mindy herself—what she honestly felt was best for the child. She knew that Jonathan was right. This could destroy the little girl.

Oh, if only there was some other way. . . . Virginia reached a hand to her aching head. She felt warm and feverish. "Jonathan," she said, her voice unsteady, "we must get the children home. It is already past their bedtime. I imagine . . . Mindy"—her voice caught—"has entertained them as long as possible."

Jonathan rose, nodding his agreement. "Can I drop in and talk with you tomorrow?" he asked his father-in-law.

"If . . . if this thing goes to court . . . you might need a lawyer with more experience in such cases," answered Drew solemnly.

"Well, at least I'd like your advice on some preliminaries—more as a father than a lawyer."

Drew nodded. "How about around eleven?"

It's already started, Virginia groaned inwardly, her head throbbing in pain. *Oh, God—where will it end?*

They managed to change the tone of their conversation before collecting the children for the ride home. James was already sleeping, curled up on a pillow in a corner. Olivia was stacking blocks while Martha, tongue protruded slightly, concentrated on a new picture for Grandma Belinda. Mindy finally had been able to curl up in a chair with a book.

Virginia could not wait to get home to her own bed—hopefully to sleep. "Here," her mother the nurse said as she slipped a small packet into Virginia's hand. "These tablets are very mild, but they will help you sleep."

"My head aches so I can't—"

"They'll help that too."

And then they were all tucked in the car and on their way home through the night. Virginia looked around at the sleepy little ensemble. She was thankful they were all together—with Mindy. She had not known that morning if . . . But she shook the thought from her mind.

Oh, God, she prayed silently, *make Jenny change her mind. Please—don't let her go through with this. She'll destroy us all.*

———

The next weeks were miserable and emotionally wrenching. Virginia felt hopeful one day and despairing the next. No word had come from Jenny. Virginia dared to hope that she had indeed decided not to go through with her threat, but Jonathan cautioned her that things moved slowly through the court system. Silence did not necessarily mean they were now safe.

Virginia woke each morning, the tension of the previous day leaving her weary and strung out. Jonathan was being very wary. She could see it in his face, feel it in his body. Each day he delivered Mindy to school and picked her up at day's end. The teacher was surprised but did not ask questions when she was instructed that no one else was ever to pick up the child. Not even her grandfather Woods.

Virginia wondered if Mr. Woods was aware of Jenny's plans. His manner toward them had not seemed to change when they met in church on Sundays. But perhaps he was adept at hiding his feelings. She could not be sure, and she found herself always on guard—looking for little things that might give some awareness of Jenny's intentions.

Because they did not want to chance any word getting back to Mindy, they did not let anyone else know except for Belinda and Drew. This put further strain on Virginia, who felt she always had to carefully guard her words when talking to Clara or Francine, or when writing to her brothers.

It seemed the whole world had changed. Instead of living in a relaxed, warm world of caring family and friends, Virginia now resided in some dark pit of frightening doubts and suspicions. She watched, she listened, she suspected evil to come from any direction at any moment. The whole situation left her strained and pale.

She tried, she desperately tried, to leave it all with the Lord. To pray for peace and confidence that His will be done. She would struggle through until she came to some kind of settlement on the issue, then something new would happen and she would find herself almost paralyzed with fear again. She scolded herself over and over for her lack of faith—and that only worsened her plight. The guilt added to the tension that characterized her days.

———

The letter, delivered by the usual mail, was addressed to both her and Jonathan and was from a city lawyer, stating that they were to appear in court to hear a child-custody case against them. It had happened. Their worst nightmare had come true.

It meant a trip to the city. It meant making arrangements for the children. It meant train fare and hotel rooms and legal fees and all manner of unforeseen expenses. And it meant a terrible toll on mind and body.

Jonathan quickly sold one of the young brood mares to a farmer who had been anxious for some months to buy her. He did not get the price she was worth, but he hoped it would be enough to pay the initial expenses.

Belinda moved out to the farm to care for the children. The four were both excited and puzzled. Their folks had never left them and gone to the city before. To the smallest ones, "city" was a word they did not know or understand. Mindy, from her years of schooling, had some idea. "It's like a big, big town," she informed them, making their eyes grow wide.

"Can I go too?" Martha asked.

Virginia informed her that she could not—not now. Maybe someday.

"Why are you going?" was the next inevitable question.

"We have some . . . some business."

"What city are you going to?" asked Mindy.

Virginia had hoped this question would not be asked. But she named the city.

"That—isn't that the city where Mama Jenny lives?"

"Yes . . . yes, it is," Virginia admitted.

Mindy's eyes lit up. She was still faithfully praying for Mama Jenny.

"Will you see her?"

"I . . . I think we likely will," Virginia said, busying herself with something to avoid eye contact with the child.

"I'll send her a little note," said Mindy, running to get some paper and a pencil.

Oh, no, thought Virginia. *This might not be good. If the judge thinks Mindy is attached, is in touch with Jenny, it might influence the decision.* Yet, could she turn Mindy down? Could she take the note and then "forget" to deliver it? No—she couldn't be deceitful. Yet if Jenny ended up in court waving a note from her child, what would it mean?

"Why . . . why don't you wait . . . with your note," she said when Mindy reappeared. "You can write a much longer one—later—when you have more time. It's time for you to be leaving for school soon."

The note truly would have been rushed. Mindy nodded in agreement and went for her school bag.

Virginia felt like weeping. She had been so careful in all Mindy's growing-up years to instill in the girl a respect for the mother she did not know. Now it seemed she was having to tear to shreds the very foundations of truth and genuine care she had worked so hard to build. It was true that Mindy, to date, knew nothing of the traumatic shift in relationship—but Virginia did. She felt she was betraying both Mindy and Jenny.

———

Drew traveled with them, and Virginia took comfort in having her father there. At least he knew about courts. At least he could give advice. But most importantly, he was her father and had been as much a grandparent to Mindy as to her other children. She felt some protection from what lay ahead just by his very presence.

It was all confusing and exhausting and foreign to Virginia. There were court appointments, delays, questions, and endless probing. Jenny was there, sitting sullenly across the room. Virginia noticed she had used rouge on her sunken cheeks to try to hide her pallor, but she still looked peaked and drawn. Her lawyer drew his own interpretation of her physical state when he told the court the anguish that his client had been going through because of the severance from her child.

That's not true, Virginia wanted to explain, but a small nudge from Jonathan, who must have felt her tense, brought her back to her senses. One did not make such a scene in a courtroom. There were countless rules and regulations about what could be said and when.

Virginia looked across at Jenny. Truly she looked awful. Now and then spasms of coughing, which she fought to control, shook her frail frame. It made Virginia's heart ache just to watch her. Then a sudden thought brought her forward in her seat. Perhaps Jenny would die before the issue even went to trial, and they would be spared the whole ugly proceeding. Mindy would be theirs. Virginia shrank back in her place, shocked and shamed at such a thought. What a terrible thing to think. Her friend still did not know God. If she were to die now, neither Virginia's nor Mindy's prayers would have been answered—and certainly Virginia would wish death on no one in order to fulfill her own desires.

No, Jenny's demise was not the answer to their problems. Reason. Justice. Mindy's welfare. Those were the things that must guide the decision of the courts.

Virginia thought that this session would never end. She couldn't follow all the legal jargon, but at long last her father was rising, and Jonathan was pulling her up to her feet beside him. The judge was exiting the room.

"Is it over?" she whispered.

Her father nodded. "This part," he answered, his voice low.

"What do you mean?"

"You have a trial date. The case now goes to trial."

"Trial? I don't understand. We aren't making any charges . . ."

"No, *you* are being charged—in a way."

"We are?" Virginia was incredulous. "You mean . . . we are being charged with . . . with keeping Jenny's child?" she gasped.

"That's about it," said her father, stuffing papers back into his attaché case.

"But that's absurd. Jenny gave her to us."

"There are no documents." Her father sounded tired.

"But—"

"Her lawyers will say she was distraught over her broken

marriage relationship—which she was. That she was not thinking clearly—which she probably wasn't. That she agreed to leave her with you—for the time. And she now wishes to resume the mother-daughter relationship."

"But . . ."

But there was nothing Virginia could say. Her head ached again. She felt nauseated and weak. She needed some fresh air. "Please," she turned to Jonathan. "I need to get outside."

He helped her from the close courtroom. She barely noticed its richly paneled walls and straight-backed wooden benches. Down the marble stairs, past the crowd that milled about, to a bench under the shade of a tall tree. She lowered herself to the seat and took several deep breaths. As she regained some composure, the realization hung heavy over her—they had only taken the first steps. Much more still lay ahead.

———

Back home with the children and duties of wife and mother, Virginia tried to pick up the pieces and go on with life as she had known it. But it was very hard. That small date circled on their calendar seemed to loom larger and more menacing with every passing day. Jonathan and Slate worked almost nonstop with the horses to ensure they were ready for the spring sale. They would need every dollar the auction would bring to pay their legal costs.

Drew had contacted a city lawyer, experienced in such cases, and preliminary information had been passed back and forth. The attorney now was preparing their case for the court appearance. Already a sizable amount of money had been transferred to him by way of a bank loan to be paid back at the time of the spring sale.

Virginia tried to ignore the cloud of uncertainty that hung over the household. Even the task of planting her spring garden did not fill her with enthusiasm and anticipation as it had in the past. Everything—everything seemed to be focused on that one date on their calendar.

The children no doubt felt the tension, though nothing was said, even from Mindy. All the daily activities, including prayer time, seemed strained.

At night when Mindy included her usual prayer for "Mama Jenny, and help her to love you," Virginia's heart felt as if it were being torn in two. Virginia and Jonathan dared not voice their deepest concerns until in the privacy of their own room. And then in mere whispers. Virginia wondered if she might collapse under the strain of it all.

It was almost a relief when she had something else to worry about. A letter from Danny told of the birth of their child. It had been a difficult delivery, and Alvira had not gained back her strength as they had hoped. She was holding her own, but they did ask for the family's prayers.

The baby seemed to be doing fine. They had named him Robert Daniel. Virginia liked the name. She longed to be able to see this new nephew. Her prayer focus changed a bit and some of the tension left her.

Then came another diversion. Slate, who had been steadily maturing, began to court one of the young ladies in the congregation. She was a fine girl, from a good family, and Virginia smiled to herself as she remembered those times from her own youth. But Jonathan seemed troubled, though he said nothing. At length Virginia felt she should discuss it with him.

"You don't care for Lucy?" Virginia prompted after they had retired one night.

"What makes you say that? Of course I like Lucy. She's a fine young lady."

"But you don't seem pleased—about Slate. About his interest in her."

He was silent for a long time. It suddenly dawned on her that the problem might not be with Lucy. "You think—we'll lose him?"

"What I'm paying him wouldn't support a wife and family."

"But he does get room and board. It's a fair wage," Virginia reminded him.

"Well . . . he won't expect his wife to live here."

Virginia pondered. "No, no I don't expect he would. But they are still young. Surely . . . surely they aren't seriously considering marriage . . . yet."

"The boy should have a few years to lay aside—to prepare for the day that does happen," said Jonathan. "I had hoped—had planned—to offer him a partnership. Gradually let him pick some of his own stock. Work together here. Maybe even give him some acres for a house."

Virginia pushed up in bed, her eyes shining in the lamplight. "That's a wonderful idea."

"Virginia," he said, "we don't know if we'll even have any horses left when we get through this thing. Not for Slate—not for us."

She slumped back onto the pillow. There it was again. Their whole future, their very lives, depended on what would happen over the next months. "The thing," as Jonathan always referred to the upcoming trial, was a threat hanging over their heads every waking moment.

From then on, the sight of Lucy's shining eyes whenever Slate walked toward her made Virginia sigh rather than smile. It didn't seem fair that even this shared joy should be taken from them.

———

The day was warm and inviting, and Virginia decided she needed to get out. She had not visited her grandparents for some weeks. It was time for her to drop in and see how they were doing.

With Jonathan so busy with the horses, she would not ask him to take on three lively children too. She got them ready to go with her and went to inform Jonathan of her plans.

"I won't be long," she promised. "I'll be home to fix your dinner."

He nodded, his face acknowledging the fact that the outing would do her good.

"We're going to see the farm Grandma and Grandpa," called Martha excitedly. Olivia clapped her hands to indicate how she felt about the proposed trip.

Virginia smiled. Her children lived on a farm, but to them the only real farm was the one where Grandpa Clark and Grandma Marty lived. That was The Farm. The one with the apple trees and porch swing and kittens in the barn.

The motorcar started with no problem, and they were on their way. Virginia had to ask Martha to take charge of James. He insisted on standing on the seat so he could see everything there was to see. Martha wrapped her arms around him so a bump in the road would not send him sprawling into the dash.

Soon they were pulling into the driveway. Virginia was as excited as her offspring. It always felt good to be back in her grandparents' yard with all its memories of family times.

Mr. Simcoe greeted them at the door. Virginia had expected her grandmother and felt a moment of panic.

"Come in," Mr. Simcoe welcomed them, no sign of any concern on his face. "Folks'll be right glad to see you all."

"Where are—?" began Virginia, but then she saw her grandmother slowly coming up beside the man, a big welcoming smile on her face. "Come in, my dear. Come in."

"Now, why didn't you just stay put?" he scolded gently. "I told you I'd bring 'em on in."

Marty's smile deepened. "You think I want to lose even one minute of this visit? I might be slow in gettin' round, but I can still move my body to the door."

Virginia frowned as she noted the difficulty with which her grandmother moved. "Did you fall again, Grandma?"

"No, child, I didn't fall. I jest got me a hip thet don't want to work anymore. Gets stiff when I sit and sore when I don't.

Come in. Come in all of you. Here—come give Grandma a hug." She held out her arms to the children.

From the corner of the room Virginia heard her grandfather stir. He might have just wakened from a nap. He blinked once or twice, licked dry lips, and began to grin. "Well . . . lookee here," he said. "We got us company."

"We came to see you." Martha stated the obvious, then ran to give him his hug. "We wanted to visit awhile."

"That's a wonderful idea," he agreed, holding out his arms.

Olivia was right behind her older sister, and James trotted along on short legs, hopping a bit as he ran and squealing in his excitement.

"I think Grandma can find some cookies," Marty began. "May not be as good as yer mama's, but I think we got some here somewhere."

Virginia set a small basket on the cupboard. "I brought a few things," she said.

Marty hobbled across to where the basket sat and lifted back the tea towel that covered the contents. "Ginger snaps. My favorite. And some lemon cake." She smacked her lips and turned to her husband. "What do ya think of thet, Pa? Lemon cake. Haven't had thet fer a while. I'll put on the tea water."

"You just sit yerself," said Mr. Simcoe, moving to get the kettle. "I'll put on the tea water."

Clark chuckled. "They have them one awful time," he said, seeming amused. "Jest like two younguns, the two of 'em. Always jawin' at one another."

"She still thinks she's a teenager," noted Mr. Simcoe playfully.

"An' he thinks I'm an ole woman," she countered.

From his corner vantage point, Clark chuckled again. Virginia went to kiss him on the cheek.

"Where's your other one?" he asked suddenly.

At Virginia's puzzled expression he went on, "You got another one, haven't ya?"

"Mindy? She's in school."

"She in school already? My, seems she's jest a little thing. In school already. They do grow up."

Come fall, Mindy would be in fifth grade and Martha would be starting off to school. But Virginia noted that her grandfather had not seen Mindy for a while. It would not be surprising if he were having difficulty keeping all the children sorted out. She dismissed the comment as natural enough in the circumstances.

CHAPTER 14

They sipped their tea while the children played on the floor by the table. Virginia could not get used to a man moving about her grandmother's kitchen. But it did not seem to bother Marty. She wanted to talk. Talk about family. About the difficulties of another winter. About the warming of spring and the garden Virginia had planted. Eventually Virginia began to relax. Maybe life for her grandparents hadn't changed so much after all.

But yes—it had. It was evident when she bit into one of her grandmother's sugar cookies. They were not the same as in the past. It was all she could do to nonchalantly keep chewing.

"I think I got a bit too much baking soda," Marty mused. "I fergit sometimes."

Her grandfather chuckled. "Ya shoulda been here the other day," he told Virginia, his eyes sparkling with merriment. "Ma was in the midst of baking up some of her biscuits—an' the phone rang. It was Belinda, an' by the time she finished her chat she couldn't remember a thing. Couldn't tell what she had put in an' what she hadn't. An' tastin' the flour mix didn't help her none. It turned out she put in a double dose of salt—an' no sugar."

Marty laughed right along with him as though it were a

great joke on herself. "Had to throw thet batch out," she said.

Now Clark laughed aloud. "This time ya didn't try buryin' 'em in the garden."

"Oh, ya'd have to bring that old story up again," she said in mock disgust. Then she laughed too. "My, my, that was a long time ago. . . ."

The look her grandparents exchanged made Virginia's heart twist with an emotion she could not have described. *Their marriage has been such an example to all of us*, she mused.

Grandma Marty was saying, "Harry here makes a good batch of bread. I love to smell it baking. Every Tuesday and Friday—them's his bakin' days."

So Harry Simcoe baked bread. Virginia should not have been surprised. He'd had lots of years as a bachelor.

"Well . . . I do git mixed up sometimes," admitted Marty, not seeming the least embarrassed about it. "My mind jest don't stay on it like it used to."

"We ain't suffered thet I can tell," responded Clark. "I git myself any heavier and Harry here won't be able to lift me."

"I think we both put us on some pounds since Harry's come," Marty informed her granddaughter. Virginia could not see that they had, but they had both lost some weight in recent years. Perhaps more than she had realized. They had needed to put on a few pounds. Even now her grandmother's shoulder blades looked bony under the cotton housedress.

Small Martha now came across the room dragging Clark's prosthesis. "Grandpa Clark," she asked. "Do you need your leg?"

Now, where in the world did she find that? wondered Virginia, quickly rising to her feet.

But her grandfather laughed heartily and took the artificial limb from the child. "You think I need thet? Tell you what—I don't use thet there thing much anymore. Jest a nuisance. I jest use this here cane—an' Harry's nice strong arm. We git us anywhere thet I need to go."

Martha looked from her great-grandfather to Mr. Simcoe. She seemed to be thinking that this new houseguest maybe had taken away some of their fun. She had loved to help Grandfather Clark strap on his leg.

Virginia glanced at the clock. "I must get on home," she said reluctantly. "I promised Jonathan I'd be home in plenty of time to get dinner."

Marty moved as though to jump up, but a spasm of pain passed over her face, and she settled back in her chair. "I'm so glad ya come. It's been a long time since ya been over. Pa and me been talkin' about ya and wonderin' how things are goin'."

Virginia ached to be able to talk with her grandparents about the situation with Mindy—but she could not. They still could not freely talk about the court case because they did not wish Mindy to be traumatized by the whole event.

"Well, I was mighty glad to see another spring come," Virginia said, hoping her voice held a light note.

"Aren't we all," responded her grandmother. "But then, I been thet way every spring since I can remember. Yet, when thet first snow falls, I must admit I feel rather snug. Like God is tucking me in with His white blanket fer the winter. Sort of a time to slow down and ponder a bit 'bout all of the blessin's of the year past. Funny how it goes."

Virginia nodded.

"Guess He made the seasons fer a good purpose," said her grandfather, then held out his hands. "Now bring those younguns over here, and we'll pray before you go."

It had always been his ritual, this little gathering close of family members as he prayed for them before they left his home. He did so now. His wavering voice suddenly became stronger and more sure. With arms that pulled them all close against his knees, He asked God for His continued care and protection upon those they loved.

Virginia felt the tears behind her eyelids. It was a wonderful comfort to know her grandfather's prayers were as strong as ever—even though his body was showing signs of weakening.

————

Jonathan's reputation as a rancher had become well-known, and the young horses brought in more than expected at the spring sale. Virginia looked at the bank statement Jonathan brought home. What a difference it could have meant to their livelihood had it really been theirs. Much of it would go to pay the bank loan for the lawyer's initial fee. And the rest would be sorely needed for the next batch of bills. It would not go for the addition to the house as Jonathan and Virginia had previously planned. They needed more room. More bedrooms for the growing family. With Slate occupying one of the small bedrooms, three were just not enough.

Virginia wondered woodenly if the addition ever would happen. Would some other family be living in their house in the future? Would they lose the horses? The farm? Would it take everything they had to fight for Mindy? And would it even work. . . ? She shook off her frightening thoughts.

Mentally Virginia ticked each day off the calendar on the wall. They were getting closer and closer to the court date. Did she want the time to go any faster? What would it mean to all of them?

Slate continued to visit Lucy, and Jonathan let him borrow the motorcar on Saturday evenings and Sunday afternoons. Virginia hoped and prayed that the young people were not already making plans. They were not prepared to lose Slate. Nor could they pay him more.

One evening Jonathan said to Virginia, "Had a little chat with Slate this morning."

Virginia waited.

"Felt he needed to know exactly what's going on. Also wanted to be straight with him on the farm situation. Told him what I'd planned to do." He hesitated. "He seemed right excited about the prospect of being partner with us."

There was a moment's silence before Jonathan went on. "I also told him that things had sort of turned aside at the moment."

Virginia thought that was putting it mildly.

"I felt I could trust him with the facts of our situation with Mindy. He assured me he would tell no one—not even Lucy."

Virginia nodded, relieved that Slate now knew what was going on.

"He said they are in no hurry. Lucy's folks, though approving of Slate, think they are both too young to take on marriage yet. They want them to wait a spell."

Virginia was again relieved. They wouldn't lose Slate, and he wouldn't need to give up his plans either.

"He would like to get working on his house though. Says he wants to rough-frame it in, then finish as time and money allow. He's got some money coming from his grandfather's estate. Not a big sum—but it'll allow him to buy building materials and get started."

"I hadn't known," Virginia remarked.

"No, he hasn't talked about it before."

Jonathan was very quiet. Virginia knew something had him deep in thought. At last he said, "When he knew just how things were with Mindy, the costs and all—he offered the money—outright—to help pay the lawyer fees."

Virginia knew the young man's generosity had touched Jonathan as deeply as it now touched her. What a sweet and unselfish thing to do—and him courting Lucy and planning their house together.

"Of course we can't take it," she said unnecessarily.

"Of course not."

Virginia brushed away tears.

———

The trial date was upon them. Once again Belinda came to care for the children. Virginia's hands trembled as she packed their bags. She did not know how long they would be gone—nor, of course, the outcome when this was finally over. Would they still be family? Would Mindy be ordered to live in a strange new world with a woman who had no idea how to take care of a child—a woman who was dying? Virginia's heart constricted, and for the thousandth time she prayed, "Father, please help us. Help Mindy. . . ."

They said their good-byes and climbed into the motorcar. This time the roads were passable and they would drive. Drew would travel with them and be on hand to help in any way he could. Having the car would certainly give them more mobility in the city.

Virginia wept silent tears for the first several miles. The two men did not even attempt to distract her or to comfort her. *Perhaps*, she thought, *they wished they could be free to express their feelings in just the same way.*

The road stretched endlessly before them. She had thought the train ride tiresome, but it seemed that the car was even more so. It was hot, and the breeze from the open windows blew her hair about her face in a fashion she found most agitating. She yearned for a chance to get out and stretch her legs.

At length her father, who had taken a turn at the steering wheel, pulled up to the side of the road in the shade of a spruce tree. "What say we have a bit of that lunch you prepared?"

Virginia was only too glad to present the basket and focus her attention on laying out the contents. But her appetite seemed to have deserted her. She noted that Jonathan did not eat very much either.

Eventually she walked about the area. The natural breeze across the fields of barley felt much more comfortable against her cheeks than the hot wind in the moving car. She tipped her face toward it, hoping it would cool her flushed cheeks.

And then it was time to move on again. Reluctantly she

repacked the basket, replaced the lid, and passed it to Jonathan.

He touched Virginia's shoulder. "Would you like a turn in the front with your father?"

"You go ahead. I'm fine in the backseat," she answered, trying to smile.

"Go on. Sit up front for a while. You'll get a much better look at the countryside from there."

Numbly Virginia allowed Jonathan to help her into the front seat. It was cooler in the front, and the wind was not so wild.

She turned to look back at Jonathan. He had leaned his head back and closed his eyes. She wondered if he was getting some sleep. Or perhaps he was simply resting. Or praying. They had done a lot of that recently. *You love Mindy even more than we do, Lord*, her heart whispered as she watched the grasses beside the road wave in the wind. *She is your child first of all. We entrust her into your care.*

Virginia took some comfort in that thought.

Virginia had never experienced such agonizing, difficult days as those facing them in that city courtroom. The lawyers paced the floor or stood thoughtfully, droned or shouted by turn, reiterating the same material, the same charges and countercharges. Virginia wanted to tune it out. In fact, she often did.

She found it difficult to keep her eyes from wandering to Jenny. The woman's face was stoic, but Virginia wondered if she saw a shadow of pain there. Of uncertainty. But also of anger.

They had not talked. Jenny made a point of never making eye contact. Virginia had longed to approach her, but her father had cautioned that it might not be appropriate right now. There would be time to try for reconciliation after the conclusion of the trial, he said. Virginia knew in her heart that she wanted reconciliation. She did not want to hurt Jenny. But they could not sit by and let her destroy Mindy.

They phoned home often to check on the family and pass on any updates. Slate was keeping up with the chores and the horse training. Belinda reported that the children were fine and healthy. Mindy, out of school for the summer, was a big help with the little ones. Virginia longed to be home with them.

And then it was over. The lawyers presented their final arguments, the judge, after taking considerable time, brought back his verdict. Mindy was to remain with them.

They laughed and cried and hugged one another. It seemed too good to be true.

Then Virginia thought of Jenny. She must speak to her. But when Virginia rose to cross the courtroom, she discovered that Jenny had already gone.

———————

They tried to get in touch with Jenny before leaving the city, but she refused. After much prayer and discussion, Jonathan arranged a meeting with Jenny's lawyer. Virginia felt anxious and nervous, as if they were entering the lion's den, as they were ushered into a room of rich wood panels and thick carpets.

A receptionist showed them into the inner office. "Mr. Tomms is expecting you." Her voice was coolly professional.

Jonathan did not waste time after the rather perfunctory greetings.

"We have taken no pleasure in this whole affair," he began, "but we had no choice but to fight for our daughter. To have sent her away from our home would have been devastating—to her even more than to us. When she came to us she was deeply withdrawn. She would not speak for many months and was even frightened of being touched or held.

"But we do feel sympathy for her birth mother. We would . . . we would be open to letting her spend time with the child. If she wishes to come to our home, she would be welcome. Or if she would consider moving back to the area—to our town—we'd arrange for regular visits. So that Mindy might get to know her. Slowly. Over time, I'm sure a relationship could develop. Mindy already prays for her mother daily."

The lawyer listened silently, tapping the end of a pencil on his desk. When Jonathan stopped, the man shifted his position, sat forward in his high-backed leather chair and looked from one to the other.

"My client wanted her child," he said firmly, "not some convenient arrangement of your own making."

"I quite understand," said Jonathan, and Virginia marveled at his control. "The court has ruled it best for Mindy to be left where she is. We fully agree. But in recognition of the mother's feelings, we are willing to cooperate so that a relationship can be established."

"The mother does not wish your charity. She wants her child."

Jonathan stood to his feet. "Will you be so kind as to pass our proposal on to the mother . . . and let her decide?" His voice sounded strained, and Virginia knew he was fighting to remain civil.

"I may," said the man, leaning back in his chair. "And I may not."

Jonathan gave one nod and touched Virginia's arm. They turned together and left the office.

"Pompous ignoramus," Jonathan muttered as they walked from the room, past the receptionist, and down the hall. If the situation had not been so serious, Virginia would have laughed at Jonathan's unusual terminology. But she could not fault him for his frustration.

When they reached the outside, Virginia drew in a deep breath. She could finally feel it was over. They were going home. And Mindy was safe. Safe. She would not face the trauma of being torn from her family.

There had been a price, of course—besides the time and costs, there were sleepless nights, the unavoidable tensions in their home, the continual worry. But Jonathan had been right. It had been worth it all. They had not lost the horses. Nor the farm. They were in debt, but they were still young. Gradually they would be able to regroup, rebuild their operation. No sacrifice was too great to save their precious daughter.

Virginia could hardly wait to get home and hold her close.

———

Virginia busied herself with the garden and canning, and she carefully watched every expenditure for the household. Each penny she could save was one more toward paying off their debt. But she tried not to fret about money. The family was intact. She still loved Jonathan and he still loved her. Their family seemed none the worse for wear after the previous months of uncertainty and fear. God had answered their prayers in a wonderful way. They had made it. Mindy was in the family circle where she belonged.

———

Virginia now awoke each morning after a good night's rest, eager to take on the tasks of the day. The children, totally ignorant of what had just transpired, seemed even dearer, more special, in Virginia's eyes. As she looked at Mindy, she understood more acutely what it would mean to lose one of her children.

Mindy spent the last days of summer helping Virginia with chores and riding her beloved Buttercup. And before they had time to really think about it, it was time for a new school term. And Martha could not have been happier. At long last she was to accompany her big sister to school. Olivia begged to go too and found it difficult to understand why she should be denied.

"Think of James." Virginia resorted to the last argument

she could muster. "He would be so lonely without you."

Olivia considered that for a brief moment, then, "I think he's too little to be away from his mama," she said seriously. "You'll have to come to school with him." Now she had them all on their way to school.

"Olivia," said Martha, her newly acquired status making her sound even more big-sisterly, "you need to be six—or almost six like I am," she added importantly, "before you can go to school. You're not six yet."

Olivia, quite aware of how old she was because she had been counting fingers since she was two, responded, "I could be six if I put all of these and one from this hand." She held both hands out in front of her.

Martha's tone was frustrated. "Mama—s'plain to Olivia it doesn't matter how many fingers you put up. You are still just as many old."

"Are not."

"Are to."

"All right, girls—enough," Virginia said, shaking her head. "Come here, Olivia," she coaxed. "You are the only helper I have now. Can you put these sandwiches into the lunch pails?"

Olivia ran to help pack lunches, feeling grown-up for the time at least.

———

Virginia stood on the porch, clothes basket in hand, and looked out over the barn, the corral, and the distant fields. *This is the most glorious autumn I have ever seen,* she mused. Never had the colors seemed so brilliant, the trees so stately in their amber-and-gold dress. Overnight a soft rain had fallen—more of a mist than actual drops, and everything looked fresh-washed and ready to be presented to the most critical of audiences. It was all Virginia could do to continue to the clothesline and the task at hand.

Perhaps it's just that I am so happy, her thoughts continued.

We are at peace again. The children are doing well in school. Olivia and James have finally adjusted to being left behind each morning. Jonathan and Slate are happy to be working together raising horses— our lives seem to be moving forward once again.

After dinner Jonathan walked in from the mailbox at the end of the lane, an unfamiliar envelope in his hand.

"What is it?" Virginia inquired.

"I've no idea." Jonathan turned the envelope over in his hands.

"Well, open it," Virginia teased. "That's one good way to find out."

He slit open the envelope with a nearby paring knife.

"Now it will smell like onions," Virginia commented, watching his face.

His body went utterly still, face pale. Virginia felt a tremor go through her body.

"What is it?" She waited motionless for his reply.

"It's from that lawyer. They have decided to appeal the court's decision. We are to appear on December the sixteenth."

Virginia felt her legs go weak. Her hand went to her mouth. "Oh, Jonathan," she cried. "I don't think I can stand anymore. Not again. I . . . I can't. . . ."

Jonathan said nothing, just reached for her—but she pushed him away and blindly ran upstairs to the bedroom. She had no strength for anything but tears.

CHAPTER 15

The preliminary hearing, now familiar, set the new trial date. Virginia felt it was like a repeated nightmare. Jenny was there, looking more worn and ill than before. Virginia could tell that the proceedings were taking their toll on her as well. She wondered if the lawyer had ever told Jenny of their offer. She wished she could speak with her, but Jenny did not even look their way.

They returned home, mentally and physically exhausted, and poorer by another large sum of money. And they had yet to face the trial, several months down the road.

Virginia knew they had to talk about their finances. The next court case would totally ruin them financially. They already had borrowed all the bank would allow.

"If we lose the stock we have nothing left," Jonathan had explained. "Selling off the stock at whatever we can get gives us nothing for the future. But if we take out a loan, at least we have the means of paying it back. It might be slow—but we'll come out of it."

Virginia had agreed that it made sense. But now there was no more money from the bank available to them. They would have to sell the stock—and then what?

Virginia put the children to bed and was finishing up the last of the ironing as Jonathan sat at the kitchen table with his financial ledger. She could tell by the furrow on his brow that the columns of figures were not producing good news. She lifted her head as he started to speak.

"Perhaps Slate would use his inheritance money for a down payment to buy the place."

Virginia wasn't sure if he was speaking to her or musing out loud. At first she said nothing. Her throat felt tight. When she found her voice, it was low and husky with emotion. "Then . . . what will we do?"

"I dunno. Maybe he'd let me work for him. It really takes two—"

"And where would we live?" Virginia interrupted. Her iron had stopped moving and was in danger of leaving a scorched patch on the skirt of the small dress. Just in time, she jerked the iron off the cloth and set it back on its protector plate.

Jonathan said, "Maybe we could find a place in town."

They would lose all they had worked for. Would Jonathan be able to support a family of six on the wage Slate would be able to pay a hired hand?

Virginia shook her head, the tears pushing behind her eyelids. She crossed to the table and lowered herself to a chair. "Jonathan—are you sure. . . ?" she began.

He reached over and took her hand, his eyes deeply troubled. She wondered if they too were wet with tears reflecting the light of the lamp—but she could not be sure.

"Do we desert her now, Virginia? Is that what you are thinking?"

"No. No, of course not. We can't. But can we just keep going indefinitely? I think we should try again to get in touch with Jenny. Make some compromise. Make sure she heard our offer of . . . of sharing Mindy. The lawyer might not have even told her—"

"She was informed," Jonathan said. "I had our lawyer draft a letter to her so she'd be sure to get it. She sent an answer. I didn't tell you at the time because I didn't want to add to your burden. She refuses to 'make any deals,' she called it. She wants Mindy outright."

A stir at the doorway made them both lift their heads. Mindy stood there, her nightie white in the darkness of the framed door, her hair disheveled, her eyes wide with confusion. "Does Mama Jenny want me?"

Virginia's breath caught in her throat. Her eyes darted back to Jonathan's. What had they done? In their own anguish, had their carefully guarded secret reached the child? They had thought her safe in bed, sound asleep—but now she knew the truth.

Jonathan held out his arms, and Mindy came without hesitation. He pulled her onto his knee and smoothed back her tangled hair.

"Yes," he said honestly. "Your mama Jenny wants you back."

"To live with her?" Mindy sounded troubled.

"Yes."

"But she's sick."

"I know."

Mindy was shaking her head, her eyes filled with fear or disbelief. "She didn't want me before."

"I know."

She pulled back in his arms. "I don't want to leave here."

Jonathan pulled her closer while Virginia covered trembling lips with her hand.

"We don't want you to leave either. We are . . . are asking the judge to leave you with us."

Again Mindy leaned back and looked into her father's face. "Is that why you've been going to her city so much?"

He nodded.

"I wondered." She looked very thoughtful. "Do you have to go again?"

"Yes . . . we do. But not for a while yet."

"Mama Jenny is sick," she repeated.

Again Jonathan nodded.

Virginia wiped at her tears and took a shaky breath. She

reached across and took one of Mindy's hands. "Honey . . . we are going to do all we can to keep you with us. Promise."

Mindy left Jonathan's side and crossed to Virginia. She threw her arms around her neck and they wept together.

Later they mopped tearstained faces and Jonathan held them both, kissing one head after the other. They were a family. They would stay together—whatever it took.

———

Though Virginia had sat at Mindy's bedside until she fell asleep again, the next morning the little face looked troubled and peaked. Virginia wondered if the child had lain awake much of the night as she herself had done. It was hard to send her off to school, but Virginia felt that school and a normal routine would be the best distraction.

Virginia watched her go, her heart breaking. Her own day had many tasks that would demand her attention. It would keep her hands busy—if not her thoughts.

Eventually she was watching the clock and the window and the lane. Soon Murphy was running toward the road, his tail wagging, his joyous yips echoing in the stillness of another winter afternoon. Mindy was coming home. Mindy with a little sister's mittened hand held securely in her own.

The two smallest ones had heard Murphy as well and hurried from the living room, where they had been playing. "They're here," shouted Olivia. "They're home. I hear Murphy saying hello."

"Murph," shouted James, just behind her.

Olivia had the front door open before the older two arrived. Her small hands clapped as she watched Mindy and Martha cross the porch. Martha was already talking.

James joined Olivia and, watching her closely, began to clap as well.

"We waited for you," called Olivia unnecessarily.

The two girls came in together in a whirl of chatter and movement. Martha flung off her hat and kicked off her boots beside the door. As usual, she had not bothered to lace them properly.

Her coat came off next. "Know what? We had another spelling bee and Mindy spelled out."

Mindy's head hung. She was usually the winner of the spelling bees. Virginia's hand automatically went out to her oldest child. "Martha," she said, a bit more sternly than she had intended. "Pick up your clothes and hang them where they belong. And watch that you don't drop snow all over the kitchen."

At Martha's quick look at her mother, Virginia's voice softened. "Mindy will get your cookies and milk." They all trooped back to the kitchen.

Virginia continued with supper preparations, and the children gathered at the table while Mindy laid out their cookies and milk. "One for you, one for you," Virginia heard her count.

"Mine is broken a little bit," objected Martha. "I should get two."

"No. One. Here's its piece."

"I want a different one. I don't want a broken one."

"Okay. Take mine. I'll have the broken one."

They traded. Virginia caught Mindy's eye and smiled approvingly at her maturity. Mindy smiled back shyly, but Virginia could tell her thoughts were really elsewhere.

The two older girls went upstairs to change. Olivia and James followed along behind. By appearances nothing had changed—but Virginia knew by the look in Mindy's eyes that nothing was the same.

———

Jonathan and Virginia were seated at the table having a cup of hot cider before retiring. There seemed so little to say—yet so much that needed saying. But both were quiet with their own heavy thoughts when Mindy again appeared.

Her eyes were dark and solemn. Virginia knew she was

deeply troubled. It was to Jonathan that the child went, standing beside him in the circle of his arm.

"Can't you sleep?" he asked her.

She shook her head.

He took her on his knee and held her close for several minutes, rocking back and forth with her as he had done when she was a frightened little child. Mindy pressed against him, her face almost hidden against his chest.

At last she spoke and Virginia was sure she had not heard the words correctly. "I think . . . I think I should go to Mama Jenny."

Virginia's "What?" escaped her lips as Jonathan pushed Mindy to arm's length, looking into her face, then pulled her back firmly against him again.

"You what?" gasped Virginia.

"I do. I want to go. For a while. I think . . . I think she needs me."

"Honey . . . you don't have to—"

"I want to."

Jonathan seemed to regain his voice. But it was husky when he spoke. Slow and measured, he said, "I think you need to give this a good deal of careful thought—and prayer."

"I did. I've prayed and prayed. Last night and today. This might be the only way Mama Jenny will learn to love God."

Virginia saw Jonathan's arms tighten around the small frame.

"I think we should pray about this together."

She nodded, her chin trembling slightly. But Virginia saw a look in her eyes that she couldn't quite identify—a resolve that spoke of perception far beyond her years.

"I . . . I think I need to go," Mindy said quietly. Then she said, her voice a mere whisper, "Mama Jenny will think I don't love her if I don't go. And maybe she will think that God doesn't love her either."

Virginia felt tears sting her eyes. What could they possibly say?

Jonathan did not forbid Mindy to go or even try to change her mind. But that night when he and Virginia retired, they talked until late into the night.

"We can't send a child into that kind of situation," mourned Virginia.

"We aren't sending her." Jonathan's voice sounded strained.

"Well . . . we can't let her go."

"I promised God."

"But you didn't know . . ."

"He did."

Virginia raised herself on one elbow and looked at Jonathan, and she could see his jaw muscle moving in the lamplight. "Jonathan . . . I don't think God . . ."

But he stopped her again, turning to face her. "Virginia, the night after Jenny told you she was taking Mindy, I spent most of the night praying. I asked God for wisdom. I . . . I sort of put out a fleece. Like Gideon. I told Him that as long as Mindy wanted to stay with us, I'd fight for her. But if she ever said she wanted to go . . . then I'd leave it in God's hands. I can't back out on that now. I can't."

"But, Jonathan, she's only ten—" Virginia's words were choked off in a sob.

"Yes . . . she is. And it worries me just as much as it does you. But God is with her. We can't let go of that. She won't be alone. And . . . maybe she's right. Maybe this is the only way Jenny will realize that she needs God. Even though I've never felt any great sympathy for her . . . I do want to see her find God."

Yes, Virginia's heart responded, *I do want Jenny to find God*. But she couldn't keep herself from saying, "Jenny is so ill. Surely—how can she take care of a child?"

"We must hope—must pray—that when she gets too ill to care for Mindy, she'll send her back to us."

Virginia sank back against her pillow and stared at the ceiling in the flickering light. *Of course*, she told herself. *Of course. If we cooperate, then surely she will let her come back home. Oh, God . . . please . . . please don't let her make any other plans . . . just out of spite. Please protect our Mindy. . . .*

Jonathan kissed her on the forehead. "Try to get some sleep," he comforted her. "We do have a God, Virginia. He knows all about this."

And miraculously, she did sleep. But even so, the next morning they both knew they carried an extra burden with them. Jonathan, with grim face and set jaw, went about his daily tasks. And Virginia had to constantly remind herself to lift sagging shoulders and smile for the sake of the children— for the sake of Mindy.

———

They asked Mindy for time and the child agreed.

"We will celebrate Jamie's birthday first," Jonathan had told her. "If—by then—you still feel you are to go to Mama Jenny . . . we'll take you."

Mindy seemed quite satisfied with that arrangement. She appeared withdrawn at times, but Virginia felt she had been getting better sleep. It was Virginia who was suffering the most. She could not imagine their home without Mindy. How would they ever live without her?

Mindy began to speak of her going. Virginia thought it might be good for the other children to be prepared, even though it was beyond them to understand it. She and Jonathan talked it over with her.

"I'm going to go live with Mama Jenny," Mindy informed the little ones the next afternoon as they sat at the table having hot cocoa and biscuits with honey.

"When?" asked Martha.

"After Jamie's birthday."

"Can I go too?" asked Olivia.

"No, you have to stay here. You only have one mama."

Olivia seemed about to object when Mindy continued. "Mama Jenny is sick, and she needs to learn about Jesus before she dies."

Virginia had not been sure Mindy was actually aware of Jenny's critical condition and the likelihood of her death. She again marveled at Mindy's perception.

"She gonna die?" Olivia looked shocked. The only death she had encountered was the rooster that Jonathan brought in for Virginia to prepare for Sunday dinner.

"She's very sick," Mindy responded.

"Who's gonna chop her head off?"

"Silly," Martha scolded with schoolgirl wisdom. "You don't chop *people's* heads off. They just die."

"Why?"

Virginia found the conversation beyond her ability to endure. She hurried to the table. "Let's get going," she prompted. "As soon as you've changed, you can go out to play for a while before supper. Mindy and Martha are to do their outside chores first—then if there's time you can work on a snowman."

The diversion worked. School clothes were quickly changed, and four children, dressed for winter, crowded excitedly out the door. Virginia could have used some help setting the table, but she felt that doing it herself was a small price for ending the dismal conversation.

———

Virginia decided to go all out for this birthday party. The entire family was invited. Mr. Simcoe brought Clark and Marty from the farm. Virginia noted with shock the difficulty with which they had to be helped, one at a time, in from the motorcar. Harry Simcoe came first with Clark, his crutch a slow thump on the boards of the porch. When her grandfather reached the kitchen, he was flushed from the exertion and breathing hard. He couldn't even say anything for a while. Virginia hurriedly pushed a chair forward, and he low-

189

ered himself into it. Mr. Simcoe stood by to see that Clark was firmly settled before he turned to the door again. Virginia let her grandfather catch his breath before speaking to him. "Welcome. It's good to see you, Grandpa. It's kind of nippy out there today."

He smiled his hello. When he spoke, his words came in catchy little breaths. "Not as spry as I used to be. Thet walkin' wears me out."

Virginia swallowed the lump in her throat and turned away to the window. Mr. Simcoe was now ushering in her grandmother. *It would be much simpler if he just picked her up and carried her*, she found herself thinking as she watched the patient progress. Her grandmother's failing hip seemed to be giving her even more trouble. And she was such a tiny thing. She appeared to be shrinking, making her look like a child parading around in grown-ups' clothes.

Again Virginia felt her emotions threaten to overwhelm her. But it would not do to greet her grandmother with tears running down her cheeks. It seemed such a short time ago that her grandparents had walked tall and straight. Virginia had innocently assumed during her own growing-up years that it would always be so. She found her heart resisting the changes that her mind now told her were inevitable.

Virginia held the door while Mr. Simcoe eased the small woman into the warmth of the kitchen and placed another chair.

"Mama and Papa should be here momentarily," she said as she kissed her grandmother's cheek. "Clara'll have to wait for Troy to get home from work, but she said he'd leave a bit early today."

"Is Francine coming?" Marty was running a hand over her Sunday dress, smoothing out the skirt with a thin, blue-veined hand.

"Yes . . . a little later. Dalton couldn't get away early. They said to save them some birthday cake."

Her grandfather chuckled and reached for her grandmother's hand. "One thing old age has done for us, Ma. We never need worry about work keeping us from fun."

She laughed gaily. "We don't worry none 'bout work at all."

They seemed to think they had a private joke on the rest of the world.

"Where's your oldest?" asked Clark suddenly.

"She's upstairs changing into her new dress."

"A new dress? Did you sew it?" wondered Marty.

"No . . . Grandma Belinda did." Virginia did not explain that she and her mother had discussed it and wanted Mindy to have something nice for her trip to the city. "She needed a special dress and I didn't have the time."

She heard another car engine. She looked out to see a green Ford pull in beside the other cars in the yard. "Here's Mr. Woods," she commented, surprised. "I wasn't sure he'd come—"

"He busy with something special?"

"No, I . . ." Virginia fumbled. She had not meant to express her thoughts aloud. "I just wasn't sure he'd . . ."

She let the sentence drop. Her grandparents did not seem to notice.

It was a lively party. Virginia found herself fully absorbed with caring for her guests. Her hostess duties helped keep the impending separation from dampening the spirit of the occasion, though her eyes rarely left Mindy's face. She was so proud of her. She was growing into such a fine young lady. She knew Jonathan shared her feelings. The young girl seemed most mature for her age. Settled and confident. One would never have known she had experienced such a troubled beginning. God had been good—to her, to them.

Virginia and Jonathan had told each other that this party was to be a grand celebration. A memory for Mindy to take with her. A memory for them. They would wait until the celebration had settled until they discussed further her plans for the future. So they were totally unprepared when Mindy took matters into her own hands.

After the opening of Jamie's gifts—with much help from Olivia and Martha—Mindy rose and took a deep breath. "This is my last family birthday party . . . at least for a while," she said, and her voice was remarkably controlled. "I have decided to go and live with Mama Jenny. She is very sick . . . and she wants me." Virginia felt the shock waves go around the circle, but she dared not look up. She was fighting for her own control. She felt Jonathan reach over and take hold of her hand. She squeezed hard, willing herself to accept his strength.

"I have been praying for Mama Jenny for a long time," Mindy continued, "and maybe this is God's way of answering my prayers. She needs to learn about asking to have her sins forgiven. She hasn't done that yet."

Virginia could not control the tears then. They ran freely down her cheeks, and no amount of blinking would stop the flow.

"Papa and Mama are going to take me there—maybe on the train if the roads are bad," she added in a matter-of-fact tone.

There was a stirring. Mr. Woods had risen to his feet and crossed to pull Mindy close. She seemed puzzled by the deep emotion of her grandfather but hugged him back in return. Virginia saw the open tears of the man. No doubt his deep feelings included both daughter and granddaughter.

The entire assembly seemed to be weeping. The young ones looked from one to another, bewilderment in their little faces.

We must stop this, thought Virginia. *They are much too young to understand. We'll have them all fearful. . . .*

Jonathan's voice was a bit unsteady, but he cleared his throat and said, "I guess we all know why this is such an important birthday party. Our daughter Mindy has . . . has given this much thought . . . and prayer. As we also have. She . . . she knows this will not be easy—for any of us—but . . ."

His voice shook noticeably, and he paused for control. "We are proud of her. She . . . she is going to . . ." He waited another moment. "She has asked to go . . . and we have agreed. She may leave us, but she will always be here—in our hearts." He stopped to blow his nose. "Now . . . I think it's time for birthday cake."

The little ones came back to life at the familiar sound of birthday cake. A cheer went up, and soon the adults were wiping away tears and attempting to resurrect smiles. Some still appeared dazed as though they could not understand or believe what they had just heard. Losing their Mindy seemed beyond belief, but if this was what she really wanted, and if Jonathan and Virginia had approved it, they would reluctantly let her go with their blessing.

Jonathan gazed soberly at Virginia. "This decision has to be one of the most difficult and important we've ever made," he said.

———

Even though the decision to allow Mindy to go had been made, they felt they should have further information regarding the legal implications. The next day Slate said he would be happy to keep an eye on the children, so Jonathan and Virginia went into town for the noon meal with Drew and Belinda.

After the homemade beef stew and corn bread, Jonathan explained what they had been thinking about and why. When he was finished, no one spoke for a time, but Belinda reached across the table for Virginia's hand. Drew's hands were steepled under his chin as he stared reflectively out the window.

"From my knowledge of the legal world," he began, "custody issues are some of the most difficult and complex the court faces. Usually there are no simple solutions, not even a clear 'right' or 'wrong' in terms of a legal ruling." Drew stood and began pacing about the room. "As you well know by now," he continued, "there are no guarantees in a court battle. As an attorney speaking to the facts of this case, I clearly see the rights of the couple who has functioned as the child's parents for the majority of her life."

Drew paused and looked at the two for a moment. Virginia was listening intently to every word, every nuance, as she knew Jonathan was doing.

"Then there are the rights of the mother to whom the child was born. Without documentation to the contrary, she can simply make the case that she has changed her mind and wants her child back." Drew returned to the table and sat down again. "The rights of the child are a significant third part to a court's considerations. What is in her best interests—for the present, for the future?"

Drew leaned forward, arms crossed on the table. "Speaking as one who has been Mindy's grandfather for a while, I want to see her remain in the family circle where she is known and loved, where she has been nurtured to become the winsome and surprisingly mature child that she is." In spite of the solemn circumstances, he smiled as only a proud grandfather could.

Virginia could feel the gentle pressure of her mother's hand on her own, and she blinked against the tears her parents' warmth and concern evoked.

"But I also know that a court 'fight to the finish' could be devastating," Drew added, his tone very serious. "Devastating to Mindy, to you and, yes, to the mother. Jenny could—out of spite—jeopardize Mindy's future by ensuring that you would never see her again."

At the involuntary shudder that passed through her body, Jonathan covered Virginia's other hand with his own. They looked at each other, understanding without having to say it that Drew's intent was not to frighten them but to help them think carefully through the various paths before them.

"It seems to me," Belinda now put in, "that Mindy's desire to go to Jenny—coming 'out of the blue' with no prompting—is an important piece here. If you were to say no to this, and if . . . and if Jenny were to die without coming to faith. . . ." She did not finish the thought, but they both could see the very negative implications of such a decision.

"As a Christian," Drew now said, "I believe the issue your mother just mentioned may be the most important at the moment. If the Lord has put this desire in Mindy's heart, fulfilling your little 'test agreement' with Him"—he turned to Jonathan—"a higher court has jurisdiction in this case." He leaned back in his chair with a faint smile.

Virginia's smile in return was a bit shaky, but she could feel a measure of peace—a *rightness*—stealing over her spirit as the four joined hands around the table to pray again for God's clear direction—to them and, yes, to Mindy—and that Jenny would turn to Him.

CHAPTER 16

*J*onathan arranged with their lawyer to contact Jenny's lawyer and tell him of the change of plans. They asked when it would be convenient for them to arrive with Mindy. His answer came back, terse and official. They were informed simply that "Miss Woods"—Jenny had taken back her maiden name—would receive "her daughter" on Saturday next, delivered to his office. Apparently Jenny still did not want them to have her home address.

There was no turning back now. Virginia had to face the wrenching truth that they would soon be losing their oldest child—for how long, she couldn't even let herself consider. If only she could hold on to the faith she had during that time of prayer with her parents.

Unable to sleep, she was sure she must be disturbing Jonathan, and she rose from their bed. Pulling her flannel wrap closely about her shoulders, she crossed the hall to the children's room.

Mindy was sleeping soundly, her childish face angelic in the light of the winter moon that streamed light through the lace of the window curtain. Feeling emotion tighten her throat, Virginia hastened from the room before her sobs would disturb the sleeping children.

She went down to the living room and huddled on the hearth. Floods of bitterness and anger swept over her. *Why,*

God? Why? she cried silently. *Why did you let her come to us if you knew we wouldn't be able to keep her? It isn't fair. We love her like she is our own—and now you are letting her be taken from us. It isn't fair. What has Jenny ever done to deserve her back? She gave her away. She has not even kept in touch. What does she care for the child? She is just being vindictive. Mean and selfish. She only wants Mindy because it will hurt us. She wants us to pay for her pain.*

Virginia spent long minutes crying out her distress. For all her discussions with Jonathan and her words of agreement with the decision, she felt God had deserted them in this hour of crisis.

Spent and cold from the chill of the room, at last she slowly pulled herself to her feet and stirred up the fire. She threw on another log and watched the blaze catch. *Why? Why?* echoed continuously in her mind.

Suddenly a voice within seemed to say, *Why? Think about it.* Virginia shook her head to clear it of the strange impression. But it persisted.

Mindy came as a frightened, suffering child, the gentle voice continued. *Had she not come to your home, where would she be now? What if Jenny had not given her to you and Jonathan? Would there have been much chance that she would develop into a whole, lovely, and competent human being who loves Me?*

Virginia sank back onto the rug before the hearth, her mind and body still as she listened.

Should perhaps Mindy never have been born? the voice seemed to ask.

That idea was unthinkable. Mindy was a special person with so much to offer. She had already brought incredible joy to their home with her unselfish ways, her nurturing attitude toward the younger children. Her fervent prayers often put the faith of adults to shame. A world without Mindy would be a poorer world for them all.

Then maybe she should have gone to some other home.

No! Virginia could not bear to think of that. They had been blessed by Mindy. She fit perfectly into their home—

into their hearts. *So Mindy needed us—we needed her*, Virginia's inner discussion continued. Yes, that was absolutely true.

So why are you agitating? came the still small voice once again.

Because I don't want to give her up, replied Virginia honestly in a fresh burst of tears. *I don't want to see her go off all alone. I love her. I want to care for her as I've always done.*

And I love her. She will not be alone.

It was then that the ultimate truth captured Virginia's heart. Mindy would not be alone. Not ever. No matter how far she went from them—she would never be alone.

Trust me, continued the silent voice.

"Trust," echoed Virginia's heart. *That is what I need to do. That is what I haven't been doing, Lord. I haven't been trusting you.*

A fresh stream of tears poured down Virginia's cheeks. What had been happening to her over the past weeks and months? Why hadn't she seen it before? She had been failing to trust God. God had not changed. Only their circumstances.

God, you are right—and I have been so wrong, admitted Virginia. *Help me to realize I cannot hang on to Mindy—or to any of our children. Mindy is your child—not mine. Help me to give her completely to you. Help me to let her go. To trust.*

The fresh tears were not ones of bitterness but tears of repentance—of acceptance. As they poured down her face, a sweet sense of peace came over her. She knew without question that there would be many days of loneliness ahead. That she would miss Mindy with an ache that would not go away. But she would also be able to thank God for the gift of the wonderful years they'd had together. The many memories that they had built. She would know with certainty that Mindy was not alone. That God walked with her—wherever she was. That God would continue to lead her and direct her ways just as He had promised. Virginia's heart reached out and received His gift of assurance—whether or not He saw fit to bring her back to their home. God's hand had brought her to them in the first place. That same hand was leading her back to Jenny right now, and Mindy's future was in the care and keeping of their trustworthy Father, who loved them all.

———

After a tearful good-bye to the three younger children and her grandparents, Mindy climbed the steep steps of the train and settled herself on the worn wine cushions, Virginia and Jonathan on either side.

"I might never come back here again," she said, her voice trembling as she looked out the window.

Virginia felt like crying along with her, but she said instead, "But you might. Maybe sooner than we think. Your mama Jenny might bring you."

Mindy shook her head. "I don't think she will."

Virginia placed an arm around Mindy's shoulders and drew her close. "If you don't come back here, we'll come see you sometime."

"Will you bring my sisters and brother?" Her voice trembled again.

"Yes. You can be sure we'll bring the little ones along with us."

"Martha will miss me. She won't like walking to school all alone. She likes to hold my hand."

"I know, but we'll make sure she gets there okay."

Silence.

"Olivia likes to hear stories. Martha can't read well enough yet. Can you read to her, Mama?"

"I'll read to her."

Mindy broke the next silence with a soft chuckle. "James is so funny. He tries to do everything we do. He even tries to wrap up the baby dolls like we do. He thinks he's a girl."

"He'll find out soon enough that he's a boy," Jonathan assured her. "His papa will see to that. Do you think he's about old enough to go fishing?"

"I would like to go fishing," Mindy announced.

The two adults looked at each other in surprise over her head, then Jonathan nodded. "We'll do that," he said.

Mindy was silent again, but her thoughts obviously were not. "Buttercup will miss me," she said very softly.

"We'll take good care of Buttercup."

"She needs exercise."

"She'll get lots of exercise. Slate and I will make sure of that."

After another silence, Virginia assumed that Mindy was still deep in thought until Jonathan spoke. "I think she's worn out. She's sound asleep."

Virginia eased the child into a more comfortable position. She and Jonathan exchanged glances, both sets of eyes shining with unshed tears.

Virginia's fingers toyed with the soft curls that wisped about the child's cheek. It was a joy to hold her. Just hold her. Silently and lovingly. Just to let the love she felt flow through to the child in her arms, without the bitterness. Without the turmoil. To thank God for the sweetness He had brought into their lives when He placed Mindy in their care. They had been blessed. So very blessed.

––––––

The three stayed overnight in one of the nicer hotels in the city. Virginia wondered if it was an extravagance they could afford, but Jonathan had made the point that their last night with Mindy should be special. They even had their evening meal in the lovely dining room. Mindy looked awestruck as she gazed about her at the white linen and shining silver.

"Ooh," she said at one point. "Did you know they had things like this, Mama?"

Virginia smiled. Perhaps Jonathan had been right.

After dinner they walked the frosty, well-lit streets, peering in shop windows and pretending they were shoppers with unlimited resources. It was a game that Mindy loved. "Look at that," she'd squeal. "Martha would love it. I'd get that for

Martha. And that. She'd like that too. And look at the doll. The one with its eyes closed. Olivia would like that. And that wagon. For James. Is he big enough yet to pull that, Papa?" At last, shivering but cheerful, they headed back to the hotel. Mindy had a nice hot bath in a big glistening tub and then climbed in between the stiff, white sheets.

"This has been a fun day, Mama," she whispered just before she dropped off to sleep. "I will never forget it."

Nor will I, echoed in Virginia's heart.

They said prayers together and kissed her good-night. She was sleeping almost as soon as Virginia had tucked the covers up under her chin.

It was too early to retire. Virginia felt restless in spite of her weariness. She had brought a book to read, but she had no interest in the story. It was proving very difficult to quiet her thoughts and relax enough to rest. She idly thought that she should have brought some hand work. Socks to darn or torn pinafores to mend. She wandered over to the window, drew aside the curtain, and looked out on the wintry night. The streets were almost empty. A few cars moved about, but the sidewalks were nearly void of people.

"Isn't this the city where you stayed with that preacher?" Jonathan asked quietly.

Virginia turned back reflectively. "Yes. Yes, the Blacks. I had quite forgotten," she answered, keeping her voice also low so Mindy would not be disturbed.

"Perhaps we should give them a ring—see if they are still around."

"I doubt he would remember me. It was such a long time ago."

"You say he. Wasn't there a family?"

"Just the minister and his mother. But the mother married and moved away."

"The minister wasn't married?"

"Not at the time. I'm sure he would be by now. Likely with a family the size of ours—or more."

"I wonder if he's still here."

"It would be interesting to know. Maybe in the morning we should try to look him up."

"We are to be at the law office by ten."

Virginia only nodded. She knew that. It still made her heart constrict—but she no longer fought against it.

"I wonder if Jenny will be there?" she mused.

"She'd better be," responded Jonathan, an edge in his tone. "I refuse to give Mindy to anyone else."

Oh, please God—no trouble, pleaded Virginia silently. *It's going to be painful enough without any difficulties. . . .*

She turned back to the window. It had begun to snow. Light, silvery-fine flakes that sifted down from the sky.

"It's snowing," she murmured.

"I'm glad we didn't try to motor."

She nodded. It would have been foolish to try the drive in the winter.

"Are you going to be able to sleep?"

She shook her head doubtfully.

"I don't think I will either. If you don't mind, I think I'll go down and see if I can find a city newspaper."

"I don't mind."

"Would you like anything?"

Yes, thought Virginia, *I would. I would like to turn right around and go home with our little girl*. Aloud she said, "No . . . thank you."

Jonathan quietly left and Virginia continued to watch the snow fall. It seemed symbolic somehow. Like a new world. A fresh start. Not a better world. Or a more desirable start. Just . . . newness. A strange unbroken path that they must now traverse—making exposed steps that would leave their mark for all to see. Would the steps be sure—confident? Or would they stumble some? Perhaps. Perhaps there would be a bit of faltering . . . but with God's help they would not fall.

———

They were ushered in to the austere offices by the same professionally cool lady. She said nothing beyond a perfunctory greeting but nodded her head that they were to follow. The attorney was no more than civil. "It's good you have realized the proper rights in this case," he informed them. "Saves us all a lot of time." Jonathan did not answer. Virginia saw the stiffness of his jaw and knew he was holding himself firmly in check.

The man turned to the child. "So you are going to live with your real mother," he noted.

Mindy did not blink. "This is my real mother," she said almost shyly yet with confidence as she gestured toward Virginia. "But Mama Jenny is sick. She needs me, so I will live with her."

The lawyer's eyes flashed, but he did not say anything.

"Your *real* mother," he said again, stressing the word, "is in my office, waiting for you. She is most anxious to have you back."

Mindy nodded. "I used to be with her," she said, her tone even, "until she gave me away."

"Who told you that," the man demanded, straightening up and staring at Jonathan and Virginia with an accusing expression.

"I heard her. I was little. But I heard her."

Virginia was shocked at this news. How could she have known? She was three. . . .

"She . . . she couldn't care for you . . . at the time," the man attempted to answer the implied charge.

"No—" said Mindy. "She didn't want me. I heard her say so. She wanted my other papa to come back."

Virginia didn't have any idea that the child had carried the ugly reality with her all this time. Her memory brought her back to that tiny, silent figure sitting absolutely still in the chair, only her thumb for security. Because she did not speak, they had mistakenly assumed that neither did she understand. . . .

"But it's okay," Mindy continued her explanation of events. "Mama and Papa taught me to love her anyway. She still needs Jesus to forgive her, and she hasn't asked Him to yet."

Virginia slowly let out her breath, not daring to move. She noticed Jonathan's hands gradually unclench as he relaxed. He reached out to enclose her trembling fingers in his firm grasp.

The lawyer was the one who now looked tense. "Well," he finally said briskly, "let's get on with it. Come—I'll take you to your mother," he said to Mindy.

Jonathan stepped forward and took Mindy's hand. "No," he said. "We will take her to her mother."

"Her mother has no desire to see you," the man announced bluntly.

"Then I guess she won't see her child either."

"This is preposterous!" he sputtered. "You said you would—"

"And we have," Jonathan answered. "We are here. Mindy is here. If Jenny wishes to take the child, she will come to receive her."

The man stood for a moment, looking from one determined face to another. Finally he went to the door of his office and instructed his receptionist, "Show them into the conference room."

Jonathan turned back to the lawyer and said, keeping his voice low, "You will understand our deep concern for Mindy's welfare, that she is fed and cared for properly, that she attends school regularly."

The man did not answer but simply stared back at Jonathan.

"We would appreciate it if you could check—"

"I will make no such promises," he said dismissively.

But Virginia noted the flicker of uncertainty in the man's eyes. She took some small comfort that this seemingly uncaring person might have just a bit of sympathy for Mindy and the unknowns of the situation into which she was headed. Maybe he would follow up on Mindy's circumstances in the near future.

The meeting room was darkly paneled with heavy brocade draperies and plush stiff-backed chairs. The soft carpet drew an "Ooh" from Mindy.

After a wait of some minutes, the door opened and the lawyer held it while Jenny stepped through. She cast one disdainful look toward Virginia, then proceeded to Mindy. Without any greeting, she said, "Let's go."

Virginia felt her throat tighten. *Just like that. "Let's go." No hellos. No good-byes. Nothing.*

"Jenny . . ." she began, moving forward. But Jenny would not even look her way.

Mindy turned to Virginia. Her arms went around Virginia's waist. She held tight. Virginia pressed the small body to hers, tears pouring down her cheeks in spite of her resolve. Jonathan lowered himself until he was kneeling on the thick carpet, his hands on the little girl's shoulders. She disentangled herself from Virginia and turned to him. "I love you, Papa," Virginia heard her say. She knew he was too moved to answer as he held her close, his hand stroking her hair.

At last he was able to speak. "I love you, Scamp," he said, using the old pet name that Virginia had not heard him use for years. "We will be praying for you—every day—many times a day. I love you, Mindy." Virginia could barely see him kiss her forehead for the tears filling her eyes.

It was Virginia's turn for one more hug. One more kiss. One more whisper of love. She held Mindy close while they both wept. Oh, she so wanted to straighten and announce, *We've changed our minds*, and walk out with the child. But instead Virginia released her and whispered one last word. "God will be with you."

"I will write you letters," whispered Mindy. Virginia had tucked paper and preaddressed stamped envelopes into Jenny's bag.

Virginia glanced at the stony-faced Jenny. Would she let Mindy write? An occasional letter would be such a comfort— just to hear how the child was doing, hopefully that she was all right.

And then she was gone. Walking by the side of a grim-faced mother, the lawyer following with the two suitcases in tow.

Virginia turned blindly to Jonathan, and they held each other and wept.

———

They did not have the energy to try to contact Reverend Black. They had a few hours before their train left, but they did not feel they could talk with anyone for the moment. They did check the phone directory and found his name with the church listing. They would want to contact him when they returned home in case he could find a way to be of help to Mindy and Jenny.

When they went back to their hotel room, Virginia slipped out of her shoes and sank on the edge of the bed, feeling absolutely drained.

"Why don't you lie down for a while," Jonathan suggested.

"I'd never be able to sleep."

"You could at least rest."

Yes, thought Virginia, *rest would be good.*

She stretched out on the bed and turned to her Lord. *God, please be with her,* she prayed for the thousandth time. *Things will be strange. So different. She'll be lonely. Be her comfort. May she be able to help Jenny understand about you. I couldn't do it, Lord—as much as I have tried. Jenny's always rejected what I had to say. She has turned away from you. May Mindy be able to say what I could not. She's so anxious to bring her mother to you. Be with her, Lord. Be with our precious girl. . . .*

She was surprised when she felt Jonathan touch her arm.

"I think we'd better get ready to catch that train," he said. She had actually slept.

Already it was dark by the time the train pulled into the station. Drew was there to meet them with the car running to keep the vehicle warm for the drive home.

"It's snowed a fair bit," he told them. "Your mother phoned earlier from your house to suggest that you stay at our house for the night, but I think the roads will be passable."

Virginia hoped so. She wanted desperately to get home to her family.

They had no problem with the roads, and when they reached the farm the house was warm—and quiet. All the children were in bed. Virginia went in to check on them. They slept peacefully, Olivia snuggled up close against Martha. The bed where Mindy should have been was conspicuously empty. Virginia felt her throat tighten, and she softly touched the cheek of each sleeping child.

"And how was our girl?" asked Drew when Virginia had returned to the kitchen.

"She did extremely well," replied Jonathan. "We both were so proud of her."

"It's not going to be easy," Belinda whispered, wiping at her eyes.

"No—not for any of us," Virginia whispered back. The two women held each other a long moment.

There was silence, and then Virginia asked the question that had been on her heart for many days. "Papa—what happens when—if Jenny dies?"

"She will need to prepare a will—naming a guardian."

With Jenny as angry as she was, it didn't seem likely she would be naming them as Mindy's guardian.

"And if she doesn't?"

"Mindy—if she is underage—will become the ward of the state."

"And that means?"

He shook his head. "Who knows?" he answered honestly. "It will depend on what attorney is involved. Jenny's attorney seems rather . . . antagonistic."

Yes, thought Virginia, her heart sinking, *he certainly does*.

They settled into some kind of familiar routine, even though everything had changed. Daily Mindy's name was mentioned in their prayers. Every day Virginia hurried down the lane to the mailbox, hoping, praying for a letter, but every day she walked back with empty hands and an aching heart.

Many times the children asked for their older sister. Even little James looked around questioningly when her name was said.

"Murphy looks so sad when he comes down the lane," insisted Martha. "He's just a dog. He doesn't know why she went away. He still wants her to come home."

I want her to come home too, Virginia's heart mourned. But she bravely hid her deep sorrow and asked Martha to get the cookies and milk.

CHAPTER 17

*C*hristmas was a very difficult time, with so many memories washing over Virginia. She remembered little Mindy's excitement over her sleigh ride through the snow. That first Christmas tree Jonathan and Mindy had brought home. Christmas morning when she had been so wide-eyed upon finding her Christmas stocking with its simple toys. The bittersweet memory of her generous offer to share her baby doll with her expecting mama, since the new baby hadn't made an appearance yet. The now-worn nativity set that she had arranged and rearranged with so much tenderness and pleasure. The kitchen table where the tiny tot had rolled—and eaten—cookie dough meant for the oven pans. Her squeal of delight—to everyone's amusement—when at her first Christmas program she had pointed to the manger and baby for which the Magi were searching and called out excitedly, "There he is. Right there."

Then there were the later years as Mindy had grown and the other babies had joined the family. The shared excitement of Christmas morning. The many times she had read the Christmas story to her younger sisters and James. The small crew of youngsters tramping through the snow with Jonathan to get another tree for the corner of the living room, bundled so warmly they could scarcely move, yet calling to one another in their eagerness.

Now Christmas must be celebrated again—but without her.

The children singing the Christmas carols at the annual Sunday school program, without Mindy in her usual spot between the two Harding girls, brought fresh tears to Virginia's eyes. Everywhere she turned there were memories of Mindy. *But what if we had no memories of Mindy at all?* she thought. *We are far richer for having them, painful as her absence from us is,* she decided.

What kind of Christmas will she be having? Virginia's silent contemplation continued. *Will her thoughts be on home?* Virginia ached for some contact. To send a gift. Some of the child's favorite cookies. Her love. But she had no address. No way to get in touch, except through the lawyer. And she and Jonathan were nearly sure that would be a dead end.

Virginia fought to maintain the real meaning of Christmas. Both for her family and for herself. She was comforted to know that Mindy had the Christ of Christmas. Jenny could not take that from her.

———

Jonathan and Virginia did write to Reverend Black, briefly explaining the situation. His return letter indicated his delight to have this contact again after so many years. He had already made some inquiries as to the possible whereabouts of Jenny's apartment. He had not discovered any leads yet, but he would continue the search and would let them know immediately if he found Jenny and Mindy.

Please, dear Lord, help Reverend Black, Virginia prayed quietly as she held his letter close, taking some comfort from the warm words and his obvious care and concern.

———

"Slate will be going home," Jonathan said to Virginia as he sat on the edge of the bed before sliding under the covers.

Oh, no—not Slate was Virginia's first thought. *Surely we won't lose him too.*

"He had a letter from his folks, and they are settling the estate of his grandfather. They'd like him home for a visit," Jonathan explained.

"Just a visit?"

Jonathan looked up. He had heard the tremble in her voice. "Just a visit. He plans to be back."

"How long will he be gone?" she asked, relieved.

"A couple of months at the most."

"The children will miss him."

"He's hoping to pick up a few more horses when he's there. We need to get some new blood in the line. He's going to watch for a stallion."

Virginia knew Jonathan had hoped to bring in a new stallion earlier, but with the legal debts hanging over them, it had not been possible.

"He wants to get away soon so he can be back in time for the spring sale."

"So when will he leave?"

"Next Monday."

Virginia thought that sounded awfully soon.

"I was wondering just what we might send along—to the folks," Jonathan said reflectively. "To let them know we're thinking of them."

Virginia's head began to spin with ideas. What could they send? "I'll give it some thought," she promised.

"Good." He seemed ready for sleep with that bit of news off his mind. He leaned over to kiss Virginia and said his good-night. Soon she heard the soft breathing that announced he was in slumberland. But Virginia did not join him there very soon. Her mind was much too busy thinking of what she might include in a parcel to Jonathan's family.

———

Slate left as planned with Virginia's hastily prepared parcel of canned items from her garden and homemade jams held carefully under one arm. He kissed each member of the family good-bye and promised he would be back soon. That was not good enough for the young James, who insisted he should go along. He whimpered long after the train had disappeared around the bend.

"Our table is getting littler and littler," Martha remarked as she set out the plates for supper. "I hope nobody else goes away."

I hope so too, thought Virginia. It would be strange not to have Slate's good-natured teasing of the children, or his discussions of the stock and related subjects with Jonathan at their supper table.

"Is Slate really coming back?" asked Olivia solemnly.

Jonathan assured her that he was.

"Good," she said, her face brightening, " 'cause I'm gonna marry him."

Martha gave her a look of big-sister knowledge. "You can't, silly. He's gonna marry Lucy."

But Olivia was not at all bothered by the announcement. "Yeah," she said, her round face beaming. "Lucy and me."

Martha's snort of disgust nearly made her parents laugh aloud, but they merely looked at each other and shook their heads.

––––––––––

It began to feel like spring again. There was a new warmth to the air that even a stiff breeze did not totally dispel. Jonathan spent from dawn to dark with the young horses that would be heading for the spring sale. With Slate away, all the work fell on him. He came in very weary at the end of long days.

"I had no idea how much work that young fella does," he noted. Virginia smiled. They were all missing Slate.

"Shouldn't be too much longer now," she said, looking at the calendar. "Only two more weeks until the spring sale."

"Well, it can't be soon enough for me."

Slate arrived on the following Thursday, the occasion for all manner of excitement. The children were thrilled when he handed them a package from their grandparents in the West. Even a gift for Mindy had been included. "You can forward it to her or keep it until she comes back," said the little note, and Virginia swallowed a lump in her throat. *Will Mindy really be back?* she wondered.

The children's excitement was perhaps exceeded by Jonathan's. Slate had bought a new stallion, a magnificent animal. Sleek and muscled and finely sculptured. "Like a piece of marble," Jonathan said, his eyes gleaming. And Virginia had to agree. The animal was beautiful. He did not walk, he pranced—head high, ears forward, eyes bright, and nostrils flaring. Though he was all muscle and high energy, the most wonderful characteristic to Virginia's way of thinking was that he was easily handled. Even the children were allowed to pet the shiny coat.

"He handles like a charm," boasted Slate. "Never seen a more well-behaved horse."

"Well, that's sure something we can get along with," answered Jonathan. "I'm getting a little too old to be fighting lead ropes."

Slate also brought three new mares. A wonderful addition to their stable.

As soon as the new stock had been settled in their quarters, the family ate their delayed supper. Slate seemed in a particular hurry to get through the meal. He came down later wearing a new suit, his face shining from being scrubbed, his hair slicked back into a smooth pompadour.

"Okay if I borrow the car?" he grinned sheepishly as he asked.

Jonathan chuckled and nodded. "Off to see Lucy, are we?"

"Well, I don't know none about you—but I sure am."

"Are you gonna marry Lucy?" Olivia piped up.

Slate turned beet red.

"Martha said you are."

"So . . . Martha's got it all figured out, has she?"

"Marry Lucy *and* me," the child went on, reaching out for Slate's hand.

"Is this a proposal?" asked Slate, lowering himself to a crouch beside the little girl.

"What's a 'posal?"

He ruffled her hair. "You'll know soon enough," he said and straightened, "but I sure do hope that Lucy's somewhere near as eager as you are." With that comment he was gone. Virginia could hear him whistling as he headed out to the car.

The next morning at breakfast, Slate, with a grin that covered his entire face, announced that Lucy had agreed to become his wife.

They gave him their warm congratulations, which Slate accepted with much pleasure. "And when is the wedding to take place?" asked Virginia.

He flushed some but shifted on his chair. "I'm afraid it depends how fast I get that house built. We have decided not to set a date right now but to see how things go. Once I get things in order, then we'll set the date."

Virginia thought back to her own beginnings of married life. They had been so anxious to be man and wife that they didn't wait for the house to be built. It had been a difficult time—but looking back now, she was glad they hadn't waited. Those extra months with Jonathan were cherished. She looked at the happy young Slate and nodded. "We'll try to give a hand with that house," she said.

He seemed most anxious to get started.

————

Slate's inheritance turned out to be larger than any of them had expected. Over several evenings, Jonathan and Slate spent many hours at the kitchen table with balance sheets and columns of figures scattered before them, working through the new arrangement for the farm. The partnership would mean equal returns, equal responsibilities. Since Jonathan had invested the initial amount and still carried the lion's share of the stock, Slate would contribute an amount that would even the balance. Each partner would set aside an equal amount for future development or, if need be, to cover future losses.

The money that Slate paid to buy into the partnership helped significantly in reducing their bank loan. The debt was pared down to a size that the Lewises could honestly hope to see paid off in the future. But they would not touch the amount that the two men had agreed on as capital for continuing the running of the operation.

After the two had talked it through, Slate decided against building his house on the acres that Jonathan offered. "We might need more land for the stock in the future. Pasture and feed. I think I'd better try to get hold of some nearby land of my own."

In the end he was able to purchase the land adjacent to their own, a lovely piece of property with its own small creek. Both men were pleased that there would be access to water for any stock that might be put out to pasture.

"We just might need to hire us a hand," Jonathan remarked to Virginia with some satisfaction as they retired one night. "There's almost more than the two of us can do to keep up."

"That shouldn't be too difficult. Lots of young fellas around."

"It's not quite as easy as that. Neither of us wants just anyone handling the horses."

Virginia knew that both Jonathan and Slate were very particular about how the horses were trained. "You spend lots of hours doing work other than handling the horses," she said at last. "Why don't you hire someone to do that?"

"Like?"

"Like feeding, watering, cleaning out the stalls, laying in

the bedding—all sorts of things."

Jonathan seemed to be thinking on it. "Why not? Doesn't take a great deal of skill to do the choring. I'll talk to Slate about it in the morning."

And that was how the young man named Jacob Mooring came to be a working member of the horse farm.

———

Virginia rushed out the door after the phone call had come.

"Jonathan! Jonathan!" she called.

He must have noticed the panic in her voice and left what he was doing to come to meet her. "What is it?"

"Jonathan," she said, her voice trembling. "We've got to cover the watering troughs."

He removed his battered hat and looked at her, his expression questioning.

"We've got to make sure they are covered whenever they aren't in use. When there isn't someone around."

"What are you—?"

"You know how James is," Virginia rushed on. "He climbs on everything and tries anything. He could—"

"I've never seen James near the watering troughs."

"Maybe not yet—but he'll get there. There's nothing . . ." She slowed to a halt and clasped her hands together in front of her.

Jonathan stepped forward and touched her shoulder. "Wait a minute," he said. "Let's back up. I'm not following this at all. We can't cover the troughs—you know that. The horses come to drink all day long. What's happened?"

Virginia took a deep breath. "Mama just called. The Birdsalls—they just found their two-year-old . . . drowned . . . in the watering trough." Her last statement was barely above a whisper.

Jonathan reached out and pulled Virginia close. "Oh, Virginia," he said into her hair.

He didn't ask for particulars. They both knew community folks would pass on the word. There would be various accounts of the tragedy, some of them undoubtedly stretched— some false. But there would be reports of what had happened, how the baby was discovered, the reaction of the grief-stricken parents to their loss. Jonathan just held her.

"We'll look after it," he comforted Virginia.

"Jonathan, I don't think I could bear to lose another—"

"Shh," he said, gently putting a finger against her lips. "I'll look after it," he said again. "I'll go into town today."

And he did.

They could not cover the watering trough, he explained to her as he unloaded a roll of stout chicken wire. He nailed it all around the corral that held the trough. A small, exploring boy would not be able to get himself into danger.

And Virginia determinedly pounded boards across the top of her rain barrel.

———

James's stout little legs and active imagination did keep them busy. Not only was he mobile, but he had amazing speed. One minute he would be playing near Virginia as she weeded the garden or hung out the washing, and the next he was nowhere in sight. He loved to follow Murphy and would run after the dog wherever Murphy decided to lead. And he was always poking something into any available opening— sticks, rocks, or grass stems.

"That boy is going to get himself in trouble for sure," Virginia said to Jonathan, shaking her head. "One of these days he's going to shove something in someplace where it doesn't belong."

That very afternoon she heard Jamie's screams and ran to find him at the woodpile, his finger firmly stuck in a knothole. She managed to extricate him but not without some injury to the finger.

"Maybe you'll learn," she gently scolded. "You don't go

sticking your fingers in places like that."

Two days later she heard an awful ruckus. Murphy was yipping and James was hollering at the top of his lungs. She lifted her skirts and ran toward the end of the garden.

Even from a distance Virginia could see angry bees buzzing all around them. She could do only one thing. Run into the swarm, grab up the child, and flee.

Even so she received several stings herself. After putting baking soda on Jamie's and her own bites, she went to check on the dog.

"Murphy—you dumb dog. Don't you know enough to stay away from the hives?" she scolded the dog, who was still rolling on the ground, his face buried in his paws.

Virginia looked back toward the hive. A long, slender stick hung limply from the opening. James had been poking again.

When summer came and they still had heard nothing from Mindy, Virginia felt a growing impatience. *Why doesn't Jenny let her write? She doesn't need to be that spiteful*, she fretted. *She must know how anxious we are.*

But perhaps Jenny didn't. She had never been anxious herself when the small girl had been with them all those years. Perhaps Jenny truly did not understand the normal response to parenthood. Maybe she had never learned. Virginia wondered if even now Jenny understood what mother-love was all about.

After discussions with Jonathan, the two decided Virginia would write to Mindy in care of Jenny's lawyer. They had no assurance he would send the letter along, nor any that Jenny would let Mindy have it.

Please, Lord, Virginia prayed as she worked over the letter, *please let Mindy know how much we love her and pray for her. . . .*

Virginia filled the pages with family news and daily happenings of the community. "Murphy and Buttercup send their love too," she concluded, hoping it would bring a little smile and good memories to Mindy.

Jonathan included a cover letter of his own to Jenny's lawyer, politely requesting that he forward the letter and reminding him of his ethical, if not legal, responsibility to make sure Mindy was all right.

They did not hold out much hope that the lawyer would comply with either appeal. All they could do is once more entrust Mindy—and Jenny—into the loving care of the heavenly Father.

––––––––

Virginia turned to her garden. It kept her hands busy, if not her thoughts.

She was expecting her fourth child, and she was experiencing morning sickness. *This is hardly the time for that*, she scolded herself. *What with everything there is to do and trying to keep up with James . . .*

It did help that Martha was out of school for the summer months. She took over much of the supervision of James, trying to keep him from chasing the chickens with sticks or filling the feed dishes with dirt from the flower beds. But even Martha's vigilance could not protect them from all Jamie's misdemeanors, and often there was a call for Virginia to "Come quick!" and she knew that James was in some sort of trouble again.

Gradually the morning sickness subsided, but by then the summer was almost gone. Leaves were beginning to show a change to yellow and fall flowers were blooming profusely in the flower beds by the walk. Garden produce needed to be harvested, and Virginia had little energy left after the routine tasks of the day.

Belinda came often during those weeks of early September, and Virginia was thankful to have assistance from her mother. Her hands helped to fill many quarts of canning jars. Their conversations helped to make the jobs much more enjoyable. Virginia looked forward to the times spent together.

"I can't wait for Danny and Alvira to get home with that new little one. Just think—he'll be past a year before we even get to see him," Belinda commented.

"Have you heard from Danny again?"

"No—not for a few weeks now. It takes such a dreadfully long time for mail to get back. But they are due to return the first of the year. Unless of course his organization asks him to stay longer."

"Are they thinking of that?"

"There have been some suggestions. But I certainly hope not. It's been such a long time. I keep reminding myself of the parents whose children have gone to distant countries as missionaries. What a sacrifice they make."

"Maybe it would be easier if he were there as a missionary," observed Virginia. "At least then you'd feel the sacrifice had a real purpose. Not that studying animals is not a purpose—but it does seem that, well—that people over there could be doing it."

Belinda nodded. "I suppose he's learning a lot," she finally said.

"I suppose."

They snapped beans in silence for a few moments.

"I'm not sure how long I can let things go at the farm," Belinda said, almost to herself.

Virginia looked up in surprise. She had thought things were being handled nicely at the farm with Mr. Simcoe now installed.

"Is there a problem?" she asked. "Isn't Mr. Simcoe—?"

"Oh, he's fine," her mother was quick to say. "He has worked out well. It's been such a blessed gift. His being there has given the folks longer time in their own home. But now . . ."

"Now?" Virginia prompted when Belinda did not finish the thought.

"Now . . . Mama's arthritis is worse. It's bothering her

shoulders now. She can barely lift her arms above her head. It's becoming increasingly hard for her to dress herself. And Papa has his own problems and can help her only a little."

"I didn't know," said Virginia sadly.

Belinda sighed. "You know Mama. She says no one is going to be doing for her what she can do for herself."

"I don't blame her."

"No, I don't blame her either. It's hard enough to have another *woman* helping you dress and giving you baths. I wouldn't expect Mr. Simcoe to be doing that for Mama. Nor would I expect her to allow him to."

Virginia thought back to the years of caring for Grandmother Withers. Bed care certainly left one little privacy.

But she still felt that inner resistance—surely, surely things were not that bad. There must be some way to leave her grandparents in their own home. To remain as they had always been.

"I . . . I hope we don't have to . . . to rush with a decision," she finally said.

"Rush? My dear girl," said Belinda with a soft chuckle, shaking her head, "we've been dragging our feet for the last five years. The folks should have been off the farm long ago."

———

"Would you feel okay about Martha riding Buttercup?"

Virginia was surprised at Jonathan's question.

"She's awfully young for horseback riding, isn't she?"

"Well . . . maybe. Maybe not. She's been in the saddle since she was a mite."

"But not alone."

"No, not alone."

"Is it for her sake . . . or the horse's?" she said, her tone teasing.

"Well, Buttercup could do with the riding," he answered a little sheepishly.

"I thought you or Slate were seeing to it that she got exercise."

"Exercise isn't the problem. We can take care of that all right. But she should be keeping in contact with children. It's not quite the same as with adults. If she's going to be a child's horse . . ."

"I see."

"We won't send her alone. At least not yet. We'll ride along with her until we're sure she can handle things on her own. Mindy wasn't so much older. . . ."

Virginia pondered the question. She did not like to see Martha grow up too fast. However, she did not wish to see Mindy's horse become fit for only adult riders. And she knew Martha would be thrilled with being able to ride alone.

"I guess it would be okay," she finally agreed. She saw Jonathan smile.

CHAPTER 18

A sharp wind was rattling the downspout at the corner of the kitchen, whipping the limbs of the birch tree outside the window and sending sprays of falling leaves dancing across the newly plowed garden. Rosebushes and flowering shrubs already had been put to bed for the winter, the garden produce had been gathered, and the ground fresh-plowed to work in all of the cuttings, peels, and plant tops. Autumn was in the air.

Virginia listened to the blowing wind outside, glad for the warmth of the home Jonathan had provided. She was placing cream in her butter crock, setting it out for the next day's churning, the last task of the day. She would prepare hot cider for Jonathan and Slate, who discussed farm business in front of the large living room fireplace. She could then stretch out her feet toward the blaze and take up her knitting while the sound of their voices filled her with a sense of peace.

But she had not poured the last of the cream before a quite different sound caught her attention. Lights reflected off the side of the chicken house, then swung in an arc toward the porch. A car had come down the lane and was pulling to a stop near the back gate.

Virginia frowned. *Who on earth? And at this time of night.* Her eyes glanced at the clock—almost a quarter to ten. No neighbors—nor family—came calling at such a time. Unless of course, something was wrong.

Virginia felt fear clutch her heart. "Jonathan—someone's here."

Jonathan quickly joined her, peering out the window into the darkness. Steps sounded hurriedly across the porch boards, and Jonathan moved to open the door before the caller had a chance to knock.

Mr. Woods stood on the threshold. Virginia could tell by his face that the man was distraught. *Jenny*, her heart whispered and her hand went to her throat.

"Come in," nodded Jonathan. "I take it . . . you've heard something."

For an answer the man held out a single-page letter. "This came. In today's post. I just now found the time to go through my mail."

Jonathan turned the letter toward the light, and Virginia stood beside him to read over his shoulder.

> *Dear Grandpa Woods,*
>   *Mama is very sick and I don't know what to do. Can you come?*
>   *Respectfully,*
>   *Mindy*

Virginia's eyes lifted from the page. It was the first anyone had heard from the child. Strange—the mixture of childish concern and careful formality. Under different circumstances Virginia might have smiled. All she could think of now was that Jenny was very ill. Mindy was alone with her. The poor child. The poor little child.

"You're going," she heard Jonathan saying to Mr. Woods. It was hardly a question.

"There was no return address," the man said and his voice sounded hollow. Worried.

"Isn't there some way to—?"

"I'll have to find some way. I can't just . . ." His voice drifted to a stop.

Slate had joined them. He stood back, his face concerned, listening to what was being said.

"How about the police?"

"I don't know."

"Maybe the hospital staff if she's been under treatment."

"I don't know," he said again. "But I'll find her. Some way. I just hope I'm not too late. I . . . I thought you'd want to know," he said as Jonathan returned the letter.

"Of course," said Jonathan, running a hand through his hair. "Of course."

Virginia became aware of tears running freely down her cheeks. She fumbled for a handkerchief. "Is there anything we can do?" she heard Jonathan asking.

"Pray. Please pray. That I find her in time to . . . to say a proper good-bye." He looked so anguished. So suddenly old that Virginia's tears increased.

"We'll pray. You're leaving on tomorrow's train?"

"I'm on my way now. I'm driving. I . . . I just can't sit around and wait for tomorrow."

"You're driving through the night?" Jonathan sounded shocked. He looked out the window. The wind still howled around every corner of the house, shaking with an angry violence anything that it touched.

The man just nodded and folded the letter, putting it in his pocket.

"Would you like another driver?" Jonathan offered. But Mr. Woods shook his head.

"No, thanks, I'll be fine. But I appreciate it."

"We'll pray for your safety," Jonathan added.

The man was turning to go when Virginia stepped forward. "Please—please," she begged. "Keep us informed. And give Mindy hugs from us."

"I will," he promised and then he was gone.

———

"I'm sure Jenny is not allowing Mindy to write to us,"

Jonathan said to the question in Virginia's eyes after Mr. Woods left. "She probably said, 'I'm going to write to Grandpa Woods,' and Jenny must have let her."

"And she forgot about putting a return address on the envelope," Virginia added, thinking about the preaddressed envelopes Mindy had not been allowed to use. "Oh, Mindy," she wept. "Our poor little girl. . . ."

They held each other a long time.

———

It was two days before they heard anything. Two long, anguishing days. "I found them" were his first words when the phone call came. "It took me some time and I went down countless blind alleys—but I found them."

"How is she?" Virginia asked, feeling both relieved and apprehensive.

His voice sobered. "Mindy was right. She is very ill."

"How is Mindy?"

"She's a real little soldier. Don't know how she has managed for so long. Do you know she has been taking care of her mother for weeks? Jenny has been confined to her bed for almost two months."

Virginia wanted to weep. Mindy was only a child. It wasn't fair. She swallowed the lump in her throat.

Finally she asked hopefully, "Have her prayers been answered?" She did not have to explain her question to Mr. Woods.

"No . . ." he said soberly. "But Jenny is much, much more open, more mellow. I think she was even glad to see me. Relieved. She did not fight against me—at all. Made no resistance when I insisted we get her to the hospital. I think she knows . . ." He stopped, then started again. "I think she knows it is near the end. She . . . she couldn't not know. She's so weak. So frail."

"She's in the hospital now?"

"She is."

"And Mindy?"

"She's here. She'd like to talk to you. Is that all right?"

"Oh, yes." Virginia could hardly believe it. She prayed inwardly that she would be able to do more than weep over the phone.

Soon Mindy was on the line. "Hello, Mama."

It was almost too much for Virginia. She fought for control.

"Hello," said Mindy again. "Are you there?"

"Yes," she finally was able to say.

"How are you?" asked Mindy, sounding very grown-up and concerned.

"We're . . . we're all . . . just fine. How are you, dear?"

Virginia took a deep breath and began to get hold of herself.

"I'm fine. Mama isn't, though. She's very sick."

"I know. Your grandpa told me. I'm sorry."

"I don't think she's going to get better."

"We'll pray."

"Mama . . . she still hasn't asked Jesus to forgive her." The child sounded very sad. "But . . . but last night she said . . . she said she wished she knew how. She wished she hadn't been so stubborn. She said that. Does that count?"

"Yes, I think . . . I think that it's a . . . a very good sign," answered Virginia. "Perhaps she is . . . thinking seriously. We need to keep praying—"

"Mama," Mindy stopped her. "There isn't much time to pray for her any longer."

It was all Virginia could do to finish the conversation. She assured the young girl that they were thinking of her. Had been praying for her. Loved her very much. She heard Mindy's tearful good-bye. She wanted to go to her room and cry. Or pray. Or both.

Mr. Woods came back on the line after Mindy had said her good-bye. "I've been in touch with Reverend Black," he said. "He promised to go over to see Jenny. He's not even going to wait for morning—he said the hospital will let him in tonight."

Virginia was greatly relieved. *Please, God*, she prayed, even as she continued to speak to Mr. Woods. *Give the pastor the right words. May your Holy Spirit take those words and make them believable for Jenny. Open her eyes to truth, Lord. To you.*

"I'll call you," said Mr. Woods. "I'll keep you informed."

"Yes. Please. Please. We will be so anxious to hear."

The phone clicked. Virginia stood a long time holding the receiver against her heart.

———

Virginia jumped whenever the phone rang. One call was from her mother, asking if there had been any news. Then Clara called to let her know they were praying. Then her grandmother.

The familiar voice and her years of experience, of faith in God during incredible sorrows and loss, made her words of encouragement particularly meaningful to Virginia.

"Oh, Grandma . . ." Virginia's voice broke. "I hardly know what to pray anymore. . . ."

"God doesn't ask fer us to know the right words, honey," Marty said. "He only asks fer us to trust Him. And He knows even that isn't easy all the time—when we can only see jest what's around us."

It was late afternoon before the call came that she had been expecting and dreading. Even so, Virginia felt the shock of its finality. "Jenny's gone," Mr. Woods said simply.

"It seems . . . it seems so soon," Virginia murmured.

"Yes . . . we didn't have much time." There was a pause. "Here," he said, "Mindy wants to talk to you."

"Mama . . ." Mindy was weeping and Virginia had to strain to make out her words. "Mama . . . she did it. Mama Jenny asked Jesus to forgive her."

Virginia felt her knees go weak. "Honey—that's wonderful news," she was able to say. "I'm so glad." But Mindy was crying so hard that her grandfather had to take the receiver again.

"She did," he assured Virginia, though his voice was unsteady. "Pastor Black went through the Scriptures with her, and she made her peace with God. She . . . she even called me in and . . . and asked my forgiveness. Imagine that. She asked my forgiveness. I'm the one who needed to ask for hers."

He was so broken he could hardly speak.

"It's not been an easy life for my Jenny," he eventually said, "but she's at peace at last."

So many emotions washed over Virginia. She was so happy. But she was very sad. She rejoiced, even as she sorrowed. *If only . . . if only*, her thoughts kept repeating. *If only she had done it years ago—had saved herself . . . and others . . . all of the years of pain. If only she had taken a different road.* Her friend Jenny with the bright red hair, the flashing green eyes, the quick wit and even quicker temper. Virginia had loved her. Had been exasperated with her. Had quarreled . . . had made up . . . had worried and admired and wished to shake her by the shoulders. Oh, if only . . . if only she had been able to say good-bye.

Mr. Woods was speaking again. "She wrote you a letter. At the last. She had to dictate it . . . but she wanted so much to let you know . . . how she felt. She struggled . . . with her last breath . . . to get it said. Then she . . . she had me take her hand and . . . and help her sign it. She was too weak . . ." He couldn't go on.

Virginia sank down onto a chair near the telephone, openly weeping.

A new voice came on the phone. Virginia recognized it immediately. "This is Pastor Black. How are you, Miss Simpson? No, it isn't Miss Simpson anymore, is it? Forgive me."

"First of all, I am so sorry I was unable to locate Mindy and her mother sooner—"

"Oh," Virginia quickly responded, "we are awfully grateful that you tried."

"Mr. Woods has asked me to give you some information. He will be bringing Jenny back to be buried near your little church. The funeral arrangements haven't been made as yet with your pastor but will be announced as soon as things are settled. Mindy will be traveling with him, of course. She is quite a girl, your Mindy. You must be proud.

"Jenny had some last requests. She would like you to let your mutual friend Jamison know that she accepted the Lord's forgiveness before her death."

Virginia was surprised. "Jamison?"

She had not kept close touch with Jamison and his Rachel over the past few years. He was no longer playing professional football. After four good seasons he had hurt his knee and turned to his other profession. He and Rachel had settled down in a small town in the Midwest and were busy raising a growing family and serving in a local church. She assumed the address she had would still reach him.

"Of course," she heard herself saying to Pastor Black. "I will be . . . glad to inform him."

"She also had a message . . . for your mother."

Virginia waited.

"She said your mother was the only mother she ever knew. And she envied you . . . dreadfully. But she wants your mother to know that, in her own way, she loved and respected her, and she was always grateful for her concern and—I believe she said—her therapy."

"Yes," said Virginia, "she likely did."

There was a brief pause.

"And how have you been keeping?" asked the minister.

"We are . . . doing well," Virginia said, not quite sure how to answer under the circumstances.

"And your family?"

"We are all fine. Jonathan—my husband—is very busy.

And I'm pretty busy also with four—well, three of our own—we always count Mindy."

"This all must have been very hard for you."

"Yes . . . yes, it is. Very hard."

"She's a wonderful little girl."

"And . . . you?" asked Virginia, now feeling more calm and able to talk. "Are you still at the little community church?" she asked.

"Well . . . it's not so little anymore. It's done a good deal of growing since you were here. We've had to build."

"That's wonderful. And your mother?"

"She is still keeping well. We were to see her this past summer. Very happy."

"That's good news." She had noticed that he had said "we." "You . . . you have a family?"

"Yes. Yes . . . I married one of the young ladies from the congregation. Elsie Blakewell. You likely don't remember her, being here just the one Sunday. A wonderful woman. We have two little ones—with a third due next month."

"Congratulations to you both. That's nice. We are expecting another as well."

"Wonderful. Those little ones really give life meaning, don't they?"

"Yes, they really do."

They said their good-byes, and Virginia hung up the receiver. She felt much better after chatting with Pastor Black—and then she realized that was likely what the last part of the conversation was all about. After he had relayed the emotional messages, he knew her thoughts would need to be redirected. Had to be focused beyond the tragedy to more pleasant things—like family. She had the impression that Jonathan would approve of Pastor Black. It was a shame they hadn't had an opportunity to meet one another.

But as she turned back to the cupboard to continue the supper preparations, her one thought was Mindy. What was going to happen to Mindy now?

"I've been wondering," said Jonathan after they had retired, "what steps one takes to apply for guardianship."

"I've wondered the same."

"I don't know if it's another lengthy business with court
hearings and all, or what. I suppose the best place to start is
to talk with your father."

"Yes, he would know something about it—at least could
get us started."

Silence.

"If . . . it does take that . . . what are your feelings on it?"
Jonathan wondered.

Virginia stirred. "I've been hoping we could get that loan
paid off." She shifted again. "But I can't imagine the future
now without Mindy."

"You mean . . . go to the courts again?"

"Right."

"That's what I've been thinking too."

More silence.

"Do you think our girl has changed?" Virginia could not
help but ask.

"I suppose she has. I don't see how a child could go
through what she's just been through and not change."

Virginia knew in her heart that he was right, but she did
hope their Mindy had not changed too much.

The funeral service was held on a Wednesday afternoon
at their church in town, the one Jenny had attended as a
young girl. Virginia was surprised at the number in atten-
dance—but she should not have been. There were many folks
in the town who had known Jenny during her school years,
and Mr. Woods was considered an important member of the
community and his newspaper a significant asset to the town.
What surprised her most was to see Jamison there, seated

with his family. She had gotten his phone number from his parents and had phoned him to let him know as Jenny had requested, but she had not expected him to make the long trip back for Jenny's funeral.

Mindy walked in with her grandfather Woods and was led directly to the front pew where she sat silently. She looked pale and much slimmer than she had been. Taller too. With a lump in the throat, Virginia felt she was looking at a different child. She started to rise from her seat to go to the girl, to hold her close, but the organist began to play. The service was about to begin.

Mr. Woods put his arm around Mindy's shoulders, and Virginia sank back into the pew. She would wait, though it was so hard. Their minister shared some of his memories of Jenny—the auburn-haired, free-spirited schoolgirl. His description was so vivid Virginia could once again see her friend flashing those green eyes, tossing her red hair, jutting out her stubborn chin. Then the pastor went on to tell the congregation about Jenny's last days and of her turning to God before her death. A hush fell over the gathering. Several reached for handkerchiefs to wipe wet eyes. In great rejoicing, they lifted their voices at the close of the service to sing "The Old Rugged Cross." Then the group quietly filed from the church to follow the casket to the cemetery next to the building.

Virginia was not aware that Jamison was beside her until she heard him whisper, "Well, Virginia, you did it. She finally made the right choice."

"I didn't do it. I never did seem to be able to make her understand. No . . . it wasn't me. I think Mindy had a great deal to do with it. She taught her what love was all about. But it was Pastor Black who helped her to understand and believe the Scriptures. To realize that God loved her."

Jamison touched her arm gently. "Scriptures tell us that one sows, another waters, and still another reaps the harvest."

Virginia nodded, awed by the thought. "Perhaps," she

said. "Perhaps it took all of us. Thank God for His faithfulness in never letting go of Jenny. Our prayers were finally answered."

"She had so much potential," Jamison commented. "It's so sad she waited this long."

Virginia looked over and glimpsed at young Mindy, clasping tightly her grandfather's hand. "Yes," she said. "Yes, it is."

Her tears fell freely then. Jamison pressed her hand and moved on, and Jonathan stepped closer to put an arm about her waist. Through her tears she watched a pale-faced little girl place a rose on her mother's coffin. Then Mindy turned and buried her face against her grandfather's dark coat. Virginia moved to go to her, but Jonathan placed a hand gently on her arm. The minister was speaking again.

By the time she pressed her way through the milling throng of people, Mr. Woods and Mindy were climbing into his motorcar. He must have been anxious to get the child away from the dark scene of the gaping grave.

Virginia's call caught in her throat. She was not yet to comfort the little girl as she so longed to do.

———

Virginia and Jonathan went home without getting a chance to talk with Mindy. They both felt bereft. Confused. Had it just happened because of the solemnity of the funeral, or had Mr. Woods deliberately kept the girl away from her former parents? Surely—surely they would not be barred from the child.

Jonathan is right, she thought with determination. *We need to take steps quickly to appeal to the courts for guardianship.*

They were just finishing their supper when the phone rang. Slate hurried to answer it, no doubt hoping it would be Lucy. She could tell from the one-sided conversation that it was not.

"Yes. Yes . . . they're home. Yes . . . I think so. Tonight. I'll ask."

He held the receiver against his chest and turned to them. "It's Mr. Woods. He wants to know if it'll be okay for him and Mindy to come out."

"Of course," answered Jonathan. Virginia was not even able to speak.

"Yes. That'll be fine," Slate said into the mouthpiece. "Yes . . . they'll be expecting you. We are all anxious to see her again. Yes. Fine. Bye."

"He'll be here in about half an hour," Slate said as he turned around. He was grinning. "Did you hear that, Martha? Olivia? Mindy's coming!"

A cheer went up from the little gathering at the table. Even James cheered, though he could not have known why.

"Mindy's coming home," squealed Martha, grabbing hold of Olivia in her excitement and giving her a little shake. "Mindy's coming."

Virginia felt her heart sink. Would the children understand that this was no doubt just a visit?

CHAPTER 19

$\mathcal{L}$ike a girl welcoming her first beau, Virginia's heart was pounding as she watched Jonathan open the door to their visitors. What had all the months apart meant? What might Jenny have done? Have said? There had been no letters. Was it because Mindy had decided not to write or truly because Jenny had not allowed it?

The two stepped inside. Mr. Woods was chatting comfortably with Jonathan about the change of weather. Mindy stood, just inside the door, her eyes scanning the room, taking everything in. "It's the same," Virginia heard her whisper.

Virginia moved forward, slowly, one hand slightly extended. "Hello, Mindy."

The child looked at her, her eyes large and haunted. "Hello."

Virginia found herself inwardly crying out to God that the gulf wouldn't be too great to cross. That somehow they would be able to reach her again.

The children, who had been playing in the living room, suddenly realized that their guests had arrived. They rushed into the kitchen, led by Martha, Olivia, and James following close behind.

"Mindy," shrieked Martha, throwing herself headlong at the girl. "You're home!"

A light came on in Mindy's eyes. She held out her arms

to Martha and the two embraced. The other children piled in, arms outstretched, and the next thing Virginia knew she had joined the little huddle and they were all hugging and laughing and crying together.

It took some time for things to settle into some kind of order. At last Mindy allowed herself to be led away so the children could show her everything new they had accumulated over the months she had been absent. It seemed time for the adults to talk. Virginia served hot cider and sliced some pumpkin loaf, and they gathered around the table.

"I haven't had a chance to give you Jenny's letter," Mr. Woods said and drew an envelope from his pocket.

The letter, thought Virginia. *I'd forgotten all about it.*

She accepted it with trembling hands and unfolded it carefully. *This isn't Jenny's writing*, she found herself thinking and then remembered Mr. Woods had said that Jenny had dictated the missive to him. Her eyes fell first to the shaky signature at the end of the script. *Jenny's*—though barely discernible.

> *Dear Virginia,*
> *You've been a good friend. I know I haven't always been.*
> *You have done a good job of raising my girl. I'm proud of her.*
> *I was wrong. You were right. He does forgive.*
> *I'm sorry for all the hurt I've caused you. Please forgive me.*
> *I'll see you in heaven.*
> *Jenny*

Virginia folded the letter carefully again and tucked it in her pocket. *Of course I forgive you, Jenny*, her heart cried.

"We've been wondering," Jonathan was saying. "We don't quite know the procedure for guardianship. How to apply. Do you know if Jenny had taken any steps—if she was well enough to think about it? We don't know where to start."

"You want her . . . again?"

"Oh, yes," said Virginia quickly.

"I thought—hoped—you would." He sounded relieved. For a moment he hesitated. "There will be some new adjustments," Mr. Woods said carefully. "What she has been through, no child should ever need to suffer."

They nodded, faces serious. There would be adjustments.

Suddenly Virginia couldn't help but put her face in her hands, the tears falling through her fingers. The terrible burden of the separation, the uncertainties—and now, in one moment, it seemed to be over.

"I'm sorry . . ." she tried to choke out over her sobs.

Jonathan quickly moved his chair closer and put a comforting arm around her shoulders. He said to Mr. Woods, his tone apologetic, "Virginia has suffered—"

"Oh, I know she has," Mr. Woods responded fervently. "Let her weep . . . I understand," he added, wiping his own eyes.

Virginia eventually was able to get her emotions under control. "Has . . . did Mindy . . . say anything . . . to you . . . about her future?" she asked hesitantly.

"She hinted. She—I think she's worried," Mr. Woods responded. "She said something that made me think she believes she'll have to go back to her mother's apartment."

"Alone?"

He nodded.

"But surely—"

"I'm afraid I don't know what's been going on in recent weeks any more than you do. I was too busy trying to track Jenny down—then finding her like I did—and knowing that she was dying. Making arrangements for the funeral and packing up Mindy. It's all been . . . so . . . so upsetting I haven't really had time to think. I want you to know—right off—that I'd like you to have her back. This is where she belongs. You'll have my full support if you petition for her. As her grandfather, I should think I'd have a great deal of influence. If you need to go to court, I'll back you all the way."

Jonathan and Virginia exchanged glances, sure that would be a great help.

"We know nothing about how to proceed. But we'll find out."

"In the meantime," asked Virginia, "what happens to Mindy?"

"Well . . . I guess that's up to you . . . and Mindy." He smiled softly.

From where they sat they could hear the children chattering excitedly. ". . . and I've been riding Buttercup—for you," Martha was explaining. "Daddy didn't want her to forget about kids."

"I can't wait to see her," they heard Mindy's voice.

"Will you read us a story?" coaxed Olivia.

Mindy must have agreed, for the next moment Olivia squealed, "I'll get the books," and then things were quieter.

"Can she stay—now?" asked Virginia, wondering even as she asked if they were pushing things too quickly.

"I have her suitcases in the car. I'll bring them in."

After he had left, Virginia turned to Jonathan, her hands clasped together tightly. "Are we doing the right thing? Bringing her back now before we know how things will be? If we have to go through this all over again, I don't know if I can . . ." She paused to take a breath. "I don't know if Mindy could bear another separation."

"We can't not take her back," said Jonathan. "We'll just consider every day as a gift from the Lord and trust Him for the future."

There was that "trust" word again. She would hang on to it for dear life.

———

"We've got one of those fancy official letters again," Virginia told Jonathan, a tremor in her voice.

"What do you mean?" he asked, turning from the sink where he was washing up for supper.

242

"Well . . . it looks like it's from that law office."

"What have we done now?" He crossed to her.

"I hope nothing. Here—you open it." Her hand was trembling.

"Maybe he's heard we have Mindy."

That was exactly what Virginia feared. But they'd only had Mindy for two days. How could the man have heard of it so quickly and gotten a letter through the mail?

Jonathan scanned the contents. "There is something here signed by Jenny," he said.

"Jenny?"

"Yeah. There's all this legal stuff, but this here has her signature. It's to do with Mindy, all right. Jenny must have done this before she got so desperately ill."

"Do you think we should go to Papa?"

"Just let me read through this—then we'll see."

He took the letter to the table and sat down. Virginia crossed with him and took the chair opposite. She watched his face as he read.

"Well—I'll be—!" He sounded surprised—but not alarmed.

"What is it?"

"Jenny. Jenny has left Mindy to our care. As her legal guardians."

Virginia could only stare at him.

"It's right here. She wants us to raise her daughter. She is naming us legal guardians. She . . . she even wants Mindy to share our name. Right here. She's already changed it—legally—herself. It's Mindy Lewis now. Right here. Look."

But Virginia could not see where his finger was pointing. She couldn't see through her tears, this time ones of joy.

———

There were adjustments—but they were not too difficult. As far as the younger children were concerned, things were right back to where they had been. But Mindy found it a bit more difficult. Her eyes still looked haunted at times, as though she could not forget those dreadful days of trying to nurse a dying mother.

They decided that time was their best ally. Time and plenty of love. "But she needs to talk about it too," said Jonathan. "Say what she's feeling. Get it out."

Virginia agreed—but she didn't want to push her too soon. "Do you think she'll know when the time is right? Do you think she'll come to us?"

"I don't know. I understand so little about these things."

Virginia admitted that she too knew little about them.

Mindy started back to school with Martha. She had missed much of her studies in recent months, but Virginia was sure she would be able to make it up. The teacher, aware of the situation, offered extra help as well. They would not put pressure on her, but they would help the girl make up the lost lessons. Mindy was smart and no doubt would have little trouble catching up to the class.

School seemed to be good for her. Virginia did not know if it was because it was a familiar routine or because it kept her mind busy. But she seemed to be more like herself as she went off with Martha at the beginning of each day and returned down the lane, lunch box swinging at her side, at the schoolday's end.

————

One evening the younger children had been put to bed and Mindy was seated at the kitchen table, eating an apple and working on lessons. Virginia, seated across from her, was darning one of Slate's socks.

Mindy closed her books. "I'm done," she announced.

"Good."

"I guess I'll go to bed."

Virginia nodded. "You know, it might not be too long until you can have your own room. Slate has been working really hard on his own house. When he moves out, we'll have the extra bedroom back. I've already decided that you—"

"I like it in with Martha and Olivia," she said quietly, lashes lowered.

"Of course," said Virginia, noticing the look on the child's face. "I just thought . . . your room's so crowded . . ."

"I like it crowded."

Virginia smiled. Maybe being all together was a comfort. For the time being she would not press Mindy to make the change.

"I don't like Slate to go away," Mindy said.

"He's not going far. Just across the fence. He will still be working here—every day."

"But it won't be the same. He won't be living in this house—having supper with us." She sounded so sad.

"I know. I'll miss him too." Virginia tried to brighten her voice. "But that's how life is. There are always changes. Things just keep . . . being different. People grow old—new people are born. Children grow up. Nothing stays the same for very long."

Like Mindy, she dreaded change. Had always fought against it. It would not do to let Mindy know her own thoughts and fears. "But changes are good too." Virginia tried to sound confident. Then she had a sudden realization. In all the turmoil, they had not yet told Mindy that the family was to increase. "Did you know . . . that we are going to have another change here?"

Mindy shook her head.

"We are going to add another baby to the family."

"Another one?"

"Another one. Do you know what Olivia said when we told her? She said, 'What are we going to do with Jamie?' "

They both laughed.

"We told her we were going to keep James too, and that made her feel better."

"You'd keep them all, wouldn't you—no matter how many you had?"

Virginia, surprised by the question and the earnest tone, quickly said, "Yes. Yes, of course I'd keep them all."

Mindy seemed to think about that for a long moment. "Mama Jenny loved me," she finally said quietly. "After we had . . . been together . . . she loved me then. She told me. She said she was sorry she'd given me away."

"I'm sure she was."

"She said you loved me too. And Papa. She said that was good—to have so many people who loved me. She said I was fortunate." Her tongue tripped slightly over the word.

"What was it like—the days with Mama Jenny?" prompted Virginia gently. "Do you want to talk about it?"

And Mindy did. She poured out all her fears, her frustrations, her lack of knowledge of how to run a home, care for an invalid, and live in a city. She concluded by saying, "Mama Jenny wouldn't let me write you or phone you, and I didn't know anyone else and I didn't even know where to get food or what Mama Jenny could eat. I was really scared. Then, at last, she said that I could write to Grandpa Woods. I was so glad."

Virginia just held her while they both wept. She felt the shiver pass through the small frame. "You did very well," she informed the child. "Many grown-ups would not have been able to do what you did. You were so brave—and I'm very proud of you. Your Mama Jenny was proud of you too. Papa and I both love you—very much."

From then on the haunted look seemed to fade from Mindy's expression, and she settled confidently back into the Lewis family.

————

"The folks have finally agreed to leave the farm." Belinda sounded so relieved. Virginia said nothing.

"I was out to see them yesterday, and Mama brought the subject up herself. She said they had talked about it and decided they couldn't be stubborn any longer. They know that things can't go on as they have been. Even poor old Mr. Simcoe can no longer care for all of their needs."

"They're moving into town—with you?" Virginia finally found her tongue.

Belinda nodded. Her face had lost much of its strained look.

"When?"

"Just as soon as we can get them moved. I plan to go out and pick them up the early part of next week. I'll just bring their personal things. We can empty the house at our own convenience."

Empty the house, Virginia's mind echoed. *Empty the house. Just as if it were only . . . ordinary things. Not years and years of precious memories. How can you empty that?* she mourned. *How do you sort through and discard what has been part of your life? In which pile do you toss the worn baby shoes . . . the faded petals of handpicked bouquets . . . the pictures crayoned by childish hands?* Virginia could not let herself think more about it. "Maybe I could help . . . some," she said when she could speak again.

"There's no hurry, dear. Nobody will be moving into the house. At least not right away."

————

All through the day Virginia carried the news about her grandparents like a heavy load upon her shoulders. She retired that night with the burden still there. She still did not want it to happen—but her mother was right. It was for the best. It had to be.

Life keeps changing, she heard the echo of her own words to the troubled young Mindy. *Things never stay the same. People grow old.*

Yes, yes they do. I hate it—but they do. They grow old . . . and more precious. But we can't stop time. We have to let them go. We have to.

Virginia's heavy heart kept her from immediate sleep.

The next morning she decided to head for the farm. It was

a Saturday, and the children were home from school. Jonathan promised to work inside so she wouldn't have to take the children. She wanted one more time when she could visit the farm while her grandparents were still there to welcome her. One more chat around the familiar kitchen table. One more opportunity to feel the love and the warmth as she had known it for all of those years. *Please, God, once more.*

She cried on the way but managed to get herself under control before she pulled into the driveway. She gazed at everything through new eyes. The old barn that housed the new kittens, the apple tree where she had sat and read and munched on green apples, the swing where she had played with her cousins or chatted with her grandfather. It was all so familiar—yet today so strange.

She was welcomed as she always was. With arms of love and bright faces. This time she was the one who prepared the tea and placed the cookies she had brought on one of her grandmother's china plates. It was the first time she had noticed the little chips along the edge. Many years of service had left their mark.

"Pa said this mornin' thet we should have a goin'-out party," chuckled Marty from her spot at the table. "He said folks are always talkin' 'bout comin'-out parties, so maybe we should have a goin'-out one."

Virginia looked across at her grandfather. He was chuckling too.

"I says to him, 'An' who's gonna do the cookin'? Me or you?'" They both laughed again as though it was the funniest joke they'd heard.

"He didn't volunteer none, so I guess this is it, huh, Pa? This is our goin'-out party."

Virginia was relieved that her aging grandparents could face the great change in their lives in such good humor. At the same time she wished to stop them and say, *Don't you know what this means? Don't you understand that everything will be different—and there's no going back?*

But of course they knew. They knew far more about life than she. They had lived through the tough times and the good times. They knew all about changes.

She took her seat at the table and reached for the frail, soft hands on either side of her and listened once again while her grandfather prayed. She had no cause to worry about a man who could pray like that—or the woman who sat across the table, *amening* every petition to the Lord. They might be weak of body—but, oh my, they were so strong in faith. Virginia chastised herself for her gloomy thoughts and decided to enjoy this last visit.

"Mama is excited," she heard herself saying.

Her grandmother's eyes sparkled. "Is rather exciting. I says to Pa, 'Jest think, the next move we git to make might be to glory.' I'm lookin' right forward to thet. These old bones, all they know to do anymore is to ache."

Virginia looked up at her grandfather, who was nodding his agreement. "No wooden legs up there," he said, and his eyes were shining with unshed tears.

After all her time of denial—of fighting—of resisting this moment of change, suddenly Virginia was able to nod her head in understanding and acceptance. In her heart, because of her love, she released them to God.

———

It was an absolutely beautiful day. The sun shone down as though smiling on the world, warm fingers caressing childish heads at play. The breeze played hopscotch. Lifting a flower head here, whispering a secret there, dancing its way through the yard. Virginia sat on the step, drinking in the day. She had just finished pegging the last of the washing to the line and now was taking a bit of a rest. Not totally because she needed it, but more because she enjoyed it. Before her the children played. Martha busily scolded James for some childish offense. Olivia sang a little tune she had learned in Sunday school as she scooped sand into a red pail that had lost both its color and smooth sides over the years of play. Nearby Mindy was brushing the silky sides of Buttercup, who had just taken her for a ride. Murphy lay on the ground, pretending to be finding nourishment in a well-chewed bone. In the distance Virginia could hear the faint *thump-thump* of hammers as Jonathan and Slate busily worked on the new house.

Virginia sighed. For the moment her world seemed perfect. Mindy took Buttercup to the corral and slipped off her bridle. The horse flicked her tail and moved off but turned to look at the girl as though reluctant to leave her. "Go on," Virginia heard her say. "Go join the others."

"James, don't put dirt on Murphy," Olivia's voice cut into the silence, and she set to work awkwardly brushing at the dog's coat. Murphy just turned, rolled his eyes, then went back to chewing on his bone.

Mindy crossed to where Virginia sat and lowered herself beside her. "Tired, Mama?"

Virginia put out a hand and brushed back Mindy's hair. "Not really," she smiled. "Just sitting . . . enjoying. Everything is so . . . so just right."

Mindy looked around as though only now noticing the sunshine and the playing children and the contented horses feeding in the corral beyond.

She turned again to Virginia and nodded her agreement that everything was perfect. "I was afraid that you were tired . . . because of the baby."

Virginia *was* tired because of the baby. The due date was getting near. It was hard to move about and keep up to her usual tasks.

"A little," she admitted. "But it's worth it."

Mindy smiled, seeming to understand. "Do you know what?" she said after a moment of silence. "I'm getting kind of excited. About the baby, I mean. It's going to be fun to . . . to find out who it is and if it'll be like Martha or Olivia or James."

"Maybe this one will be different—than any of them."

"That would be fun too."

Virginia reached out a hand and drew Mindy up against her side. "I've been thinking—about the baby. We need to pick a name. I was thinking . . . if it's a girl . . . I'd like to call her Jenny. What do you think?"

Mindy's eyes began to shine. She nodded her head. But she did not speak.

Virginia pulled her closer and the girl's hand reached out until it rested on the growing baby. Virginia knew her oldest child had already claimed this new little one—whoever it turned out to be, as an important and already loved member of the family. Her family.

EPILOGUE

We have traveled for many years with the Davis family, sharing the joys and the heartaches, watching the family grow—and diminish. The steadfast faith that they have shared is an echo of my faith testimony. God can be trusted.

And now, in response to requests from many readers, "Please don't let Clark and Marty die," we must leave them in the hands of God, as we must do with our own families. For life moves on. Years bring change and the inevitable must eventually happen.

Some of life's lessons are not easy. It helps to know that God has a plan—for our good and His glory—and if we are obedient we can walk the way, however long or short, rocky or flower-strewn, confident that He is with us.

It also helps to know that we can entrust our family members to Him as well. Through each generation, each individual must discover a personal faith for himself or herself. But that faith is available—it is within reach. As parents and grandparents, we must try to instill in them—our followers—a desire to reach out, to accept, what God is so anxious to impart—salvation through Jesus Christ, our Guide and Comforter for whatever life holds.

Children's Books by Janette Oke

Making Memories
Spunky's Camping Adventure
Spunky's Circus Adventure
Spunky's First Christmas

Classic Children's Stories

Spunky's Diary
New Kid in Town
The Prodigal Cat
Ducktails
The Impatient Turtle
A Cote of Many Colors
A Prairie Dog Town
Maury Had a Little Lamb
Trouble in a Fur Coat
This Little Pig
Pordy's Prickly Problem
Who's New at the Zoo?